Caribbean

Layoff

C. Michael Lance

Caribbean Layoff

Part 1

Chapter 1

Grand Prairie, TX
April 3

Paco squatted on a wheel well inside the back of the nondescript white van. Its faded, sixteen year old chassis concealed a recently rebuilt engine, drive train, and suspension. Watching through darkened rear windows, he awaited the final delivery. At almost one p.m., it was a cool spring day. Texas weather wasn't oppressive—yet. Otherwise, closed up in here, he'd be melting.

Half a block down, on the other side of the street, the Medina cartel safe house squatted beneath a canopy of untrimmed, mature trees. He'd dropped a load of drugs there two hours earlier. Others had dropped off cash. Only he knew it had been Paco's last job as a cartel "mule".

The neighborhood was transitioning downward from lower middle class. Foreclosed, unkempt houses spoke to the economic meltdown and job loss. Extra activity at the house went unnoticed amidst greater troubles haunting the area.

The money transfer funded a nationwide "Cash for Gold" operation. Medina's accountants came up with the scheme to launder the operation's massive cash infusions. The drugs Paco had brought would be distributed through the tentacles of the cartel network.

Until recently, Paco had headed up Jorge Medina's security team. A role he'd filled since they were teenagers together in Medellin, Columbia. Jorge had the brains, experience, and savagery to develop one of the largest cartels in Mexico when Columbia became too hot.

Jorge was recently assassinated in what looked like a rival cartel's attack while Paco was on vacation. Two things convinced Paco that Esteban Medina was behind the hit. First—the smooth way Esteban stepped into the cartel power vacuum after his father died. Second—Esteban had convinced his father that Paco needed the long overdue vacation—against Paco's wishes.

He'd kept his thoughts to himself, like always. Perhaps because of that, or since Esteban grew up fearing Paco, he didn't get rid of him. Instead Esteban demoted him. Now he was a delivery boy. Paco's teeth ground together. But Paco still had influence. He'd use it today.

The schedule called for a last drop off shortly after one p.m. At two o'clock, the cartel armored car would arrive to pick up the money assembled at the safe house. That left Paco a window of an hour.

After his morning delivery, Paco had switched from the cartel delivery truck to his one-year old black Cadillac Escalade. Arriving back in the safe house neighborhood, he'd parked two streets over and two blocks down, leaving keys in the ignition when he climbed out. In this neighborhood, the Escalade would be gone in under an hour.

He walked a small dog he'd picked up at the pound yesterday. A man by himself prowling the streets might be noted and reported; not a man walking a dog. Once he'd arrived beside the stolen van in which he was now sitting, he'd set the dog free to make acquaintance with the dogcatcher, again.

Old trustworthy, legendary Paco was about to take his revenge and collect a pension from the cartel for himself, Estralita, and the kids. His white teeth flashed in a grim smile.

Chapter 2

Grand Prairie, TX
April 3

Six armed men guarded the house. Paco needed them together. If scattered around the house, those furthest would be warned and spoil his plan.

An unmarked van rolled down the street past Paco, slowed, and turned into the safe house driveway. It vanished from sight as it pulled to the garage in back. Delivery number five.

Paco shrugged his arms into a specially made harness. Two shotguns hung straight down below his arms. Shoulder holsters held two .45 pistols. His signature duster went on last, concealing the armament.

The shotguns were twelve-gauge automatics, based on the AA-12 Atchisson Assault shotgun designed at the end of the Vietnam War. At 300 rounds per minute, they provided tremendous firepower in close combat situations. Perfect for what he had to do. Each had the slimmer, eight round magazine with one in the chamber. The thirty-two round drum magazine was too bulky to conceal.

The delivery van pulled back into the street and drove away. It was time. He buttoned the duster's middle button. Two pinches and snorts from the baggy set aside earlier gave him a familiar sense of power as the cocaine flooded through his system.

He slipped out through the side door. Keeping the van between him and the safe house, he walked to the end of the block. After crossing the street he paced toward the small, red-brick home, glancing back at the van occasionally.

A concrete porch covered by a faded white and green-striped tin awning with rusted edges fronted the left side of the house. Peeling shutters flanked the picture window on the right side. Rumpled, stained drapes guarded against light and curious neighbors' glances.

Two cracked and broken concrete ribbons separated by scraggly brown grass ran along the left side of house to the garage in back.

Paco opened the sagging chain link fence gate and turned up the front walk. A man stepped out onto the porch. He held a pistol hanging from his hand on the side away from the street. Another man stood just inside the doorway with an assault rifle.

Paco raised his hands at the foot of the steps to the porch. "It's me. Don't shoot." He kept his hands up as he climbed and gestured with a thumb over his shoulder at the van up the street in which he'd been hidden. "I think there's someone in the truck."

Paco saw a man twitch the front window drapes aside to look at the van. "Don't look!" Paco hollered.

He pushed open the door and walked in. "Stay away from the windows." He headed for the kitchen. "Don't let 'em know we suspect somethin'."

"Ever'body in here," he bellowed—taking charge. He stopped and gestured for two men to precede him. He couldn't let anyone bump into him and feel the guns, or worse, have one go off.

Herman, a tall, muscular black in charge of the crew, was already in the kitchen. "What are you doing back here?" he asked.

"The old white van across the street. I reported to Raoul that I saw movement in it this morning when I arrived and again when I left. He told me to come back and check it out. He thinks DEA might be monitoring cell phones so he sent me instead of calling. Stay off your phones. I can't tell if anybody is inside the vehicle. The windows are dark."

Four other men—another black, two Hispanic, and one white—crowded into the kitchen. Two had pistols. The others hefted assault rifles.

"We need to check it out. Is everyone here?" Paco asked.

Herman, leaning against the refrigerator, surveyed the crew. "Everyone except José."

A sleepy voice echoed from the hallway. "I'm here."

"Get in here." Paco turned to the window and moved the ragged, soiled curtain aside. In the window's reflection, he saw everyone standing in a half circle behind him. José stood in the doorway. The two with assault rifles were on either side of him.

The kitchen was empty except for a folding card table, four folding chairs, and the refrigerator. The other black man pulled a chair out and sat. Playing cards lay scattered on the table. A soiled rectangle on the linoleum floor outlined where the stove had been. A chipped and stained sink under the curtained window and cracked tan tile with brown grout completed the décor.

Still facing the window, Paco unbuttoned the single button holding his coat closed then reached into and through the cutout inside his right coat pocket. He wrapped his hand around the shotgun. His finger laced through the trigger guard.

"We have to check out the van. Decide what to do if somebody's in it." Paco said while turning toward the men arrayed behind him, He raised the shotgun through the front of the coat. As it rose, he grabbed the forestock with his left hand and pointed it toward José, framed in the doorway.

Two shots erupted—sounding like a single explosion. One round caught José in the chest, blowing him across the hall. The next slammed the man on the left into the wall. Buckshot at close range tore bodies open and shattered bones.

He swept the gun back to the right. With the next squeeze, two rounds smashed into the other assault rifle bearer. Paco continued swinging to the right toward Herman—the most dangerous. Herman had snatched a gun from his holster but hadn't brought it to bear. Two shotgun blasts hammered him into the refrigerator.

Paco dropped his left hand from the forestock of the shotgun as he turned to the last two, before Herman hit the floor. The white guy almost had his gun up. Paco squeezed the trigger again. Two shots thundered. One hit the man in the gun arm, nearly ripping it off—starting a fountain of blood. The second went wide.

With only his right-hand grasping the shotgun, the recoil knocked it from Paco's hand. But he'd already flipped the coat out of the way and raised the shotgun on his left. The last man aimed his pistol as he rose from the chair.

Paco squeezed the trigger of the shotgun planted against his left hip. Four shots roared. A pistol bullet plucked at Paco's coat. He blasted the other man in the groin, chest, and face as the gun barrel climbed. The shots shredded the black man and knocked him into the card table. It collapsed. Playing cards fluttered down. A red mist and the acrid smell of gunpowder filled the air.

Footsteps clomped in the echoing silence as Paco stepped over to the wounded man still twitching on the floor. He drew a pistol and shot him in the head twice.

Paco's wheezing echoed in the quiet. He looked around at the bodies. Not much different from what he'd done numerous times for Jorge Medina. His gaze rested for a moment on Herman's body crumpled in a pool of blood spreading on the linoleum. Not a friend, but he'd known and respected him for years. "Sorry, man. It's for family."

Gunshots weren't unheard of around this area, but not this many all at once. Neighbors would call the police. Move.

He raced to the van he'd left on the street, jumped in, and backed it to the house—engine racing. He whipped the wheel to send the van weaving backward down the driveway, around to the

6

back. Brakes squealed. Sweat ran into his eyes. He felt weak, dizzy, and couldn't catch his breath. He crossed his arms on the wheel and laid his head on them. When he looked up, colorless spots floated in front of his eyes. Leaving the van running, he pulled on the door handle and heaved with his shoulder to open it. "For Estralita," he muttered.

Stacked boxes of money and cocaine filled most of the laundry room at the back door. He pushed the lip of a two-wheel dolly under a chimney of five boxes. He rolled it down one step and ten feet to the van. Paco shoved the cartons into the back of the van and returned for more. Six more trips filled the back of the van. On the last trip, he threw the shotguns, duster, and harnesses on top of the boxes. He'd left many boxes of drugs behind. He only needed enough for personal use. The money was what was important. Finished loading, he leaned forward and put his hands on the floor of the van, gasping raggedly. He shut his eyes, but dizziness forced them open when nausea surged.

Pushing erect with an effort, he started to shut the van's back doors but stopped. He thrust his hand into a box and dragged out a powder-filled baggie, then closed the door. Walking around to the driver's side, he maintained an unsteady balance with his right hand against the van. A lacy curtain fell back into place in the house next door. Hurry. He placed the van in gear, drove to the front of the house, and accelerated into the street.

As he made his turn toward the freeway heading north, sirens whooped.

Chapter 3

North Texas
April 3

Still laboring for air, Paco began the eight-hour drive to Estralita's home near Kansas City. He'd stay away from I-35 and follow lesser-traveled highways from Dallas, past the Lake Texoma dam, then through small Oklahoma and Kansas towns.

In a Walmart supercenter parking lot he changed to the license plate he'd stolen the last time he was in Kansas City. When done, he hunkered in the driver's seat for two minutes—trying to catch his breath. He'd been up almost twenty hours, running on nervous energy and cocaine.

He was in worse shape than he thought. But with a pinch of powder from the baggie in the passenger seat, two sniffs, and he was ready to go. Between the cocaine and energy drinks, he could make it.

He planned to pick up Estralita and drive north to Canada. Canadians had good healthcare.

———

Paco's mind wandered as he drove. Forty years ago he began as street muscle for the Medellin cartel in Columbia. Jorge Medina, then a minor player, first saw Paco playing soccer on the streets in Bogota. After a few tequilas, Jorge would tell listeners that he wondered why a man was playing with kids. Paco had towered over the rest of the boys. At sixteen, Paco was already six feet four inches and, although slim, had a massive frame. He played goalie, protecting the space between two broken-down, rusting cars. Jorge said Paco had reminded him of a jaguar.

Jorge had come at Estralita's request to look after her *little* brother. Six years older than Paco, she took care of him after their parents and two siblings died in drug wars. With no skills, other than an attractive face and a voluptuous body, she sold herself to raise money for food and housing in this rundown section of Bogota.

Her pimp made the mistake of hitting her in front of Paco. He beat the pimp to death with a nicked and dented cricket bat he'd found in a trash heap outside the Bogotá Cricket Club. He left it on the man's broken body along with his dreams of becoming a cricket hero, and wearing the brilliant white uniform like he'd seen through a hole in the Club fence.

Fearing reprisals from the pimp's large family, Estralita fled Bogotá leaving Paco in the streets.

Jorge, her ex-customer, thought he'd find a scrawny teenager he could put to work picking coca leaves. Instead he discovered a hulking teenager who took to violence like a coyote to baby chicks.

Jorge's rise within the cartel, based on native cunning, accelerated when backed by Paco.

Paco developed expertise in a wide range of weaponry including knives, handguns, rifles, shotguns, and machetes.

Foreseeing that the Columbian government, backed by US weapons, money, and men, was going to crush the Medellin cartel, Jorge moved to Mexico. He took over distribution organizations falling apart along with a failing cartel. Paco headed security.

After Jorge died Paco was demoted to transport mule.

———

Estralita called two months ago. "*Hola, Paco.*"

"*Hola hermana, cómo está?*

"*No es buena,*" she replied.

"*Qué?* What have they done?" Paco immediately feared that one of his nephews was in trouble, maybe in jail.

"*Cáncer.*"

Paco inhaled and his breath froze in his chest. "Who?" He breathed out.

Estralita explained that the disease was spreading through her body. She and her husband didn't have insurance. They were using up their life savings on cancer treatments, which weren't working.

After she'd left Columbia and snuck into the US, relatives helped her find work cleaning homes, offices, and hotels. She met and married a cook who dreamed of opening a Mexican restaurant. While he cooked, she cleaned.

She and her cook eventually moved to the Kansas City area to open a restaurant with a cousin in Lawrence—not known as a hotbed of Mexican cuisine. They filled a gustatory niche by downplaying Mexican spices for Midwestern tastes. The restaurant grew successful—so successful Estralita quit cleaning homes except for her own.

Paco visited them whenever he could, which was infrequent. He swallowed his disappointment when he couldn't interest his nephews in cricket. Since they excelled at *fútbol*—soccer in the US and a game he'd only played a few times on the streets in his youth—he learned their sport.

Estralita's news devastated Paco. In her early sixties, she deserved many years to play with grandchildren. He had to help her and the boys—like she helped him. The best medical care possible was what she needed.

Paco had no retirement plan, no health insurance. Most people in his line of business never needed them. A pre-purchased cemetery plot was more realistic.

But what could he do? He had no savings. He'd always spent everything he received—and that was a lot. Liquor, whores, gifts, and shit he didn't need and most of which he didn't have anymore. Now when he woke up in the mornings it took a half-hour of creeping and creaking before he could walk without supporting himself on the furniture and walls.

He'd made up his mind after talking to his sister to take what the cartel owed him.

Chapter 4

Oklahoma to Kansas
April 3

Paco drove the van through North Texas into Oklahoma. Twenty-five miles inside Oklahoma, he stopped on a bridge over the Blue River. When traffic cleared, he dropped the shotguns over the railing into the river. They disappeared from sight. Shotguns were too much trouble to smuggle into Canada. He'd keep the pistols.

Back in the van, he panted again from the small exertion. After another pinch of cocaine he pulled onto the highway and continued north.

As he rolled down the highway, labored breathing made his chest hurt. He needed rest but couldn't stop. A dash of cocaine every hour sustained him.

He stopped for gas. Stepping from the van, Paco slapped white powder from his shirt and pants. He rubbed a dusting from his lips and chin as he trudged inside and laid two fifties on the counter. He waved his hand over his shoulder. "White van, fill up." Back outside he went through the gasoline ritual—flap, cap, nozzle, trigger squeeze. He stared at the unresponsive nozzle. "Damn." He turned to select a grade of octane. He leaned his forehead against the van while it filled. The cool metal felt good on his head.

Returning inside for his change, he snatched up a hotdog along with a six pack of Red Bull.

Four and a half more hours to Estralita's. By the time he got there he'd have been awake for almost thirty hours. He couldn't stay at her house. The cartel may already be after him. A few cartel friends knew Estralita. He'd take her to a motel where he could sleep. Her husband could sell the restaurant and follow to meet up with them later.

He popped the top on a Red Bull, took another pinch of cocaine, part of which drifted down to dust his clothes, shifted into drive, and steered back onto the road. The drugs in back would keep him going until he could quit them. The money would be enough for Estralita and the kids.

Driving grew harder. He panted for air. Sweat ran into his eyes and soaked his shirt. When the buzz wore off, he caught his eyes drooping closed. He took more finger squeezes of powder.

His left arm throbbed. He rubbed it as he drove. Must be sore from the shotguns.

It was dark before he turned west toward Lawrence. He was within thirty minutes of Estralita's when the arm ache intensified, spreading to his shoulder, neck, and chest.

Talons of pain clutched at his chest. Doubled over in agony, he was oblivious when he jerked the van to the left. It ran onto the shoulder, dipped down in the middle of the grassy median, then shot back up on the other side; airborne for moment.

It landed on the wrong side of the road, running at an angle toward the far shoulder. He didn't have on a seat belt. The bounce had thrown him between the seats. He barely registered lights coming toward him.

Hauling on the steering wheel, he pulled himself back, and wrenched the van left. He slid out of the seat onto the console again. The guardrail passed within inches on the right. Blurred images flashed by. A wall of rock appeared in his headlights. He tugged the van back right. Metal crunched and squealed.

Searing, tearing pain gripped his chest and arm as his vehicle rolled forward. Fingers clutched at the source of his agony. A jolting bounce slammed him against the dashboard. Trees materialized in the headlights. He stretched his leg to stop, missed the brake pedal—stabbed the gas instead. The front of the van rotated downward as the ground dropped away. Paco floated off the seat. A hand clutching the steering wheel was his only anchor.

Everything moved too fast. The van hurtled toward a too small gap in the trees. The rear view mirror rushed at him. He jerked his head sideways to miss it.

No chance for a last thought about Estralita. A blast of pain and his world winked out.

Part 2

Chapter 5

Rural Kansas – Near Kansas City
10:10 p.m. April 3

Steve flung the Taekwondo uniform into his gym bag. He couldn't catch a break. The bag hung limply from his hand as he shambled to the exit. His brow furrowed. It seemed like more shit kept getting shoveled onto the pile of his life.

As the door swung open, the frown relaxed His mouth pulled into a smile. Bobby and his dad, Frank, were waiting in the parking lot for him. "Great match today," Steve said. He extended a fist. "Sorry it went so late."

"Thanks coach," Bobby said.

Steve's fingers flared in a mock explosion when Bobby's fist touched his. The corners of Bobby's lips twitched upward and he ducked his head.

"Thanks, we stayed to watch yours," Frank said. "Too bad. You were winning."

Steve shrugged. "Master Lee told me the difference between a red and black belt is control. I have to learn."

Frank draped an arm over his son's shoulders as they turned toward their car. "Remember, no punches in the nose."

Steve waved goodbye before pitching his gym bag into the back seat of his Land Cruiser SUV. He jumped in, started it, and flicked on the seat heater. It may be spring, but it felt like winter.

15

Despite his earlier depression, Steve's chest swelled with a deep, satisfied breath. The kids he'd trained did well. Three of the four kids he brought tonight had won their age group. Bobby, the youngest at twelve, hadn't, but he showed marked improvement. If he kept improving he had a chance to medal next time.

Steve had done well and like Frank said, he might have won his own match if he hadn't been disqualified. He'd punched his opponent—a younger black belt, a level higher than his own red— in the nose.

He shook his head. Taking satisfaction in a loss—it summed up the way his life was going. He blew out a heavy breath.

Yes, the head was off limits in matches, but that guy unleashed a combination of punches and moves that left his nose hanging like a piñata. Steve instinctively whipped out a backhand, smashing his first two knuckles down into the bridge of the opponent's snout as he'd been trained to do. He wished he could take it back as soon as it made contact.

Well, it was a lesson for both. Steve would learn not to take every available opportunity. And the black belt would learn to keep a guard up—after his broken beak healed.

Steve swung his SUV out of the parking lot and headed home. He pressed the icon on his cellular for home. It rang three times.

"Done with the games?" Jen answered.

"The kids did well. Me not so much."

"Did you set up any interviews today" She demanded. Jen blamed all their troubles on his inability to find work.

"I made about a dozen calls," he said. "Tried for decision makers, but mostly got shuffled off to HR. Did catch one VP at lunch. He didn't sound happy to hear from me." He'd tried to explain that jobs for fifty-nine-year-old quality control engineers these days were as mythical as baby dragons. It was like talking to a wall.

"But you have time for martial arts," she said frostily.

"You know Master Lee gives me free lessons and workouts if I teach these classes." When Steve was going to drop out because he couldn't afford it anymore , Master Lee told him "You good teacher. Kids like you. Leave me time for better students. You teach—your lessons and workout free."

"It's not about the cost," Jen said. "It's the time wasted."

"You said it would be hard for me to find a job looking like the Pillsbury Doughboy. That it made me look older," Steve said in exasperation. Years ago he'd slipped easily into the sedentary suburban life style—his riding lawnmower had a beer cooler on the back. "I work out so I look fit and energetic—like you said I needed to be." He'd dropped forty-five pounds in the last fourteen months by dieting, exercise, and taking up Taekwondo again. Now, Jen complained that he was wasting time better spent looking for work.

"I saw the letter from the bank. It warns of foreclosure," She said, changing subjects. "What are we going to do about that?"

It looked as if a job didn't magically appear they'd have to sell the house. At least they weren't upside-down like so many others, but they wouldn't make much if anything. He'd tried to convince himself that it was better than letting the bank foreclose. "Let's talk about options tomorrow." Steve said. "I'm bushed."

"Alright," she said and disconnected.

He hoped Jen would be asleep when he got home. Their marriage had gotten rocky since his layoff at the beginning of what the media now called the Great Recession. Maybe hit-the-rocks was too mild an expression. It was more like falling off that giant rock at Yosemite—El Capitan.

The only good thing about being laid off—he was now in the best physical shape in twenty years.

But he needed some way to vent his frustration—his opponent's broken nose was the result. Damn.

Driving this desolate Kansas highway gave him too much time to dwell on his problems. Tonight, dark, dense clouds stole all celestial light. No cars were in front or behind and few passed on the other side of the wide, undulating median that divided the four lane roadway. He raced along the tunnel that his headlights carved through the darkness. Only the dashed lines whipping by on the road gave any sense of speed.

"Holy crap!" His hands clamped the steering wheel. Headlights charged across the median from the other side of the highway, dipped down out of sight, and then shot into the air. They bounced, tipped at an angle, banged back to level, and headed right at him.

Chapter 6

Rural Kansas
April 3

Steve stomped on his brakes. The ABS system moaned as his three-ton SUV decelerated to halt on a bridge. Two east-bound lanes enclosed by guard rails left little room to maneuver. He shifted into reverse, preparing to take evasive maneuvers. But the oncoming headlights passed across the road at an angle. Barely missing the guardrail, it left the roadway on his right.

Jouncing high beams charged toward fractured bands of limestone climbing a rocky cliff. The light colored van swerved sharply to avoid a head-on collision with the stone wall. Metal squealed as its side scraped against rock. It rolled erratically down the long slope toward the creek—dropping out of sight.

He tracked its progress by jittering flashes of light on trees as it bounced down the incline.

Lights winked out with an abrupt crunch.

Steve drove across the bridge and parked along the right shoulder. A semi-truck whooshed by in the fast lane. It was the first vehicle he'd seen on this side of the divided highway since leaving the tournament.

He jumped out of his SUV and waved his arms at dwindling tail lights. The truck kept going.

Steve shut off his headlights and flicked on the flashers. Didn't need two accidents in the dark tonight.

After hustling around the SUV to the guardrail, he looked toward the wreck. It was a pale form in the darkness of the trees lining the creek.

On the other side of the rail, between the highway and rocky cliff, the ground descended toward the creek. A narrow concrete drainage ramp followed the incline down.

He needed to call for help. Report the accident first. Then check on the passengers. He retrieved his phone from the console and punched in 911. Silence. He tried again. Still nothing. He squinted at the screen. Shit! No bars.

Steve ran along the road and rechecked twice more—the signal still flat lined. Drive to somewhere with reception?

No. Check on the passengers. He had Red Cross certification. He could administer first aid or CPR. Maybe someone stopping would go for help.

Steve grabbed the first aid kit from the emergency bag he kept in the back of the SUV "in case." He yanked on his leather gloves. There might be jagged metal or broken glass.

Carrying the first aid kit and his flashlight, he strode to the guardrail. He swung his legs over and jogged down the grade toward the creek. Branches of lightning danced across the clouds. "One, two, three... ten, eleven...." His instinctive count matched the slap of his right foot on the concrete drainage ramp... "fifteen...." *BOOM!* The lightning was three miles away. Close.

Steve ran up behind the van and swung wide to see what he had to work with.

Steps he taught in Red Cross first aid classes for the Boy Scouts raced through his mind—look around, make sure the area is safe. Rescuers often rushed in, turning themselves into victims. All his first aid training came from the boy scouts. His army training was short on emergency medicine and long on killing. Sniffing the air, he detected the sweetish smell of antifreeze, but no gasoline.

Two thick trees growing from the creek were all that kept it from falling in. He heard the roar of rushing water. It must be raining upstream.

The ground upon which the vehicle rested descended precipitously. And then it fell away. The undercarriage just behind the front wheels rested on the edge of what he estimated to be a twelve-foot drop. Front wheels dangled in space.

Lodged against the trees that had smashed it's front end, the van appeared secure. Steve tried to open the back doors. Locked. He shined the flashlight through darkened rear windows. He saw a jumbled cargo of boxes—no passengers.

The loading door on the right side was also locked. The impact had buckled the front passenger door. It didn't look like it would open without the Jaws of Life.

He circled to the driver's side. Although the ground was steeper, there was less damage in front. That door might open.

Steve glanced up at the bridge. Red flickers from his emergency flashers reflected off the bridge rail. Any traffic sounds would be inaudible over the rumbling water. The bridge was at least thirty feet straight up. No one could see the van down here unless they leaned over the rail.

Maybe someone would stop for the blinking lights. If they did, would they think to look down here? *Please, someone stop and look.*

He eased beside the van, down the steepening grade toward the driver's door. Steve kept a hand on the vehicle's rain gutter for security in case he slipped.

Leaning forward, still gripping the gutter with fingertips, he grabbed the door handle. The handle moved but the door didn't open. Stuck.

His flashlight played over the driver. A man was out of the seat—stomach draped over the top of the steering wheel. No seat belt. Deflated airbags sagged below him. His head and neck stuck through the top half of the broken windshield.

Steve used the flashlight to trace from where the man's thigh lodged against the bottom of the steering wheel down to his foot pressed against the front of the seat bottom. It wasn't a straight line and the angle was in the wrong direction. Some part of that limb must be broken. The way it was wedged perhaps was all that had kept him from flying through the window to the creek below.

Steve stretched his left leg until his toes rested on the edge of the bumper. Re-gripping the rain gutter with both hands he took a deep breath and lunged with his right leg, positioning those toes on the bumper, too.

The left shoe started to slip, but he shifted weight and planted his foot against the sycamore tree holding up the van. The sole slid on the smooth pale bark and then caught on a knot on the trunk. He held a death grip on the rain gutter with his fingertips. This was crazy.

Breaths coming in short gasps, Steve glanced down toward the thundering water. If he fell, they might find his body ten miles away—or not at all.

He inhaled deeply. Thank god the tree was sturdy—an eighteen-inch diameter colossus growing from the bank. It arched over the cascade below.

Two feet away, the driver's head protruded through the shattered windshield. Steve flicked the flashlight back on.

Fractured, laminated glass bulged outward where the man's shoulders had slammed into it. His head and neck sagged crookedly out of the hole they had ripped through the windshield. Steve grimaced. Necks shouldn't bend like that. But, it wasn't like he had a lot of experience with dead bodies. All his military scores in Vietnam had been at long range.

He dragged off a glove and pressed fingers against the carotid artery on the neck just below the jaw. No pulse. Was it his imagination or was the dark olive skin already starting to cool?

The rear-view mirror dangled—touching the driver's shoulder where it pressed against the torn opening. Steve reached his fingers into the hole. His glove scraped glass edges. With a tug, he pulled the broken mirror loose.

No fog formed when he held it under the driver's nose. "May God receive your soul," he whispered.

He dropped the mirror and watched it bounce off the rocks. Water swept it away.

Steve shined his flashlight beam at the churning water. All this for a dead man. He started to ease his way back to firm footing. Then he stopped.

Could there be a passenger? Shining his light around the right side of the cab, he noted that a box had broken open and spilled its contents between the seats. He must be a craftsman. It looked like a scattering of tiles or small bricks. Steve held the light still and squinted. His heart surged. "Holy shit," he gasped. The flashlight revealed packets of money scattered all over the floor.

Chapter 7

A Creek in Kansas
April 3

There was no way to reach the money through the window. Not with the guy's head and its dark, oily looking, gray-salted hair hanging out.

Lightning brightened the surroundings.. Thunder came on the heels of the flash. If it rained, his perch would become more precarious. He edged back to firm ground and then scrambled up the steep slope to the back of the van.

Why would someone dressed in T-shirt and jeans have a box full of money? It looked like it might be thousands of dollars.

Oh man, what he and Jen could do with that money.

Steve looked around and picked up a stone about the size of his fist. With his second blow the tempered glass window shattered into a rain of glass pebbles. Because of the vehicle's tilt, the rear was raised three feet in the air—tires barely touching the ground. He grabbed the bottom of the window frame with a gloved hand, and hopped up on the bumper.

Reaching inside he popped the lock open. He pulled up on the door and shuffled sideways on the bumper to let it swing wide.

He glanced up at the bridge. *Please, no one stop and look!*

He slid down the metal floor to the cargo piled against the seats. Boxes blocked access to the money in the passenger compartment. He dragged one back to shove it out of the way. The top gaped open. His light shined on the contents. Steve's breath froze in his chest. More money packets.

Lifting one, he saw a fifty dollar bill on top. Ruffling it revealed the packet contained all fifty dollar bills. He grabbed another stack—more fifties.

The next box contained packs of twenties. One more had baggies of white powder. *Drugs? Is it cartel?*

Steve grabbed another box, pulled it close, and jerked it open—more twenties.

He collapsed against the front seat. All these boxes contained money or drugs! His arms and legs felt weak. Call the police? What good would they do with it? If he takes some, no one will know it's missing—except the cartel—and they don't deserve it.

Crap! He heaved his body upright. *The Toyota Land Cruiser had its flashers on.*

He scrambled up the smooth floor, swung his legs around, slipped, fell out on the ground twisting his ankle, and charged up the drainage ramp toward the road at a hobbling run.

Chapter 8

A Creek in Kansas
April 3

Steve yanked open the SUV door and punched off the hazard flashers. He glanced back down the road for traffic. Nothing. Thanks.

Without headlights he drove forward past the guard rail. He shifted into reverse. Backup lights provided the only illumination in the inky darkness. It wasn't much—barely enough to see—but enough to be seen from the road.

As soon as the SUV backed far enough to be out of sight from the road he stopped, jumped out, and opened the rear hatch and tailgate for a better rearward view. Interior lights came on and he flicked them off. He continued backing the SUV until its tailgate was three feet from the van's rear doors.

Steve laid his head back against the headrest and took a deep breath. His heart thumped at an accelerated rate. Don't have a heart attack now.

Before climbing back up into the van, he scanned the bridge above. No lights going by. Then he brushed broken glass out of the van onto the ground. His gloves protected him from cuts. Hoisting himself inside, he slid feet first down the steel floor to the muddle of boxes. He grabbed the first box, saw cash inside, and pushed it up the floor to the open doors. It slid back down. This time he pushed it out of the door until it rested on the edge of the floor and the up-tilted bumper. It held.

The next box contained baggies filled with white powder—drugs. He shoved it to the side and looked into the next box. Money. He pushed it up to the door opening.

When four cash boxes were poised on the lip and bumper, he climbed around them, dropped to the ground, and loaded them into his SUV. He kept eyeing the bridge as he worked. Only once did a passing set of lights flicker along the railing.

Back in the van he repeated the process. Push drug boxes to the right. Shove the cash upward. This time he stacked a fifth box on top of one of the others. That stack began to tilt out. He lurched to grab the top box, but bumped the one beside it. That one shifted forward and fell to the ground. Damn.

After loading the other four boxes into the SUV, he knelt and placed the spilled money packets back into the fallen box. He heaved it into his vehicle, turned, and climbed back. Four boxes at a time.

Thunder rumbled. Rain burst from the sky. Its drumming on the van roof reverberated inside.

Streams of water started running down the floor. The tilted rear opening faced into the wind. Rain poured in. Should he stop now? Five boxes were still jammed against the front seats. Finish it.

He transferred the last boxes in a deluge. Soaked clothing plastered to his body. Even his shoes squished. He leaned on the SUV tailgate. The raised hatch sheltered him somewhat. Rain hadn't abated. Only the money in the front of the cab remained. Eleven boxes of bagged powder rested against the right wall. He climbed back inside and slid down to the front seats. Streams of water made the floor slicker.

He leaned between the two high backed seats. The driver was big. Steve could smell him. Sweat and blood. To climb into the front for the money, Steve would have to push him aside. He couldn't do that. It wasn't right to disturb the dead man. Maybe it was silly, but he couldn't do it to him. Instead he pulled the wallet out of the corpse's back pocket. It reminded him of recovering comrades' dog tags in Vietnam. Later he'd go through it for ID. If the guy had family, maybe Steve could do something for them.

There were a couple of money packets within reach, but Steve backed up, turned to the rear, and climbed out. White light blinking between the railing supports above indicated a car passing. Lightning flashed, illuminating the surroundings. The crack of thunder followed less than three seconds later. It was almost on top of him.

Ready to shut the door, he looked back inside. Drug boxes stacked along the van sidewall didn't look realistic for a wreck. Steve scrambled in and heaved the boxes against the back seat. He nodded—pleased with the disorder he'd created.

He slammed shut the van doors, the SUV tailgate, and hatch. With four wheel drive in low, he slowly accelerated. A widening stream of water flowed down to the creek behind him. The ground was mostly rock, but a deep patch of dirt, turned into mud by rain, could strand him. As if to prove him right, the SUV fishtailed and then straightened. His heart caught in his chest. He patted the dash. "C'mon, do it, baby."

Thanks for full-time four-wheel drive.

Continuing up slope, he steered through several squirrelly spots where his tires spun before catching again. Finally, he bumped over the raised edge of the paved shoulder. Arms trembled and his knees felt weak. He stopped and looked back. In the distance a halo of headlights brightened as they approached the top of the ridge.

Steve didn't want anyone to come to the assistance of his standing vehicle. He accelerated onto the roadway. The car behind swung into the next lane and overtook him before the SUV reached the posted speed. Steve's stomach plunged. It was a

Highway Patrol cruiser. It slowed to match speeds momentarily. Don't stop me now.

The officer looked him and the Land Cruiser over and then surged ahead. With a whoosh, Steve exhaled the breath that had lodged in his chest. Too soon. As it pulled in front, the Patrol car decelerated. Steve lifted his foot off the gas pedal.

The Highway Patrol vehicle pulled away then accelerated. Steve's body went limp with relief.

Chapter 9

Rural Kansas
April 3

Steve ran ten miles under the speed limit until the Patrol cruiser was out of sight over a hill.

Get off the road. He turned onto the next exit. His body shook and hands trembled on the wheel. He turned right at the road that crossed the bridge. Within a mile, he steered into a gravel turnout fronting a pasture gate.

Despite the heated air blasting from the vents, Steve couldn't control his shivering. He was soaking wet on a cold spring evening. Nerves played a part.

The Taekwondo uniform in his gym bag was dry. He'd hardly raised a sweat before being disqualified.

He struggled in the front seat to change out of his sopping clothes and into his gear. He was too old and out of practice to undress in a car. He tried to remember the last time he and Jen— whatever, it was a long time.

Heat seeped back into his body. Tremors subsided until he wasn't afraid of chipping teeth.

The drenching rain had turned into a drizzle. He got out and walked around the SUV to see if there was anything unusual that warranted the Highway Patrol officer's scrutiny other than parking on the road late at night. Nothing appeared amiss, just twenty-two file-size boxes in back. Mud splattered the sides behind the wheel wells—not unusual for a four-wheel drive SUV.

Back in the driver's seat exhilaration flooded Steve's body. Just when he thought his life had turned to dog crap this fell in his lap. He'd done it. Opportunity presented and seized.

There could be a hundred thousand dollars in the back. His palms drummed a rapid beat of happiness on the steering wheel. The released tension made him feel light-headed.

He started the car. Before putting it in gear, he wanted to touch his prize first. Reaching back he opened the top of a box pressed against the passenger seat, and lifted out a money packet. His mouth dropped open. Hundred dollar bills were on top. A quick thumb through revealed all hundreds. Twisting in his seat to look into the box he saw nothing but hundreds. He laid the packet reverently on the console. Maybe there's *several* hundred thousand dollars. Maybe they wouldn't lose the house.

He swung the SUV around in a U-turn. Home again, home again. Cruise control set at the speed limit, he kept watch for other official vehicles.

Guilty thoughts fermented in his brain overwhelming the elation. What had he done? He always told the kids not to steal. Stealing was the worst thing you could do—taking someone else's hard earned gains. Here he was with a truckload of stolen money. But it was drug money. Wasn't it? Was it wrong to take money obtained illegally? Big companies stole from each other all the time—people, intellectual property, whatever.

Shit, he could spend weeks—years rationalizing.

He did it. *Deal with it.* Move forward. But his brain still roiled.

If they caught him, would they send him to jail or just make him give the money back? What would it be like to wear the same orange jumpsuit every day and have a roommate who gave him the choice of being the husband or the wife?

If it was drug money could he get a finder's fee? Jen was the lawyer. He needed her advice.

The nervous chatter of joy then depression oscillated in his mind all the way home. As the garage door rose, revealing Jen's Camry, his thoughts focused on what to do with the money. How would Jen react to the load of boxes in the rear of the SUV? Should he take them out tonight? And do *what* with them?

Wait, Jen would leave early tomorrow. She had an interview. She'd be in a hurry and probably wouldn't notice. Grabbing a tan tarp from a shelf he covered the boxes.

He needed to talk to her but didn't know how to break the news. Now wasn't the time. If he dumped all this on her it would mess up her mind before the morning meeting. She needed to be on her game—one of them needed an income or the house would be foreclosed. But he knew that wasn't the real reason. Guilt and shame washed out the elation he wanted to feel.

Inside the master bedroom walk-in closet, he changed into pajamas. He'd shower in the morning. He'd barely broken a sweat in his match and the rain soaking washed that away.

When he came back out Bozo, his Scottish Deerhound, cracked an eye from where he was stretched out like an area rug on the carpet and then shut it when he saw it was Steve. Jen didn't move when he crawled into bed. Usually not a good sign. She slept like a cat. He'd deal with it tomorrow.

Steve's thoughts turned to the driver. He probably died quickly—neck snapped like a brittle pasta noodle. Who was he? Why did he have all that money? What about Family? Kids? His restless questions kept him awake. He forced himself to make his mind a blank slate—a technique he'd learned in Taekwondo. Sleep finally came.

Chapter 10

Overland Park. Kansas
April 4

Steve woke after a fitful night—surprised he'd slept at all. Thoughts started warring inside his skull—elation, shame, and fear. Were the dead man, van, and the money a vivid dream? That would fit the path his life has been taking. At fifty-nine he could start collecting Social Security in a few years, not that he wanted to. Not after what the economy had done to their savings. He needed a job. And now both of them were out of work.

In the kitchen, Steve started to open the door to the garage when Bozo surprised him with a nose nudge in the butt. Dark blue gray, he moved like a ghost in the predawn shadows.

The hound looked at the French doors to the back deck, then back at Steve as if to say, "Time for my morning constitutional." Steve smiled and ran his hand over the dog's back as it padded out the door.

He liked a dog you didn't have to bend over to pet. Thirty-four inches tall at the shoulder, one-hundred and fifteen pounds, and a foot long head which was mostly mouth and teeth could make even a dog lover pause. But Bozo's fearsome aspect disguised a couch potato nature.

Steve returned to the garage door. His back and legs felt sore. Was it Taekwondo aches from last night? He faltered before turning on the light—fearing that it was a dream but dreading it wasn't.

His breath puffed out through parted lips. A tan tarp covered the boxes in the back of the SUV. He didn't dream it. He lifted the hatch, pulled the tarp aside, and opened a box. It was full of cash. He lifted a cash packet, and fanned it. All fifties. After laying it back, his hand rested on the box's contents, savoring the feeling.

He shook his head. "What the heck did I do?" He yanked his hand away and looked around as if afraid someone would hear. He tugged the tarp to re-cover the boxes.

Stay with his routine. In the basement he climbed onto the elliptical and flicked on the TV. Morning news presented the spring feast of weather, traffic, auto collisions, and shootings. Last night's storms had passed through. It would be a nice day. Nothing about his wreck. He cut his routine short at twenty minutes and skipped the weights completely. Back upstairs, he let Bozo in and started coffee.

Jen was in the master bathroom. He showered upstairs. Jen was dressed and applying makeup in the master bath when he finished. He watched her from the dark of the bedroom for a moment. She still made his heart race. While his belly looked like Garfield's, she kept trim even after two kids. Yoga, diet, and good genes. Steve had long ago traded in his six-pack on a beer keg. Maybe now it was down to a pony keg.

The weight he had lost helped—kind of. A recent interviewer said Steve had considerable experience for someone his age. Steve assumed the guy was saying he must be older than he looked. He held his temper and didn't invite the interviewer to consider having intercourse with himself. He didn't get a call back from that company. But it'd only been three weeks. Chin up.

Steve opened a drawer to get his sweats out. Elf, Jen's Papillon, raised his head, oversized ears perked forward, from where he ruled the bed. An undersized growl issued forth. Steve shushed him and Elf settled his head on outstretched paws. Bozo the Scottish Deerhound continued his post-constitutional nap.

In the kitchen, he poured a cup of coffee.

Footsteps approached. Steve schooled his face. Don't look guilty.

"Pour me one too?" Jen said as she entered the kitchen.

Steve's eyebrows rose after he turned to pull another cup from the cupboard. They were talking today. That's a good change. He turned and handed her the cup filled with black coffee—like he drank it. Another of the many things they shared through thirty plus years of marriage.

She smiled, took a sip, and turned back toward the bedroom for her finishing touches. The barely audible patter of Elf's feet on the hardwood followed her out.

Jen returned, buttoning her suit jacket. "How do I look?"

He took a moment to appraise her. "You'll knock 'em dead."

"Thanks. I'm going from the interview to the women's shelter. There are two restraining order requests I need to work on for ladies there. I'll be back later this afternoon. Will you be home?"

"Nothing planned."

"Good. We need to talk," she said.

Steve's eyebrows knitted. "OK?"

She blew him a kiss. "Wish me luck."

"Luck," he said to the closing door.

Chapter 11

Overland Park. Kansas
April 4

Steve switched on the television while he waited through the whirring and rattling of the garage door a second time. He'd wanted to tell Jen she didn't need to worry about the interview. But until he wrapped his head around what to do with the cash he needed to keep his mouth shut.

The weatherman, who usually popped on screen only to say he was going to tell about the weather in a few minutes, finished babbling about the fine clear skies for the umpteenth time. Then— more breaking news—yet another auto collision.

Steve tensed when the image switched to an on-site reporter. *His* wreck was in the background.

He tried to focus on the words. "... at the scene of a single-person fatality discovered this morning," said the reporter standing beside the guardrail on the bridge. There was brief mention of police interest in possible drugs found in the vehicle.

"I knew it." Steve slapped the marble countertop. "Drugs."

The scene cut to a view of a wrecker pulling the van out of the creek. Now he didn't feel bad about who lost the money. It wasn't baggies of talcum powder and cash from Social Security checks for widows at the old folks' home.

The reporter didn't mention money.

The cartel that lost the drugs wouldn't file a complaint with the police about missing money. How long would it take the drug lords to find out about the wreck? Could they find him? Could they trace his tire treads? The TV video showed a wrecker pulling the van up the hill. Wouldn't both vehicles tires obliterate his tracks?

It didn't make him comfortable to admit it, but perhaps he'd committed the perfect crime. He wore gloves. There weren't any witnesses. The police didn't suspect anything and had compromised the site's evidence.

But maybe the police tracking him down was the least of his problems.

Was it a Mexican drug cartel? He hoped it wasn't, then he threw his hands out in exasperation. "It's not a Canadian drug cartel," he growled to himself in annoyance The closest Canada came to a cartel were drug companies that ship prescription drugs made in America back to the US at a lower price. They don't move baggies of white powder.

This was as bad as not having enough money. Finding the money made him happy, but he couldn't stop worry and guilt from battering his euphoria. Up and down like a teeter-totter, but he couldn't see what was balanced on the other end, a pot of gold or the Predator.

Stop anguishing over it. Get busy. First, figure how much there was, and get the money away from the house. He recalled his dad's words, "Put your money in land, but put it in a tin can first so it doesn't rot." A slight smile pushed his lips up on one side.

A storage facility would be perfect. A place for the money— and a place for junk from the basement. Besides her passion for helping battered women, Jen had a zeal for decorating. Their basement was a lost graveyard of ornamental bric-a-brac, enough holiday decorations to outfit the White House, and replaced furniture. The junk would provide cover for the money.

That answered the question about where.

———

The first box had two rows of twelve banded packets across the top. He picked up a packet and fanned it. They were all twenty dollar bills. He counted one hundred. The next packet was the same; one hundred twenty dollar bills—two thousand dollars. The math wasn't hard but he struggled to believe his answer. Forty-eight thousand in the first layer.

The next layer was the same. Twenty-four packets of twenties.

There were twenty layers in the box. He did mental calculations three times because he couldn't believe it. "Nine-hundred, sixty thousand in this box alone," he whispered. It was stupefying. He had to revise last night's estimate up—way up.

There were twenty-two boxes—*almost twenty two million.* His knees weakened and he slumped to sit on the bumper. "Holy shit! I can stop buying lottery tickets." Then he sobered. People killed for this kind of money.

He hauled out the rest of the boxes and checked them. The packing was consistent, two hundred and forty packets of one denomination in each box.

When finished, there were five boxes of twenties, seven of fifties, and ten full of hundreds. Not trusting mental math at this point, he placed his laptop on top of one of the boxes and entered the data into a spreadsheet. It totaled $34,800,000. The counting process had kept him focused, but now butterflies galloped in his stomach. He slowly collapsed to his knees on the floor.

More than his wildest fantasies.

When the shock wore off, he rose to his feet and reviewed his numbers. The spreadsheet didn't lie.

On the front and back of each box he'd penned the denomination and total. Jen had christened him anal. He preferred to think of it as the thoroughness of an engineer.

They'd need access to money that didn't require a trip to storage. Money that couldn't go into a bank. He filled a black trash bag with packets taken from several boxes and placed others onto his driver's seat. Tally marks went on each box to indicate the number of packets removed. He reviewed his work. Jen's accusation might have a basis in fact. But he'd never admit it.

Folding overhead stairs led from a closet on the second floor to the attic. He and the trash bag ascended into the dark.

Using a flashlight he negotiated the ceiling joists until he was above the upstairs bath. He knew there was an empty space between two of the walls from the time he installed an exhaust fan. With heavy twine wrapped below a knot tied in the neck of the garbage bag, he lowered it into the empty space and replaced the insulation he'd removed. The excess length of string, looped over a convenient nail head, would make it easy to retrieve. That took care of any urgent needs for cash once the rest was in storage.

In the kitchen, he Googled storage facilities, selected one nearby, and reserved a room on the first floor in their climate controlled building. He didn't need constant temperature for the cash, but he didn't want a room that could be seen by everyone driving by. The one he selected was one of many inside a multistory air conditioned building.

Returning to the garage, he put the packs of fifties and hundreds he'd left on the seat into the SUV console. A two-wheel dolly went into the back on top of the boxes. A heavy duty lock he'd used to secure the ski-boat he'd sold cheap to raise money to live on went on the passenger seat. With the address programmed in his GPS he backed out.

At the storage office, he paid for six months and bought another lock with cash. When given a choice of accommodations, he selected one in a short, dead-end hallway two units from one of the building entrances. Easy access with little or no tenant traffic. No one was in the area as he quickly rolled the boxes of money into the building and then into the room. All the security cameras would see was file boxes being moved.

When finished piling boxes at the back of the space, he surveyed his work. Adding boxes of Christmas decorations, lamps, surplus end tables, and other basement relics in front would give the impression of just another pack rat homeowner's collection. He shut and double-locked the door.

Back home in the basement he surveyed the clutter. Many of the boxes probably hadn't been opened since they were moved from their former home years ago.

He filled the back of the SUV with basement relics. Muscles told him it was time to rest. It wouldn't be long until Jen arrived home. The problem with slowing down—it gave him time to think and worry again.

Now he had to figure out how to tell Jen. Would it begin to heal them or add to her anger over his stupidity?

Chapter 12

Mexico City
April 4

Esteban Medina slammed his hands on the desk and screamed *"Que?"* His lips drew back in a snarl. He leapt up. The chair bounced off the shelves filled with antiques and artifacts behind his desk. A rare pre-Columbian pot fell to the thick carpet but didn't shatter. He stalked around the desk. The messenger who had delivered news of the raid dropped to his knees and raised his hands in supplication. Perhaps groveling saved his life.

Esteban whipped the barrel of his .45 revolver across the messenger's face, knocking him flat on the floor. He waved the pistol toward the door. *"Fuera,"* Esteban barked.

The messenger scrambled to his feet. Blood streamed from beneath the hand he held to his cheek. *"Gracias a dios,"* he muttered as he scurried out.

Esteban watched the man leave and pull the door shut. Despite what his professors at Yale Business School had said, he found terror to be an excellent management tool.

Back at his desk, Esteban considered next steps. The raid meant someone knew the details of his operation. It was a major glitch in the, until now, smooth running Cash for Gold program. In this depressed economy millions of people needed cash and were willing to part with their jewelry, coins, and other artifacts. The perfect way to launder money.

A bigger issue than penetrating his operation was the lack of respect it demonstrated towards his organization. His power was built on fear more than greed.

Despite having spies in all major US enforcement agencies he'd received no word of the raid. He phoned a source who worked out of the Dallas FBI office. Switching to fluent English he said, "There was a raid this morning in your area. Do you know who did it? Was it an official operation?"

"Hang on." After a few moments, Esteban heard a door close, then, "Heard something about it. Someone escalating a war with you?"

"Perhaps. They stole drugs and millions of dollars."

"Then it wasn't law enforcement. That kind of bust would already be in the media if it were. The bigwigs want favorable press. Large cash seizures justify funding requests. Rumor is it's a squabble between cartels. It was a massacre—lots of bodies."

"We will find them." He disconnected.

Loss of the money was an issue, but with the billions generated by the cartel, it wasn't major. Lost employees' lives was a cost of doing business. There were plenty of others. However, disrespect had to be punished. Others must be afraid to attack. Only strength ruled.

———

One of Esteban's best informants was agent Juan Santiago. Born in a US hospital to illegal immigrants, he'd leveraged his U.S. citizenship, hard work, and affirmative action programs to win scholarships to UCLA. Graduating at the top of his class with a degree in Public Policy, specializing in Drugs and Crime, he joined the US Drug Enforcement Agency. The DEA valued his bilingual capabilities. He spoke English with a Southern California accent and Spanish like a Mexican.

Juan had made a name for himself as an investigator. He combined above average intelligence, an intuitive flair, and dogged determination. He specialized in the Medina cartel.

He'd continued his education, earning a master's degree part time while working.

A little over two years ago, the girl he loved left him to marry a rich hedge fund executive. His DEA salary couldn't buy her the lifestyle she craved. Soon after, he sent a message through his informant network requesting a meeting with Esteban Medina.

When he finally met with Esteban, Juan said he wanted to retire early in a comfortable style. Government work wasn't going to provide it. If Esteban could make it happen, Juan would be a conduit into the DEA's plans.

Esteban realized that turning Juan into an asset would be a major coup. His investigations had been putting pressure on the cartel. Esteban asked for a demonstration of good faith. Juan did it by exposing an undercover agent in the cartel's operations.

Esteban picked up the phone and gave orders, while staring Juan in the eye, to kill the undercover agent. Juan shrugged.

As a result, the first deposit went to Juan's offshore retirement fund.

Juan's continuing leaks had done well by both. Juan was building up his offshore retirement fund. The Medina cartel always stayed one step ahead.

———

After considering all other options, Esteban called the secure phone Juan used. There was no answer. He didn't leave a message. Juan would see the incoming number and call him back soon.

His phone rang within five minutes.

They never used names on their calls. When Esteban answered, Juan said "Yes?"

"Did you hear of the incident with my operation in Grand Prairie, Texas?"

"I just heard they retired all on-site operatives. Was anything taken?"

"Mostly money, some merchandise. The people aren't important, but lack of respect is. Do you know who did it?"

"No. Local police assume it was either internal or a war with another organization. They notified us because of product in the house, but because of all the deaths local police are handling the case. It isn't high priority to us because of the small amount recovered. I know the people were from your organization. But they're insignificant players. I guess we're in agreement about that."

"They took over thirty million."

"Oh...," Juan breathed out. "That's big."

Based on all the problems Juan had caused him before switching sides, Esteban knew Juan was the best investigator he could find. "I don't care about the money, but they must pay. Find and punish them."

"I can try, but I don't know if I can get assigned to what looks like a minor internal skirmish."

"No. I *need* you to find them."

"Believe me, I'd like to help, but my value to you depends on maintaining a low profile which I'm not ready to jeopardize. My retirement savings haven't matured yet."

"I want this done," Esteban growled. "I'm moving up your retirement plan. I'll deposit two million in your account today. You can have half of the money you recover. I don't care about the money. It's about respect. I want them destroyed"

Juan was silent for long moments. Then he said "Half of thirty million? I'll have to leave my organization. There are already rumors about a mole. My activity would cause fingers to point."

Juan paused. "If I leave, I won't be able to continue to sell you information. If I find them but can't recover what they've taken, my retirement plan will still be underfunded."

Esteban squeezed the phone. He felt he was being played, but he had to have this like an addict wanted a fix. "What is your number?"

"Another three million if I find them, plus half of whatever I recover."

"Done."

"I'll call you after the money is deposited in my account."

"Give me an hour."

They disconnected and Esteban put his accountants to work. Forty-five minutes later Juan called back. "OK, I have it. I will begin immediately. I can find whoever took it, but I'll need two men who can follow orders to handle dirty work."

"You can have two of my best men—smart enough to follow orders, but big and very mean. They hurt people for me. They will call you. Find who did this and punish them." Esteban disconnected.

Chapter 13

Overland Park, KS
April 4

Steve retrieved the money he'd hidden in the SUV console and stacked it inside a shoebox. After returning to the kitchen, he covered the box with wrapping paper and affixed a glued, pre-tied bow from Jen's gifting stash.

At four-thirty-five he glanced nervously at the clock. Jen would be home soon.

It demanded a celebration. He poured the last of his hoarded single malt scotch into a glass. The woody velvet of port barrel aged Balvenie rolled over his tongue.

Since his layoff, he drank bargain brand scotch and Jen had box wine. There was an upside—quality beverages they used to drink tasted so much better now.

For Jen he opened a 2001 Switchback Ridge Petite Sirah to let it breath. It was one of the last three bottles stowed in the basement for special occasions.

Today qualified—one way or another. He worried about how Jen would take his news. Also, there was her *need to talk*.

A hum sounded from the opening garage door. Steve poured a glass of wine for Jen and carried it to greet her. When the door opened, the look on Jen's face doused his cautiously festive mood. Her hazel flecked, blue-green eyes were red rimmed. Mascara streaked her blotchy face.

"What's wrong, honey?" He reached an arm out for her and she began crying into his chest. A glance over her shoulder didn't reveal any obvious damage to her Camry.

"What's not wrong? One of my ladies is in the hospital." Her voice quavered and broke.

"Oh no, that's terrible. What happened?" He held her and stroked her hair—careful to not spill wine down her back.

"She went home to pick up her things. Her husband was supposed to be at work. Before she finished he showed up drunk. Beat the hell out of her. He knocked out teeth, broke her nose, cheek, and wrist." Jen's words were punctuated by sniffles.

"I guess a restraining order doesn't count when she goes to where he lives."

"No, but he'll go to jail for assault and battery. The son-of-a-bitch left her unconscious and bleeding. Luckily, a neighbor heard shouting and saw the bastard leave. He found her and called 911."

She stepped out of his arms and retrieved a Kleenex to swab her eyes and nose.

Steve said, "I know it hurts. You've invested a lot in your ladies. Will this be another one you bring home?" They'd opened their home to a number of battered women over the years. It was a good place to hide them from abusers. The only time one tracked down his abused wife, Steve was home. The abusive husband's eyes grew wide and he beat a hasty retreat when all six foot three and two hundred and thirty pounds of Steve charged out. Apparently, smallish women were all the coward could handle.

Jen shook her head and reached for another Kleenex, tears still running. "No. She has a place to stay and family to help. Besides, we're not in any shape to take care of someone else."

"We can always help somehow. Why don't you go change and wash your face? I have some interesting news for you. Here's a glass of wine to take the edge off."

She took a taste and her eyebrows rose. After rolling it around in the glass and inhaling the bouquet, she admired the deep ruby color. "This is very nice. Is there a special occasion that I forgot?"

"Go change. Then we'll chat."

"Did you get a job?" she asked eagerly.

"I'm not talking until you wash your face, change, and drink half of that glass."

"OK." She drew out the word as if it had more than two syllables and cocked her head with a quizzical expression. "You've got me interested."

———

In the bathroom, Jen cringed at the ravages left from her sobbing. She scooped cold water onto her face. She and Steve needed to talk, but she needed to put a better face on it—literally.

As she lathered up a washcloth, she thought of her lunch conversation yesterday with Marge, a lawyer she met through the clinic and her wisest advisor.

"Steve's driving me crazy with all the nagging about money," Jen told Marge. "That and the need to find a job. He said we'll have to sell our house. The bank has threatened foreclosure. I'm trying to close my last few cases and I feel guilty taking that time away from my job search. I just want to rip his head off every time he digs at me."

"You married for better or for worse." Marge said. "This is definitely a worst. Try to put it in perspective with all the betters you've had together."

Jen brushed crumbs back and forth across the table cloth with her knife. "Yeah, we have had a lot of those."

"You're both under a lot of pressure. You feel guilty when you take time away from helping ladies at the shelter to look for a job, and vice versa. I'd guess you're blaming him for your feelings."

Jen flashed a moue and shrugged.

"He's always been Mr. Breadwinner," Marge continued. "He encouraged you to go back to school and finish your law degree. He supported your choice to work at the women's shelter. Your salary there is barely enough to pay for your nice suits, much less a decorating addiction."

Jen grimaced and tapped the knife rapidly. "Yeah, I know."

"Now he's not in control. Jen, he's a good guy. And not hard to look at. A lot of women our age would happily trip him and beat him to the floor. Try to discuss things with him, instead of growling back."

"Talk? That's his weakest area. He doesn't."

"Well, he's a man."

"Worse. He's an engineer."

"But you love him."

Jen looked up from the knife in her hand, shrugged, and nodded. Yes, they had to talk—without anger.

———

Jen smiled wryly at the memory as she applied a thin layer of makeup to cover the shadows below her eyes. She inspected her face in the mirror. It would have to do.

After taking another swallow to get the glass down to half-full, she returned to learn Steve's news.

He stood and refilled her glass. "Feeling better? How was the interview?"

She sat down and tucked bare feet under her thighs before she said, "Typical interview. They'll let me know in a couple of weeks. Pros—some of lawyers who do pro bono for the clinic recommended me. Marge is one of them. Cons—I don't have experience for most of the work they do. And, although they can't say it, I'm old to start learning." She gave him a wry smile. "Enough about me. What's going on?"

"Have some nourishment." He waved at the hors d'oeuvres plate. "And I'll tell you a story."

She smiled sadly and picked up a cracker. "I hope your story has a happy ending."

He told her about seeing the wreck, the van in the creek, and stopping to render aid. He described the lack of cell phone signal, the dead victim, and checking the vehicle for survivors.

"I hope no one else died."

"No one else was in the van, but I made a strange discovery in the back."

"What?" Jen asked. "Don't keep me in suspense."

He extended a wrapped package to her. "Look at this." She dropped the wrapping to the floor and lifted the top of the box. Her eyes locked on the contents. It couldn't be what it looked like. She reached in tentatively and pulled out a packet of money. A one hundred dollar bill was on top. She fanned the bills in the packet. They were all hundreds. She looked up at him. "What is this? One thousand dollars?"

He gestured emphatically with a cracker slathered with pate and a small pickle. "Actually, that packet is ten thousand. It has one hundred, one hundred dollar bills."

Her eyes widened and her heart rate picked up. What did this have to do with the wreck last night? She looked back into the box "*Get out.* How much is in here?"

"That box has ninety-five thousand."

"Where did it come *from*." She gasped. "Is the money ours?"

Steve raised a hand. "Can you hold your questions?" A grin stretched across his face. "I need to show you something in the attic. I could tell you, but you have to see it."

"The attic?" This is getting weird. Where did he get that much money? We're broke. Did he rob a bank? Or involved in drugs? Had the financial pressure finally taken its toll? She felt ready to explode, but she'd hang on to her questions like he asked—for a few minutes.

"Yes, that's where it is." He stood and headed to the stairs. Looking back he said "Come with me little girl," with the comical leer he used sometimes.

A small smile stretched her lips. If he was going to kill her he'd do in the basement where there are drains. She shook her head. Steve's sardonic humor had rubbed off on her.

She followed Steve to the upstairs closet where the folding attic stairs were down.

He went up ahead of her with a flashlight. When she reached the top, she took the hand he extended and sidled from the stairs to sheets of plywood laid out like stepping stones on the attic floor.

She looked around as he flashlight moved through the space and shivered. "It's really yucky up here. Look, there are spider webs, wasp nests, and dust. I hope the surprise is worth it." She treaded cautiously after him as he shined the light to guide her feet.

He pointed to the plywood. "I put these down today so we can walk up here. Watch your step. If you miss the boards you'll fall through the ceiling."

She stopped walking. Steve's hand tugged her forward. "Come on. I want you to see this, in case you need to do it, and I can't for whatever reason."

Shuffling along, she watched out for cobwebs. One tangled in her hair and she almost screamed. She brushed wildly at it. Steve placed a hand on her side to steady her until she ceased gyrating.

He shined the flashlight on the ceiling. The sloped roof with tarpaper was within her reach. A wasp nest clung to a roof beam. She shuddered.

He handed her the flashlight, reached into the dark, and then pulled his open palm toward her into the flashlight beam. "See this string? It's connected to something at the bottom of the false space in the bathroom below," Steve said.

She pulled her eyes and the flashlight from the wasp nest. Lying against his extended fingers was a string. She swung the shaft of light to follow the string to a loop tied around a nail sticking out of the same roof support as the nest. The other end disappeared below into the insulation.

He pulled the string up from the floor of the attic, hand over hand. A black plastic bag rose from below through the insulation. He set the bag down and untied the string. Spreading the top, he pointed in. "Look."

Jen pointed the light in and gasped. It was full of more money. "How much is that?"

"About $600,000."

"Holy shit!" Was he kidding or had he gone crazy?

He snorted. "That statement captures my feelings precisely." He tied and re-lowered the bag back into the space. "Let's go back downstairs." He took the flashlight back.

"And leave that money up here?" Maybe he *was* unhinged.

"Now you know how to get at it if you need it. It's an emergency stash. Let's go downstairs and talk."

A thousand questions raced across her mind. She cautioned herself to practice patience—not the easiest thing—before she blurted out something hurtful like *did he steal it*. It could be an inheritance, or from a lottery ticket. He'd always been honest and trustworthy.

Following him, she glanced back several times. The string wasn't visible in the dark attic when she looked back from the top of the stairway. They could use it now. Their current finances were an emergency.

Steve waited at the base of the steps with a hand extended to assist her. Back on the carpet, she brushed her arms, pants, and hair—making sure there were no cobwebs or spiders.

Chapter 14

Overland Park, KS
April 4

Jen perched on the edge of the couch seat, picked up her wine glass and rotated it as a way of steadying feelings clamoring for expression. She leaned forward waiting for the rest of Steve's story as he requested. Wanting to ask, but fearing what his answers would be.

He told her about discovering money in front of the van and even more in back, along with drugs. "The news this morning confirmed my suspicion of drugs." His gunmetal blue eyes looked at her steadily as if watching his information sink in. "I counted it this morning. There's over thirty million dollars."

A sense of unreality washed over her. The number was too big to comprehend. Even in daydreams of winning a sweepstakes, she'd never imagined that big.

"So what are your thoughts?" he asked. "This is a lot to dump on you. I'm coming to terms with the amount myself. And conscience and logic are still playing tug-o-war in my brain."

Jen stared at him and then looked in the shoebox again. Her mind felt anesthetized. He was right. It was wrenching. Both of them laid off, despair cresting. Now he's talking about lottery kind of money; big lottery money. Theirs for the taking, but it didn't feel right. She was numb. "There's thirty million in that bag upstairs?"

He smiled. "No, the boxes took up the whole back of the SUV; the money wouldn't fit in a single garbage bag. That's six hundred thousand upstairs."

She rubbed her face and forehead with both hands then shook her head. "Right, you said that. It's still sinking in. Have you got it squirreled away in other parts of the house or in your gun safe?"

Steve, like her father, was an avid hunter and had an expensive and diverse gun collection.

"No, I rented a storage facility nearby. The money is there. I kept back the two stashes I showed you, the shoebox, and the garbage bag. There's a lot more where I got that. How do you feel about me taking it?" He looked like a small boy afraid of her response.

Jen looked at Steve while trying to comprehend the ramification of his questions. "It's stolen money," she finally said. "Instead of taking it, you should have called the police."

Steve hung his head. "I know. Like I told you, I tried multiple times—even before I found the money." She saw anguish when his eyes rose to her. "The situation grew and I lost control. We need money so bad. First it was a box of cash in the front seat. Then boxes of money, then of drugs. I thought it was a few thousand, then a few hundred grand. I had no idea how much until today."

"I'm an officer of the court," she said. "I have to report it or I'll be an accessory."

"I want you to be my lawyer. Isn't there lawyer client privilege?" Steve asked. "Besides, you're my wife. Doesn't that mean you can't testify against me?"

"It's not about testifying. It's about doing the right thing."

"What *is* the right thing? It's drug money. It was on television today," Steve said. "Do we give it back to the cartel? If the police take it, what good will they do with it—if anything? Give it back to the druggies the cartel sold to?

"What should I do with it? As my lawyer, tell me—what will they do to me if I bring the money to them now? If I do, and my name gets out, what will the cartel do to me—us—our kids?"

She blew out a breath through pursed lips. Her foot bounced. They didn't cover this situation in law school. You've been told you have a fine legal mind, girl. Kick it into gear.

She focused until it felt like she'd herded her thoughts into a straight line. Steve remained silent for the two minutes she mulled.

"Now that you've done it, I don't think you should turn it over to the authorities" Jenny said. "If you had called them locus in quo, that's one thing, and was probably the right thing, but if you call them post facto, what will they do? The legal ramifications are interesting. Did you steal it? Would the owner press charges? Are there charges the police can issue against you? Would they consider charging you for leaving the scene of a fatal accident even if you weren't involved in the accident?"

She tapped the side of her jaw while she thought, her half-full wine glass ignored. "But if you report it, of course the IRS would want a large piece of it. Would someone else, like the Justice department, take it from you and, if they took it; would the IRS still want taxes from us? Deciding jurisdiction and who gets the money could generate massive legal fees and keep lawyers working for years. I'm speculating without any research, so take it with a grain of salt. But one thing is certain, we don't need more expenses because you found some money and took it while in shock over the dead person you found." She was playing with ways to form a defense.

She sat quietly, turning over thoughts, both legal and personal, in her mind. She appreciated that Steve waited patiently for her. Patience was one of his good qualities. "What do we do now…and is it dangerous?"

"Drug cartels play mean and dirty," Steve said. "We have to assume that they want to recover the money—by any means possible. That means it's dangerous."

"What do we do now? Can it be traced to you?"

Steve shook his head. "I don't think it can be traced. No one saw me. I wore gloves. The only place my prints may be is on the corpse. I took the gloves off to check his vitals. The ground was very rocky. There shouldn't be footprints. There could be tire tracks further away, but on TV, I saw them dragging the van out of the creek, which would wipe out a lot of tracks. I don't think they investigate a single vehicle accident as thoroughly as a robbery or murder." He looked pensive while he prepared another cracker. "I believe it may be the perfect crime."

He looked up to her, and then said, "In response to your first question I've been thinking, and I have several objectives." Steve held up his hand and began counting on his fingers.

Of course, he had a list.

"Get the money out of the country to somewhere safe where we can access it, hide the trail, provide for our families: the kids, our brothers, your Mom and Dad, and fund charities like the Abused Women's Clinic; but most of all, keep you safe."

She felt a chill. "Babe, I want you safe too." Worry tightened her chest.

"Jen, I'll be better able to protect myself if I know you're somewhere secure. So, let's work together to plan this out to meet all our objectives. We're a team."

"We are. That's why you aren't going to stash me somewhere, while you put yourself in danger." She said firmly.

"Honey if it gets dangerous, I'll have to take action. But my reactions will be slow if I'm concerned about your safety. I have experience and training, albeit long ago, that you don't. I can't be in a situation where my instinct to protect you might cause us both harm."

His obvious concern and practical arguments would be endearing if it didn't piss her off so much.

Jen felt anger rising and she consciously controlled it. "Let's table the discussion for now. I'm not prepared to discuss it after everything that has happened today." She held up her wine glass. "And while consuming beverages. Besides, you've had more time to think about it."

She smiled as her spirits rose and said, "But, I really, really want to see all the money. Can I see it huh, huh?"

Steve broke into the big smile that always captivated her and said, "It is kind of amazing when you think about it. All that money in what aren't that many boxes. I couldn't believe it when I figured out how much. You can help me load the other junk into storage and see the money then."

Her eyes narrowed. "What other junk?"

He held up hands as if to ward off her anger. "We have way too much stuff cluttering up the basement. I thought this would be a good chance to clean it up. I loaded the SUV today with clutter to take to storage tomorrow."

Her jaw jutted, as she demanded, "What are you taking?" He'd raised the issue of too much junk before in one of their many recent arguments. What was he doing without her guidance?

"Help me tomorrow and you'll see."

"OK. I have to protect my interests." He irritated her, but she did love him. Maybe if he wasn't always focusing on their money problems the anger that gnawed at her since their troubles started would go away.

They spent most of the night discussing options. Steve made it plain—he wanted her out of town, somewhere safe while he figured out what to do with the money. She knew she needed to stay with him and help. She'd be quietly persistent. Steve said it was like Chinese water torture; but whatever worked was fine with her.

She steered the discussion toward getting the money out of the country. They agreed on that. Oversight was too intense in the US. They discussed and planned until they fell asleep about 3 a.m.

Her last memory was of smiling at a joke he told about a genie, three wishes, and an ostrich.

Chapter 15

Grand Prairie, Texas
April 4

Juan rented a car after landing at Dallas-Ft. Worth airport, and was on his way to visit the cartel robbery scene.

He thumbed a number into his cell phone.

"Detective Richardson," a man answered."

"This is Inspector Juan Santiago with the DEA. I'm on my way to your drug related crime scene in Grand Prairie. What can you tell me so far?"

"You guys move fast," Richardson said. "I'm on site, still going over it. There aren't a lot of drugs. Normally, I wouldn't expect the DEA to get involved, but I have six dead bodies."

"It has the sounds of a cartel war. If it is, we want to get on top of it."

"Jeez, I sure hope not," Richardson said. "I have a witness that saw one man come out after a series of gunshots. Majority of the injuries are from a shotgun. One shooter sounds less like a war than a heist. He loaded a bunch of boxes into a van white van with dark windows."

"Did you get a description?"

"Hispanic. Big—tall and beefy. Wearing a long coat. He drove off minutes before our officers showed up."

"Just one witness?"

"Other witnesses reported seeing a similar van parked on the street the previous evening and yesterday morning."

"My GPS says I'm about fifteen minutes away," Juan said. "Will you still be there?"

"Not going anywhere soon."

While interviewing the next door neighbor, Juan received a call. The number was from his Detective Chief Inspector supervisor in the Los Angeles office.

"Juan here."

"What are you doing now?"

"Interviewing witnesses in Texas. There are signs that it could be a cartel war. Six bodies blown away at close range. Double ought buckshot."

"I wish they'd fight their battles in Mexico. Don't want US civilians in the crossfire," the chief inspector sighed. "We've got another incident in Kansas that needs a detective. You're closest if you can break away. The Texas job sounds more serious than I thought."

"What's in Kansas?"

"We got a post about a white van wrecked in a creek. The communication came because the van held a large amount of drugs and a little cash along with two pistols—one recently discharged."

"No shotgun?" Juan asked, disappointed to hear that there wasn't much money. Thirty million fell didn't fall into the "little" category.

"Not in the information I received."

"White van, huh? A white van was used here," Juan said. "Can you give me a number to call? I'll check it out."

His follow up call revealed that the dead driver was a large Hispanic male and the van had dark windows.

Juan hung up and booked a flight departing for Kansas City. He made arrangements to visit the morgue that evening. Upon arriving at the morgue and flashing his DEA credentials, he was taken to see the body.

"This is the big fella they pulled out of the van." An assistant coroner indicated a gurney.

Even in the body's recumbent position Juan could tell the man with the traditional Y-shaped incision on the chest had been large in life.

"It's a tossup whether the coronary or the broken neck killed him. Friend of yours?" The coroner asked Juan with a smirk.

Acquainted with coroner humor, Juan deadpanned, "I think so, but I've only seen pictures—and not high quality ones," Juan said. "I'll wait for a second opinion." The two men Esteban had promised, Hector and Edgar, would arrive in Kansas City that evening. "I've got two guys coming tomorrow who might be able to make a positive ID."

———

In the morgue Juan watched Edgar's face as a sheet was pulled back from the corpse. Edgar had been a member of Jorge Medina's security team. "Yeah, that's Paco Rojas," he said after gazing at the corpse for a moment. "I thought the *cabrón* was indestructible. It's weird he died in a car crash. Half the *policía* in Mexico tried and couldn't kill him. Everyone figured he'd die in a shootout. That guy is—was a legend."

"The end of a legend," Juan said, then smiled. "We have the chance to start our own legend if we find the money like Esteban asked."

Edgar grinned. "I'm in."

Juan met the sheriff in the hall outside. "The guns you recovered may have been used in a felony in Texas yesterday. This could be more than a simple single vehicle accident. I need ballistics tests fast. If you can't do it, I'll use DEA resources."

The sheriff looked affronted. "We'll get 'er done. I'll shoot for tomorrow,"

After the sheriff left, Juan asked Edgar, "Why would Paco be in Kansas?"

"I don't know, man." Edgar shook his head then his eyes narrowed. "Wait. I think he had family here. Somethin' about a restaurant. Y'know, the person who knowed him best was Carmen Rivera."

"Call her. Find out what she knows about his Kansas connection." Thirty minutes later, with the information Carmen provided, Juan's DEA analysts provided addresses for the restaurant and Estralita's home. They also provided him with the names of her husband and married sons.

———

Juan watched as Hector removed the apparatus and its probes from the old woman. She was slumped forward against the ropes securing her to the kitchen chair. The smell of scorched flesh made Juan nauseous.

It was strange, as if the woman wanted to die. Anyway, Hector accommodated her. Before she died, it became obvious she didn't know anything about her brother stealing from Esteban. Too bad, it seemed like a good lead.

Juan was proud of his technological prowess, but had to admit Hector knew his business. The gear appeared cobbled together, but it was very effective. Estralita screamed, cried, cursed, and even bit Hector when he ventured too close. Hector assured Juan that the equipment didn't kill her. "It's not for killin'. Specialists in this kind of stuff designed it to administer pain enough that you wish you could die, but everyone lived." He'd picked up the technique from CIA interrogators during his time at Bagram airbase in Iraq. "She died from something else, like her heart."

Juan didn't waste time waiting for the ballistics report. His instincts told him he was on the trail of the money. If ballistics placed Paco in Grand Prairie at the heist, it would only confirm his gut feeling. Over the years he'd learned to depend on instincts.

The coroner had set Paco's time of death at 10:30 p.m. It's possible he could have dumped the money somewhere between Texas and Kansas, but it wasn't likely. First, the timing would have been extremely tight. Second, if he drove into town to meet his sister, wouldn't he bring the money instead of hiding it somewhere between Kansas and Dallas? Third and most telling, when Juan inspected the van in the police impound yard, he'd noticed scratch marks on the floor of the van that were consistent with boxes dragged with glass underneath.

Some boxes of cocaine had embedded glass and lacerations on the bottom. How would glass get under the boxes in a wreck? The local yokel cops said they didn't pull anything out of the van.

Unfortunately, they had towed the van to the impound yard. The load could have shifted. Because of that, the floor scraping he saw in the van at the yard and the glass embedded in the bottom of the boxes wouldn't hold up as evidence in court. But for Esteban, he wasn't worried about the technicalities of the chain of evidence.

If Paco died between ten and eleven p.m. and the van was discovered at six a.m., it had been sitting at the edge of the creek long enough for someone to take its cargo. But, who? And how could he find them?

He demanded that the sheriff's department dust the van for fingerprints, but didn't expect positive results. When they thought it was a single vehicle wreck, they'd disregarded evidence cautions. He'd be surprised if anything turned up. His mouth curled in a sneer. Perhaps some of these hillbillies were snorting the evidence.

The information about a possible connection with a major cartel attack shook up the sheriff's department. Now they took the investigation seriously. But the newsflash happened too late for a clean investigation.

Juan interviewed the deputies who were working in the area on the night of the crash. When finished, he asked the sheriff, "What about others besides your officers?"

The sheriff gave him a blank look. "What others?"

Juan looked at him levelly. "Doesn't the area fall into other jurisdictions besides the county?"

"You mean like the surrounding cities?"

"Surrounding cities, Highway Patrol, Girl Scouts, National Guard, Jehovah's Witnesses—I don't know what other jurisdictions. That's why I'm asking *you*." Juan flashed him an irritated glance. The sheriff looked angry when he left to contact other agencies that might have information. Juan didn't care. He wasn't here to make friends.

———

Juan crouched on his haunches, picking up broken glass chunks on the rocky ground at the wreck site. Why would a rear window broken in a head-on collision with two large trees splatter fragments inside *and outside* the van?

The slap of footsteps on the concrete drain leading to the creek made him look up. A uniformed officer strode down the slope. "I'm Patrolman Ramacher, I understand you want to talk to me?"

Juan rose to his feet, craned his head up, and smiled, extending his hand. "Hello, officer. I'm Detective Investigator Santiago with the DEA."

Ramacher;s quizzical gaze swept the area. He had a much better view than Juan. At six-feet-eight inches he was a foot taller than Santiago.

"There was a wreck here last night," Juan explained. "The van contained drugs and money. I understand you patrol this section of highway. I'd like to know if you noticed anything around ten to eleven p.m."

"Hey, I'm Highway Patrol. The wreck was down in the creek." He pointed at the tree line where the now placid creek burbled softly. "It wasn't visible from the highway at night."

"I understand. What I'm looking for are any memories of a car or truck parked along the shoulder or off the shoulder nearby. Anything you recall from that night could be significant."

Ramacher looked at Santiago then up at the bridge, lips pursed. His head bobbed up and down slowly. "There was something. He pointed back toward the guard rail. "About 10:30-11, I drove by and saw a white SUV pulling onto the highway just about there."

"A white SUV? Any more details?"

"Yeah." Ramacher gave Santiago a shy look. "I'm a big KU basketball fan. I played there—a little—mostly warmed the bench and was practice fodder. But I still follow them. I have season tickets and go to all the games here and as many out of town as I can. The reason I remember the car was it had a rear UCLA license frame and front plate."

"UCLA?"

"Yeah, it stuck in my mind because UCLA was in the final four when KU won the NCAA title."

"Do you remember anything about the SUV—make, year?"

"It was one of those Toyotas or Lexus SUVs. Top of the line. You know, rugged but luxurious. Land Cruiser or LX-something. I don't remember the number. All the model years look similar. I can't tell you the year."

"It was pulling onto the highway near here?"

"Yes, I came over the hill and saw it in front of me. It was accelerating—pulling from the shoulder onto the road. As I approached it, I slowed down and swung into the other lane. I saw the UCLA license frame. When I pulled past I looked back and saw the front plate. It kept going so I did too."

"You saw it despite the headlights?"

"I saw it as I passed, before the headlights hid it."

"You don't see many UCLA license plates around here?"

"No way, this is KU country. We won the NCAA recently."

"Congratulations, that makes three titles. It'll only take eight more to catch UCLA."

Ramacher looked down at Juan with a frown. Juan gave him a toothy smile. "I graduated from UCLA."

Ramacher nodded—a sour look on his face. "Anything else you need from me?"

"No, your information is appreciated. I'll follow it up. Thank you."

————

As Ramacher toiled back up the slope, Edgar emerged from under the bridge. Juan asked, "Did you hear about the license plate and car make?"

"Toyota or Lexus SUV with a UCLA license plate? Yeah."

"All the tracks in the mud make it hard to tell what happened. More than one set of tire treads." He pointed to a set of prints slightly separate from the others. "These aren't as deep as a wrecker. They also appear wider than a police cruiser. An SUV would fit."

Edgar looked around, scrutinizing the ground. "You might be right."

"We need eyes on the street. Put word out to the local drug network. A $10,000 reward to anyone who identifies the driver of a Toyota or Lexus SUV with a UCLA rear plate holder or front license plate. You and Hector get busy."

"The dealers are coin operated. For that money, if it's here, they'll find it. Hell, I might find it."

Chapter 16

Overland Park. Kansas
April 5

When she woke up the next morning, Jen reminded herself that she hadn't convinced Steve he wanted her help—yet. Persistence usually worked. She wouldn't nag. That pissed him off and he dug in his heels. She'd pick her openings—nudge him now and then. Humor helped.

Her lips stretched into a smile as she realized the first thoughts this morning weren't about their financial issues. She looked at Steve's rumpled side of the bed and wondered if he felt the same sense of relief. They might have a new problem, but at least it was different.

Her nose wrinkled. She smelled cinnamon. Apple pancakes, one of Steve's specialties and her favorite. There'd better be some left.

She threw the covers off and swung her legs out of the bed.

Before she could stand, Steve walked in with a breakfast tray. "If the mountain won't come to the pancakes, then the pancakes will come to the mountain. Back under the covers."

The tray he placed on her lap had a four-pancake stack slathered in butter and maple syrup, two cups of coffee, and a glass of orange juice.

He rearranged his pillows, sat in bed next to her, and lifted the second cup of coffee off the tray.

"Aren't you going to have some?" she asked.

"I ate while waiting for you to wake up. I remembered the breakfast tray you used when the kids were sick. Don't know if it's been used since they left home. Enjoy." He raised his cup to her.

She cut a wedge out of the stack, swished it around in the syrup, and took a bite. The different consistencies layered together over her tongue. "Yum. Lots of apples. Did you use two again?"

"Yup. Lots of vanilla, apple slices mixed with cinnamon and folded into the batter, voilà. When you finish, the first thing on the agenda is the storage facility."

Jen nodded. "I need to check what else you plan to move out of here. Men have no concept of what things are important."

"That's true. If I decorated the house it wouldn't look as charming, but I'd be able to walk through the basement."

"This conversation is déjà vu, all over again."

"Thank you, Ms. Berra. My SUV is full of stuff from the basement. You can review it when we unload. If there is anything you desperately need to cram back into our cluttered basement, we can return it. No use arguing—it's already in the SUV. Besides, I thought you wanted to see the cash."

"Right. Can't worry about the small stuff. Let's get to the storage room. Imagine how much more I could buy for the house with that kind of dough." She clapped her hands and gave him a big grin. "We may need more storage rooms."

Steve rolled his eyes.

———

As he pulled the Land Cruiser out of the driveway, Steve said, "I want you to know I'm packing. There's a loaded pistol in the glove box, and my concealed carry permit is in my wallet."

"Isn't that a little drastic?"

"Honey, there's over thirty million dollars in storage. We have to assume it belonged to a drug cartel. No, I don't think it's drastic."

"You know weapons make me nervous."

"That's another reason I want to leave you somewhere safe—like with your parents—while I get the money out of the country. Your dad, brother, and I used to go hunting every year until your dad's emphysema made him stop. I still can't understand how his daughter developed a gun-phobia."

"It was all those school shootings. And I worried when the kids were in the house with your guns."

"They're all locked in the gun safes."

"OK, OK. Have you thought anymore about how to get the money out of the country?"

"Public transportation like airlines are out. Freight options have tightened up because of terrorist threats. You never know when they're going to open or X-ray your shipment," he said. "They weigh a half ton. Each box weighs fifty-three pounds."

"Fifty-three, not fifty. And they all weigh the same?" she asked with a cynical expression. "You weighed every one?"

"I weighed some on our scale. They all contain the same amount of paper."

She was pleased to see that he blushed as he answered her question.

"Have you put any more thought into where we should hide it?" Steve asked.

"When I've heard about money laundering, they mentioned places in the Caribbean as well as Switzerland, the Isle of Man, and Lichtenstein."

"With a boat, I could load it up and sail to a cash haven."

"Do you really mean sailing?" Jen asked. "I thought you didn't like sailboats."

"Yes, I mean sailing. Our boat was for lake sports—skiing, wakeboarding, and tubing with the kids. I think a sailboat would provide better cover. An old retired man cruising away the end of his life. Slalom skiing into Grand Cayman isn't low profile.

Smuggling makes me think of either offshore race boats or old rusty freighters. Sailboats don't fit the profile. Your thoughts?"

"You may be asking a leading question. But no, sailing and smuggling don't click. No way to run from the cops."

"OK counselor, another reason for sailing is because, for an equivalent size, sailboats are cheaper than power boats. There's plenty of money, but an oceangoing sailboat is still a large cash purchase. A lower total helps stay under the radar."

"But we don't know anything about sailing, except they're very tall, quiet, and careen a lot when the wind blows." She frowned, then grinned as she retrieved a memory from the boating safety lessons they took. "And they have the right-of-way."

Steve nodded and smiled at her. "There are places to take sailing lessons. I already have Coast Guard boating safety certification," Steve said.

"Excellent idea. But remember I also have safety certification. We can go to Florida for classes together, which will get us both out of town. Sounds like a plan."

He grinned at her. "Still working it aren't you?" Then his face sobered. "You're right, but I wish you'd get over your gun phobia. I hope to God it doesn't come to it, but if it does, you need to pull your weight if you're there to *help* me like you've said. If I have to use one, I can't be worried about your reaction."

She'd been listening to his arguments and realized this was a decision point. "You're right; I need to get over my gun thing."

Steve's head snapped back as if he'd been punched. "Holy crap! Did the earth move?"

Jen gave him a thin smile. "Comments like that could result in your having a gun permanently packed in your ass."

"That would make flatulence dangerous for everyone in the vicinity."

She chuckled against her will.

He slowed and turned into the storage unit driveway. When he stopped, he handed her a Post-it note. "We're here. This is the entrance code to the facility. Memorize it and then get rid of it."

"And if I don't, you'll have to kill me?"

"Use your imagination," Steve said with a somber expression. "What would the people who lost that money do to get it back? Then decide if you want to hang on to clues to its location."

A chill crawled up her spine.

Chapter 17

Johnson County, KS
April 5

The ballistics report confirmed Juan's suspicions. The bullets from the raid at the Texas safe house were fired by Paco's guns. He called Esteban. "I've got the information you wanted. Paco stole your money and drugs. The pistols in his van in Kansas killed your men in Texas."

"Who can I trust?" Juan held the phone away from his ear at Esteban's shout. "Paco started the organization with my father," Esteban continued in a moderated voice. "He practically raised me. He was with me when I made my first kill. I never would have suspected Paco. He's family."

"You can't always trust family."

A silent pause. "What do you mean?" Esteban's voice came in a whispered growl.

Juan remembered the rumors about Esteban's father's death and quickly changed the subject. "Our deal was I find who stole the money and you pay me. I found out it was Paco. You owe me three million."

"What about the other weapons, the shotguns?"

"They were part of Paco's MO. He must have dumped them. Even if I found them, forensics can't trace shot pellets to the weapon used."

Juan thought he could hear Esteban's brain grinding through the silence that echoed across the airwaves.

"You found Paco, but he's dead and the money is gone," Esteban said. "I want the money."

"I thought it was a matter of respect and the cash wasn't important to you. Three million is important to me."

"I want to punish those who took it," Esteban snarled, "We need to teach a lesson. Paco didn't have it with him. There must be somebody else. Paco couldn't have done it by himself. Find whoever has it—the one that helped Paco."

"I told you I can't do this for you and stay with the DEA. They're already asking why I'm working so hard on this incident. A few boxes of drugs, a couple of hundred thousand dollars, and a dead body they can't prosecute aren't important. The agency doesn't know about the rest of the money and wants to reassign me."

"Find who stole from me."

Juan's foot tapped. He wanted to throw the phone. "My bosses see it as an inter-cartel squabble, which makes it not their problem. I've done what you asked and you owe me. Everyone believes Paco pulled it off alone, even against six armed men. The legend of Paco continues to grow—and he's dead."

"Then where's my *dinero*? What about his sister? She lives near there, doesn't she?"

"She didn't know anything. I gave her to Hector. After he finished, I can guarantee she didn't know anything about the cash."

"Someone has it. I want you to find out who."

Esteban's repetition was getting irritating. "He could have an accomplice. Or, somebody took it from the wreck. Lots of possible trails. Following them will take time I can't spend. I'll have to resign if you push me to do this, and you'll lose my information on what the DEA is doing."

"I need this."

"There is one potential lead," Juan relented. "Edgar and Hector are trying to track down a car seen near Paco's wreck. They put out the word to your local drug network to find it. If anything surfaces, Edgar and Hector can track it down. But I have to get back to DEA work. The agency is running out of patience. I can't afford to retire, yet. I need this job."

"I'll put three million for finding out who did it, and another two in your account today—that's five million. When you find the money, I'll give you another million and you still keep half the cash you find."

Juan's internal cash register dinged. The extra two million would push his offshore account up to over nine-million dollars. He could walk away from the DEA with that. Then he would have time to look for the rest of the money. When he found it, he could retire like a king.

"OK. I'll turn in my notice as soon as the money is in my account."

Esteban hung up.

Now he *had* to find the SUV with the UCLA license plate.

Chapter 18

Overland Park. Kansas
April 5

Steve stopped next to a door in the three story building, got out and opened the SUV hatch.

"Why are you going into the office building? I thought you already rented the space over there." Jen asked from the passenger seat, and pointed at the row of roll up doors in the long one story building about forty feet away. "Why don't you park close to our storage unit?"

"Our storage unit is inside this climate controlled building," Steve said as he pulled the two-wheel hand truck out of his car. "Not only will it be pleasant inside, no matter the weather, there's a lot less traffic going by it."

Jen climbed out as Steve placed the first container from the basement on the two-wheel dolly. Out of the corner of his eye, he noted her scrutinizing the things still in the vehicle. "These plastic bins are Christmas decorations. We won't need them for over six months."

"Yeah. I see that." Jen looked from Steve's load to the stacks remaining in his car.

He piled three more on the cart and pulled it to the building. He paused in the doorway; "Come on," he said when Jen started to open another box in the vehicle.

"I'm trying to see what's here."

"I *need* your help."

Jen frowned but followed him in. After turning down a short corridor, Steve stopped in front of a roll up door, just like those on the storage units outside. He unlocked and pulled it up, and then wheeled his burden inside. Jen's eyes widened when she saw the file boxes stacked against the far wall.

"Yeah. That's what we're here for," Steve said.

"Wow. All that...."

Steve raised a finger to her lip, cutting her off before she said anything about the money. "Somebody needs to stay and stack these." He tapped the new containers. "And keep any nosy neighbors out," and raised his eyebrows. "Pretend that the walls have ears," Steve whispered.

"Oh... OK," Jen said—as if suddenly realizing the need for secrecy—whether or not she could see anyone around. Certain words like "cash" couldn't be said out loud.

Then he continued in a normal voice. "You want to unload the car or stack boxes?"

Jen nodded. "I'll stay here."

"OK. Leave at least three feet between those boxes and the new things, so we have access."

Steve left her planning the arrangement. He made four more trips to the car. Finishing the last delivery he suggested they pile it higher for privacy against snoops. After pulling the door down for privacy he lifted the last few up to the top of the stacks for her.

He leaned against the door and surveyed their handiwork. "Nice job. It looks like any other homeowner's excessive accumulation." She'd pitched right in. Maybe she would be a help.

————

With the door closed, Jen no longer had to rein in her curiosity. "Can I?" she said gesturing to the stacks at back of the room.

Steve gestured. "Go ahead, help yourself, dahlink. What's mine is yours."

He was funny and sweet. It reminded her of why they fell in love. Maybe they could get back to those feelings. But enough of that. She wanted to see what he had. She grabbed a box and peeled the top panels open.

It was full of twenties. She dug down and pulled out packets. They were all the same.

The next box had more.

"That end is all twenty dollar bills," Steve said. "Next to it are fifties, and against the wall on the right are the hundreds. I tried to keep it organized."

She cast a hooded eyelid glance at him. "Of course, you did," she said as she moved toward the wall.

Steve chuckled.

She froze after opening the next one. Hundred dollar bills in a layer across the top. More underneath. "Holy crap," she whispered, lifting out two handfuls.

Steve's arms slid around her waist from behind, and he drew her close. His breath tickled her neck. "It's nice to see you happy again. I'm glad I took it."

She leaned her head back on his chest. "I hate to admit it, but me too." When he nuzzled her neck she leaned forward, pulling away from him. Steve released his hold.

She replaced the packets in the box, tilted it toward the aisle, and the contents spilled out.

"What are you doing?" Steve yelped. "I spent hours counting, organizing, and stacking."

Jen knelt and spread the money around. She looked up with a sly smile. "I've always wanted to wallow in money. Join me?"

One corner of Steve's twisted up in a grin. "Hah." He lifted another box, poured it out, and dropped to his knees next to her in the piles of notes. "That's the best offer I've had in a couple of weeks."

"A couple of..."

His hands on her shoulders were warm. His smiling mouth moved toward hers. They came together gently as she parted her lips. His caressed hers with nibbling touches.

"Hmm," she moaned.

His lips pressed more insistently. Her teeth parted when his tongue ran across them, and her tongue rose to meet his.

After a moment she pushed him away, fell back, and wriggled seductively. "It feels lovely. How much is in a box?"

Steve's face was flushed. "About two million in hundreds. Two boxes would be four million." He smiled down on her.

She reached a hand up. "Haven't you always wanted to come into money? I have."

He leaned forward bracing his hands on either side of her shoulders and looked into her eyes. "Oh yeah."

When he lowered to rest elbows on either side of her, she reached up to his shoulders. They felt firmer and bigger. Perhaps working out was a good thing. She wondered what it did to his stamina. She pulled him down on top of her. She'd find out.

———

"Maybe you're right and we can do this together," Steve said as he pulled on his pants. "I could use someone to help sail the boat. It's not a short trip."

Jen flashed him an enigmatic smile as she fastened her bra.

Steve lifted the refilled box back into place, and turned to look at Jen who was placing spilled packets into the other. "There is a precondition," he said. "You have to learn to use a weapon."

"Oh, first sex and then preconditions." She chuckled, but her smile drooped as she looked into his eyes. "You're serious, aren't you?"

"Yes. If the cartel finds us, we have to protect ourselves. We can't to do it with candles and tchotchkes."

"OK, how do I become proficient?" she asked.

"I don't expect expertise, but you need to be able to point, shoot at a reasonably near target, load ammo, and put the safety on and off. You don't need to be a sharpshooter."

"Can you teach me? Dad says you're pretty good. Lord knows you and your buddies used to practice enough," Jen said.

"I'm probably not up to the standards of the Army rifle team anymore, but I can hold my own. Yeah, I can teach you."

Steve pulled a set of keys out of his pocket and held it out to her. "There are two locks. Here're your keys."

"I'm ready to work, boss, what's next?" Jen asked while staring at the stacks in the back of the room.

Steve reached for her hand and pulled her to the door. "Subservience from you concerns me. I feel like I'm being set up." He raised the door, looked both ways down the hall, and led her to the car.

"I defer to your weapons expertise. However, when you buy a boat, I'll take care of decorating it." Jen smiled and batted her eyelashes.

"You should have been a designer instead of a lawyer."

"Unfortunately, I went for the money instead," Jen said.

"Was that sarcasm?"

"I'd say irony," Jen climbed into the Land Cruiser.

"I never get that right." Steve started the car. "Alright, let's split up assignments. I'll look into boats and sailing schools. You research where to hide the money and how we cover our tracks."

"Aye, aye, Cap'n. Should we set up a business to move the dough through?"

"That's your call."

"OK. What will you be doing?"

"Besides investigating boat transportation, I need to schedule time for us at the target range. Get you a gun. We also need to be familiar with what the other is doing. I'm your backup and you're mine."

"You're becoming a real taskmaster."

Steve realized he was falling into old management habits. Driving toward a measurable objective was a good feeling after spinning his wheels all these months. "Yes, from now on this is our business. Forty hours plus a week. Whatever it takes for success. Maybe we should thank those bastards who laid us off for giving us this opportunity," Steve said with a chuckle.

"Nah. Fuck 'em still."

Chapter 19

Lenexa, Kansas
April 6

"Got a lead on the SUV," Juan said into his cellphone. "An office building. He used to park there all the time."

"*Used* to?" Esteban growled.

"His car hasn't been around for a while."

"Is that your idea of a lead?" Esteban asked. "How long?"

"Months," Juan winced when Esteban shouted the word back, and glanced across the Copa Room table at Edgar who must have heard it, too.

Edgar shoved a ravioli in his mouth and shrugged. "He used to work there. Somebody must know him."

"Someone in that building will know where he went," Juan said. "It's only one day since we put the word out and we already have a lead. That's fast."

"Money talks," Edgar mumbled around another ravioli.

"The reward is working," Juan said. It's got your drug pushers looking.

"Double it," Esteban said. "If that doesn't work in a couple of days—triple it."

"If I keep increasing it every few days, people might sit on information—waiting for the price to bid up."

"Do whatever you have to. Find that guy, or I'll find someone who can." Esteban disconnected.

Juan slowly put the phone down on the table to keep from slamming it. His jaw jutted but his lip trembled. He'd resigned from the DEA yesterday, and now Esteban threatened to pull out the rug from his financial security.

Edgar pointed his fork at the plate. "Try the ravioli Sinatra. Really good."

Juan had lost his appetite.

Chapter 20

Overland Park. Kansas
April 6

After returning from their storage unit, Steve researched charter operations, sailing schools, and sailboats that afternoon and evening. Following a short night, he was back at it again.

Boat charter companies were more interested in experience than certifications. They requested sailing résumés. He and Jen didn't have time to develop experience. However, a number of sailing schools also chartered boats to their students.

Before picking a school, he researched boat types. Catamarans were more stable than monohulls and almost unsinkable. The size that seemed most appropriate for what he had in mind—thirty-nine to forty-seven feet—could be crewed by two, included a backup engine for maneuvering, and was suitable for trans-Caribbean journeys.

Over a turkey sandwich the next day, he reviewed his research with Jen. "I've narrowed it to two schools in Florida that specialize in multi-hull sailboats thirty-eight feet or larger and equipped for ocean voyages."

"That's a big boat. We have plenty of cash, but won't a large purchase put us on someone's radar?" Jen asked.

"Yeah, US scrutiny worries me, but there are used boats for sale in Mexico, too. Oversight is less strict, and cash deals are easier."

Jen frowned. "How do we get the cash into Mexico?"

"We drive it in. I'm working on ways to hide it and cover stories for going into Mexico that will divert suspicion."

"Are you going to share?" Jen asked when Steve didn't continue.

"Let me work through it a little more. It's still sketchy," he said. "Let's focus on the sailing schools first. One school claims their week-long course qualifies a student team to charter, crew, and skipper one of their boats."

"Don't believe everything you read."

"I talked with one of their references this morning. He started their class with almost no boating experience at all. He and his wife now own a forty-two foot cat they've taken from Florida, through the Panama Canal to Acapulco and back."

Jen nodded, but looked a little skeptical.

"I'm checking with two other referrals the school provided and one that the first guy gave me. If they're as positive as the first, we'll go there. What have you found out about countries with 'less rigid' money reporting requirements?"

"Belize, Turks and Caicos, Dominican Republic, the Bahamas, Costa Rica, Antigua—any country in the Caribbean—except Mexico. In fact, every former English colony in the world has strong banking secrecy laws."

"Any preferences?" he asked.

"Not yet. Need more research. I'll put together a summary for late tomorrow or early the next day."

They worked until almost midnight. Steve collapsed into bed with a sigh shortly after Jen retired. "This is harder than working a real job," he said. "Jen?" A snorty snore was her response.

———

Checking references the next day convinced him the school could back up their claims. He wired a deposit for a customized, private, live-aboard course on a catamaran. He also reserved a charter boat for another week of sailing practice after they completed the course.

During his research, Steve found mentions of piracy off the coast of countries south of Mexico. A few of the boats he was interested in were in southern Mexico, not far from reported incidents—some of which included homicides. Depending upon weather, they could be blown south into dangerous waters off Belize, Guatemala, or Honduras. Taking weapons would be prudent.

There was another reason he wanted weapons. Paco Rojas's wallet, contained a scrap of paper with the name of a woman and a telephone number in Lawrence, Kansas. He'd kept it as a possible lead to identify Paco's next of kin. Maybe he'd even share some of the money with them.

But the news had reported a woman tortured to death in Lawrence. The woman's first name triggered his memory. He checked the name from the wallet. It was the same. The paper scrap didn't have a last name to check.

Paco couldn't have killed her. He was dead when she died. It happened the day after he found the money. Was it connected? He felt a chill.

He couldn't freak out. It had to be a coincidence. Surely there was more than one woman named Estralita—even in Lawrence. What could they do differently if it wasn't? He couldn't give the money back. He didn't know whose money it was, or even which cartel. He decided not to tell Jen. No point in worrying her. Besides, the remote chance that it *was* connected troubled Steve enough for both of them.

Because of piracy and the off-chance that someone violent was after them, the wise plan was to take guns. But, how could he import them into Mexico? Friends who'd hunted in Mexico had legally transported guns in country. He needed details.

"Señor you may only bring weapons into Mexico if you are hunting with a Mexican guide," an aide at the Mexican Consulate informed him. "The local hunting outfitter you contract with can provide you with the forms and requirements. It must specify the dates, location, type of game, and guns required."

"How many weapons per person and may we also bring handguns for protection against wolves or mountain lions?"

"Two rifles or shotguns, depending upon type of game you are licensed to hunt. You may not bring handguns into Mexico."

Mexico practiced Napoleonic law where you're guilty until proven innocent. Mexican jails weren't supposed to be pleasant. Smuggling cash was problematic enough. Rifles weren't good weapons for self-defense. Shotguns would have to suffice.

The next day Steve booked a hunting trip to bag the ocellated turkey. They were in luck that the hunting season was open. The bird, much more colorful than the any of the turkeys found in the States, was native to the Yucatan, near several of the boats he liked. In addition to giving them a reason to bring guns into Mexico, he'd find out if Jen could shoot live targets.

Later in the day, Steve took her to purchase a shotgun. "We'd like to look at twenty gauge autoloaders," he told the sales clerk.

"Automatics have reduced recoil because the energy is channeled into loading the shells," he told Jen. "That combined with the smaller cartridge, instead of a twelve or sixteen gauge results in less chance of hurting your shoulder."

"Aren't you sweet. Always thinking of me," Jen said. She tried several and settled on a Benelli Montefeltro Silver Shotgun. "It feels best in my hands," she told him. He wondered how much the rich looking walnut stock and the ornamented silver and gold colored receiver weighed in her decision.

Steve planned to take his Benelli Legacy Sport twelve gauge. If asked he would have admitted that he liked the look of its satin finish wooden stock.

When he got home he put turkey loads for both guns in his ammo carrier. Tomorrow and the next day he'd take Jen to the range.

———

After they returned from weapons shopping, Jen brought her notebook into the kitchen. A pen and a pencil were snugged in the bun she'd gathered her hair into. She laid the notebook on the granite island countertop where Steve worked on his laptop.

Jen filled her coffee cup and took a calming breath—she felt like she did when facing a jury. "OK, slave driver, here's what I have so far. The good news is that more than half the countries in the Caribbean are on the US State Department's list of Countries of Primary Concern or Countries of Concern—the two highest US money laundering classifications."

Steve had leaned back in his bar stool while she talked through her notes. He leaned forward and placed his hands on the countertop. "That's good news? What's the bad news?"

"Good because we have plenty of candidate countries and lots of organizations to choose from. That spreads scrutiny very thinly." Jen plucked the pencil from her hair and gestured with it. "The Cayman Islands have the highest density of banks. Home to branches of forty-seven of the world's top fifty financial institutions. There are close to six hundred registered in the Caymans with over two trillion dollars in assets."

Steve whistled. "Big business no matter what country it's in."

She gave Steve a crooked grin. "You can go with everything from Wells Fargo to the Bank of Louie the Weasel." She rested her hands on the island and leaned forward as if she was in front of a jury. "And, there is no shortage of companies I can use to set up cover businesses anywhere you want."

She patted her computer. "I've got all the information right here on my laptop."

Steve placed a hand on his and said, "All my data is here, too, and I backed it up to a flash drive. Here are two I got for you—a primary and a backup."

"You get the idea from the 'CIA for Dummies' book?"

He raised his eyebrows. "Matter of fact, I did."

"*Really*? They have one?"

"Sure, I read it cover to cover this morning."

"Sometimes I can't tell when you're smart and when you're full of shit."

Steve smiled "It's always good to consider both possibilities."

––––––––

The hectic week neared an end as they settled last minute items. The kids next door would watch the house and care for the yard. Steve bought a small enclosed trailer to haul the money, extra luggage, and guns to Florida.

Steve preferred to leave both dogs with Jen's parents in Oklahoma. Jen's dad, who raised Deerhounds, had given Bozo to Steve. Elf, the Papillion, was a leftover from the kids. Liz didn't take him when she went to college and try as he might; Steve had had no success in giving him back. He suspected Jen and Liz of plotting to prevent it.

He listened as Jen built her case. "We can't leave Elf with my folks. He's too little. He'd be the only small dog underfoot with all those giants. And we can't take Bozo on a boat ..."

"You're telling me? I'd hate to have to clean his mess, and I don't know if we could carry enough food."

"I've already talked to Dad about taking Bozo," she said "He wants to breed him to his new bitch. She's going into heat soon."

"Now you're playing dirty. I can't get in the way of the dog's love life. OK, we'll take Elf, but it he pees on any of my papers on the boat, I can deep six him."

"That's not funny," she said. "Don't be such an asshole. You know you love him."

"I said he could come. Don't beat a dead horse."

"Fine."

Caribbean Layoff

Chapter 21

Overland Park
April 10

Juan stood outside Applebee's with his cellphone.

"Did you double the reward like I told you?" Esteban bellowed.

Juan pulled the phone away from his ear then put it back. "Yes, three days ago." He peered into the restaurant.

Hector glanced up from the menu and raised his hands and eyebrows at the same time. Juan shook his head and turned away. It had been five days since the lead on the SUV with the UCLA license plate. All he had to report to Esteban were dead ends.

"Your way isn't working." Esteban snarled.

"Give me a few more days," Juan said. "The calls have doubled, so far nothing we can use but I expect something soon." Esteban was not a patient man. He didn't even wait for his father to retire—or at least that's what the rumors said.

"Call me tomorrow with good news," Esteban said.

Juan disconnected, cursed *"Chingadera,"* and resisted the impulse to throw his phone. Instead he hung it in the holster on his belt.

After stomping into the restaurant from the parking lot, he slumped into the booth. With a glare he dared Hector to say anything. Hector sat impassively, eyelids hooded over his black eyes.

Juan picked up his menu. "Where's Edgar? We were supposed to meet here a half-hour ago."

"He was meeting a pusher who is supposed to have news about the SUV." Hector shrugged. "Since you doubled the reward, we been getting lots of calls. Mostly false alarms, but we got to follow up."

Juan took a long swallow from his beer mug and set it down firmly. "Let's order. I'm done waiting." He snapped his fingers for the waitress.

As she arrived, Edgar walked up.

"We got tired of waiting for you," Juan said. "We're ordering."

Edgar smiled as he squeezed in next to Hector. "I think you'll be willing to wait on food while I tell you what I just found out."

"Give us a minute," Juan waved the waitress away. "He needs to look at the menu." His eyes narrowed when he looked at Edgar. "This better be good."

"Found out the SUV driver hasn't been around because he got laid off. But, one of our guys has a couple of clients who work there," Edgar winked. "He offered free samples for information. Now we have a name to go with the Land Cruiser."

Juan leaned forward. "What name?"

"Steve Henning. Still lives here in Overland Park."

"You have an address?"

"Yeah." Edgar smiled smugly. "About 10 miles away."

Juan waved his thumb toward the door. "Let's go pay him a visit."

"Can't it wait until I eat lunch? I've been tracking this lead all morning. Didn't have breakfast." Edgar looked pointedly at Juan and Hector's beers. "I need a beer, too."

Juan laughed. A weight had been lifted off his chest. "Sure, it can wait a half-hour. We need to stake it out and see what's happening. Good work, man."

Edgar looked up at Hector who nodded and shrugged with a smug look.

Chapter 22

Overland Park
April 10

A week after Steve found the money, he and Jen settled into the Land Cruiser. It was early morning. Cash, guns, ammo, dog food, and luggage were loaded into the small enclosed trailer towed behind. The dogs were in the back seat.

The family next door had copies of the house keys. Steve's story was that he and Jen were taking advantage of time off to tour the Eastern seaboard, starting in Boston and working south.

Jen rolled up her window. "Caribbean, here we come," she said with a smile. "I can't wait until we start our master mariner lessons."

"Master mariners might be a stretch," Steve replied.

"How about adequate aquanauts?"

"Aquanauts live underwater."

"Whatever," Jen said. "Don't mess with this pistol packin' mama. I'm a dangerous woman now."

Steve rolled his eyes. "A woman who doesn't know the difference between a shotgun and a pistol isn't all that dangerous."

"Just wait. Someday you'll fear me. I'm a weapons expert."

Steve smiled. He had taken her trap shooting twice and once to the pistol range. She broke fourteen of twenty-five clays in her last shotgun round—a good showing for a new shooter. The pistol range, however, was a challenge. Her accuracy was atrocious—and those targets weren't moving. He would have considered it a waste of time and ammunition, but the objective was to make her

more comfortable with weaponry. He prayed he hadn't created a
monster.

————

In the early afternoon Steve pulled into the quarter mile
gravel driveway leading to Bozo's romantic rendezvous.

At any time, Jen's mom and dad had three to ten dogs
including puppies. Right now they only had two bitches and a
dog.

When Steve and Jen drove up, the front door opened and the
two "house" dogs bounded down the steps, followed more slowly
by Molly and then Bob, Jen's parents.

Bozo had napped for most of the trip, spread like a hairy
comforter on the back seat. Elf's frantic barking at the giant
intruders woke him. Now he pressed his nose against the windows
as if eager to greet the dogs outside. Elf sat on Jen's lap growling
and trembling.

Captain, the male dog, stood with his front feet on the SUV
side windows, looking down at the passengers. Bozo, his tail
whipping dangerously, barked a greeting at his father.

Elf had spent the trip on Jen's lap. She gathered him and
greeted her parents with one armed hugs. Steve attached a leash to
Bozo before letting him out of the car. Like most sighthounds, if a
running cat or squirrel drew his attention, the race would be on.

Jen's mom held the collar of the older female. Bob called
Captain to heel. As befitted a dog with champion points in
obedience trials, Captain paced over and sat on Bob's left.

"While he's here will you work a similar miracle on Bozo?"
Steve asked Bob, pointing at Captain.

"I'll work on it, but don't forget Mimi, our new bitch," Bob
said. "The starting point in training is getting the dog's attention.
With Mimi in heat, his concentration will be elsewhere."

Once inside, Bob handed a beer to Steve and poured a glass of wine for Jen. "What's this I hear about your shotgun?" he asked as he handed the glass to her.

"Mom told on me? It's a really pretty gun."

"But can you shoot it?"

"If she keeps improving, we may enter her into competitions." Steve winked at Bob. "It must be genetic."

"This I've got to see."

"Her gun is in the trailer in the back of the SUV," Steve said. "Do you still have your clay pigeon thrower? She could give a demo."

Jen groaned and covered her eyes.

Bob nodded. "In the shed in back. Boxes of clay pigeons, too."

"How about it, Jen?" Steve said. "You've obviously been talking trash with Molly. Now you can put up."

The youngest of three and the only girl, Jen wasn't one to back down from a challenge. "OK, set it up and let me know when you're ready. Meanwhile, I'll help Mom." She turned away.

Twenty minutes later, Steve drove the four of them to an open field where he'd set up the trap thrower.

Bob and Molly oohed and aahed over Jen's new gun. Then Steve handed Jen a box of shells to load.

He started with slow throws and Jen nailed three of the first five. On the next five she hit three on the first shot and a fourth with her second shot.

Bob looked at Steve with raised eyebrows.

Jen went on to break five of the final ten on either the first or second shot and one with a third shot just before it hit the ground.

Bob got up from his seat on the SUV tailgate. "Great shooting, baby." He grabbed her in a big hug. "I'm proud of you, and your brothers will be envious." He turned to Steve and puffed out his chest. "You're right. I think it's probably genetic."

Molly looked to the sky and shook her head before putting her arm around Jen, who beamed with delight.

"Your best set yet," Steve said.

"But I had to shoot twice and even three times at some."

Molly gave her a kiss on the cheek. "I'll make sure your brothers know all about it."

They picked up the spent shells and climbed into the Land Cruiser. "Are you sure you can't stay a few days so your brothers can come over?" Molly asked. "Then you can lord it over them yourself."

"Mom, I'd love to, but we have an appointment we need to keep," Jen said.

"Is it about a job?"

Jen nodded. Steve knew she felt bad about lying to her parents. So did he, but they couldn't share their secret with anyone. Ben Franklin said, "Three can keep a secret, if two of them are dead."

"Well, that's a pretty good reason," Molly said. "I wish you the best of luck."

After dinner, Bob and Steve worked through another couple of beers. Bozo lay down with his head on Steve's foot.

"He sure seems to be your dog," Bob said.

Steve chuckled. "Man's best friend."

Steve and Jen woke up for an early start, and Bob helped Steve repack the car. "What does Jen think about your shooting?" he asked Steve. "Do you still consistently break twenty-five out of twenty-five?"

"I've never shot a full box of shells with her. It's about teaching her to shoot, not about me," Steve said. "She can't shoot a pistol worth beans, but she can really handle a shotgun."

Chapter 23

Overland Park
April 10

Juan, Hector, and Edgar staked out the Hennings' house. They moved their van to several different spots around the neighborhood. At one point, they parked next to a Neighborhood Watch sign. Edgar and Hector laughed at the words on the sign "All suspicious persons and activities are immediately reported to our police department."

"What's so funny about that?" Juan asked.

"I wanna see the look on the cop's face when they try to bust us and find out you're DEA," Hector said.

"My resignation takes effect in a week and a half. So don't count on it protecting you after that. Besides, I'd find it hard explaining why a house in Midwest suburbia is under surveillance. Keep a low profile, so I don't have to cover your asses."

"So Mr. Drug Enforcement Detective Inspector isn't so powerful after all," Edgar sneered.

"Why call attention to ourselves? Maybe I should let the police haul you in."

"Who would do your dirty work?" Hector asked. "You ain't gonna."

"Muscle is easy to come by. I'll call Esteban," Juan said.

"Seems like every time you talk to him, he's ready to replace you. Maybe calling him ain't a good idea. Muscle ain't the only thing that's swappable."

Juan frowned at Hector. Count on the asshole to remind him. Hector looked at Edgar with raised eyebrows. Juan ignored it. They were here to support him. Weren't they?

———

"Anything happen last night?" Juan asked when Hector picked him up at the hotel after his surveillance shift finished.

"Nada. Lights went on about when the sun went down and went off around bedtime. Didn't see anyone moving around."

"Did you try to look inside?" Juan asked.

"Without orders from our leader?" Hector managed to look aghast.

"Asshole."

Hector flashed a lopsided smile. "Yes, commander."

They stopped down the street from the Hennings' house in time to see Edgar walk around the side and disappear into the backyard. "What's he doing?" Juan asked. Hector shrugged.

A few minutes later, Edgar opened the front door and waved to them.

"Will he be court-martialed, commander?"

"Shithead," Juan said, got out of the car, and headed toward the house. "C'mon."

"House is empty," Edgar said as Juan walked in followed by Hector.

"Alright, spread out. See if you can find a computer, files, notes—anything. Just grab it. Don't worry about a mess. If you see anything you want, make sure it's not big enough to draw the neighbors' attention. We don't need to activate the neighborhood watch."

Hector laughed. "Damn, I need a new refrigerator. That looks like a nice one." He patted the top of it.

Edgar laughed. Juan shook his head and sighed.

Hector entered the room where Juan was going through a file cabinet. "I can't find a computer anywhere. I found a printer with one of those wireless thingies connected to it, but I can't find a computer."

Juan nodded. "Wi-fi router. They must have laptops. Look into all …"

"Who are you? What are you doing in here?"

Juan and Hector's heads snapped around toward the youthful voice. A teenage boy stood in the doorway, eyes wide and frightened.

Hector grabbed for the boy, but couldn't match teenage reflexes. He was out the door in a flash with Hector on his tail. "Hector, stop," Juan screamed. "Don't chase him. Stop."

Hector halted on the sidewalk just past the front porch and watched the boy run.

Juan hissed at him from the doorway. "Get back inside. Grab whatever you've found. Let's get out of here."

In three minutes, all three had hustled out of the house, piled into the van across the street, and pulled away. Juan clutched a pile of papers under his arm when he got in.

Edgar pointed at the house next door as they pulled away. "The kid went in there. That's him at the upstairs window."

Juan peered up at the house. "We'll have to change vehicles. I'll get a car and have someone dump this van. I found their credit card records. I'll put a trace on them."

Chapter 24

Ft. Lauderdale FL
April 12

After two long days on the road, Steve and Jen arrived in Ft. Lauderdale. The cerulean evening sky gave way to tall gray and white clouds hovering over the ocean. April in Florida was much nicer than Kansas. Familiar May flowers had bloomed at least a month early in southern Florida.

"Our hotel should be ahead on the right," Steve said.

"As soon as we check in, let's find a Cuban restaurant," Jen said. "I can already taste the tamales. If I start drooling let me know. I could eat a dozen washed down with red wine."

"Beer," Steve corrected.

"To each his own. You obviously don't appreciate the finer things in life."

"I married you."

"I stand corrected," Jen said with a small smile.

"First on the agenda is to get that trailer under cover." Steve gestured with a thumb at the trailer behind the SUV. "Storage is less than a mile away. We'll check in, drop the trailer, and then eat."

"Slave driver."

Steve parked under the canopy shading the hotel entrance. Jen climbed out with Elf and set him on the ground. With ears perked and tail plumed over his back, he eagerly surveyed his new domain.

Steve loaded luggage on the bellhop's rolling cart. Elf's kennel was balanced on top.

After checking in, they drove to their storage site. Steve backed the trailer into their unit, disconnected, and locked it inside. When he got back into the SUV, Jen's eyes had the same worried look as when they had dropped their oldest, Liz, at college two states away.

"It'll be OK here. The outside door is double locked and the trailer itself is locked," Steve said.

"Deserting thirty-million dollars in a strange town gnaws at my gut."

"Probably indigestion. Let's get dinner."

"We should check in with the Thompson kids to see if they have any questions," Jen said.

"This isn't the first time they've watched the house. Everything is fine and I'm hungry for Cuban food."

"Please. I'm hungry too, but it will only take a minute."

"OK." Steve stopped at the exit from the storage yard, dialed their next door neighbors, and then turned into the street.

Steve expected Jimmy or Jennifer to answer. Instead Andy, their father did.

"Hi Andy, this is Steve. Checking to see if your kids have any questions. Everything OK?"

"Thank God you called."

"What's wrong?" Steve asked, surprised at the anxiety in Andy's voice. He heard Jen gasp.

"Jimmy went into your house yesterday to water plants. There were men inside."

Steve pulled to the side of the road. "In our house? Who? Burglars? Is Jimmy OK?" He glanced at Jen, who stared at him with wide eyes.

"They broke in through the back door. The glass is shattered. Everything looks like it's still there. TV's and stereos are OK, and your gun safe in the basement is unopened."

"I don't care about that. Is Jimmy hurt?"

"He's fine. When he saw them, he ran. They chased him for a bit, but he got away and they stopped. There was a van parked across the street. They drove away in it. He took a picture with his cell phone and gave the license number to the police. He said that the robbers didn't have anything when they left except papers."

"Papers?"

"That's what he said."

"He must have surprised them right after they broke in," Steve said.

"I don't know. The place is pretty trashed. Files all over the floor. Trash cans dumped."

A chill ran up Steve's spine. He took a deep breath. "That doesn't sound too bad. I'm really glad Jimmy's OK."

"That's not all. Later, a man came to our house. Said he was DEA—looking for you." There was a query in Andy's statement.

"DEA? Did he have a badge?"

"Yes, but I didn't examine it closely. Do you think I should have?"

Steve held up his hand when Jen tried to ask a question. She glared at him.

"Did he say why he was looking for us?"

"No. He wouldn't tell me. He did ask if your car had a UCLA license plate on the front, and I told him it did. He asked where you were and when you would get back. I said what you told me—touring the East coast after your layoffs." There was that question in his voice again.

"Yeah, that's where we are now."

"He wanted to know how to contact you."

Steve's stomach dropped to his balls. "Do you want our telephone number in case he comes back?"

"No, I've got it, but didn't give it to him. I figured the DEA, with their resources, could find it themselves There's something else. Jimmy thinks the DEA guy was one of them who broke into your house. He had a suit on when he came here, but not when he was in your house."

Jen leaned closer to put her head next to Steve's phone.

"Jimmy said the other two guys were big and looked like gangbangers. White sleeveless shirts, tattoos. And the one who chased him had a long pony tail—like on TV. If they're DEA, they must be undercover."

"What was his name?"

"Juan Sandiego, Santana... something like that. He flashed it but I only looked at the picture and federal seal while it was open."

"Keep the kids out of the house. If the plants die, we can get new ones. "

"I'll go with them to make sure it's OK."

"Andy, it's not important. I don't want you hurt either."

After a pause, Andy said, "Steve, is there anything I should know?"

"I'm as much in the dark as you are. I'll let you know if I find out anything. Be safe." Steve disconnected and looked at Jen as she settled back into her seat. "How much did you hear?"

"Too much. Who the hell do you think is after us? If you hadn't stolen that damn money..."

Steve frowned and hung his head. "What's done is done. Why would the DEA be interested in us? I left all the drugs in the van." He scrubbed his face with both hands. "Could it be the cartel posing as cops? He flashed an ID, but Andy didn't examine it closely."

"They took papers." Jen said. "That worries me more."

"It could be information about our cars, credit cards, investments, or phones," Steve said. "But, if they were DEA they could get that info without breaking into the house."

"Right. They'd have a warrant and wouldn't need to break in."

Steve stared out the front window—not really seeing anything while thoughts tumbled. "Better stop using our phones. Take the batteries out. They can trace them through GPS. We can pay cash for unlocked world phones. Change the SIM cards for whatever country we end up in."

"Shit." Jen said. "We've been using credit cards—leaving a trail—when we have a trailer full of cash."

Steve smacked his forehead. "Yes. And hide the car. They asked about the UCLA license plate."

"If you'd gone to a good school, like USC, we wouldn't have this problem," Jen said with a wan smile.

"This is no time for our college rivalry," Steve said with a humorless sideways glance at her. He'd usually rise to the bait, but it wasn't important now.

"The car is parked in the hotel garage, on the bottom level," Jen said. "Let's leave it there, out of the public eye while we're in sailing school."

"Good idea. I'll remove the UCLA plate and throw it away, and get rid of the license frame on the back."

"Do you think they were DEA?" Jen asked.

Steve's sighed. "I'm worried they're not. Are you ready for dinner?"

"I've lost my appetite."

"Me too."

Chapter 25

Ft. Lauderdale
April 13

The next morning, as Steve and Jen boarded a taxi for the trip to the sailing school, he kept a nervous eye out for anyone paying conspicuous attention to them. He didn't detect anyone, but prickling in the back of his neck kept his head swiveling.

After paying cash for lessons, they carried luggage to what would be their floating classroom for a week. The Lagoon 450 catamaran was a boat Steve wanted if he could find one available.

Nerves calmed as he toured the boat. A spacious suite occupied most of one pontoon hull. It had a spacious cabin, a sofa and desk, a separate dressing room, and a bathroom with a shower.

The other hull had two cabins, each with its own bathroom. Steve and Jen would take the big cabin. They'd been told the instructors would occupy the other two

He saw that Jen, like him, was surprised at the saloon that spanned the two hulls. A few steps up from the sleeping accommodations, the living space was enormous compared to the few monohull sailboats they'd been on before.

Jen spun around in the galley taking in a 360 degree view of the Florida sun glinting off turquoise water. "Wow. This view sure beats a window over the kitchen sink looking out on the backyard." She ran a hand over the golden-hued teak cabinetry. "Steve, we're not in Kansas anymore."

"No, we're not, Dorothy. And if you click your ruby slippers and send us back, it will be grounds for divorce."

He'd settled on a catamaran instead of a monohull because cats had more space. Plus it was faster and smoother riding.

He sobered for a moment. They may be faster than a single-keel, but were much slower than the speedboats he'd heard that cartels used. Their best strategy was not to be found.

As they explored, their instructors came aboard. The well-tanned couple's names were Connie and Elyse. Connie, short for Conrad, was compactly built with close cropped blond hair and sea blue eyes. He looked at home on water, complete with a rolling gait. Elyse, a tall, slim, green-eyed brunette was immediately captivated by Elf. She crouched and extended a hand for an introductory sniff.

After Jen introduced them to Elf, Elyse picked him up. Elf tolerated it better than Steve expected. Although only seven unimpressive pounds, he had a mind of his own and preferred to explore on all fours.

Steve had cleared it for Elf to accompany them on the training trip, so he could adapt to sailing.

In a refresher class in the saloon, Jen and Steve recalled the basics from their boating safety certificates. From that, they jumped to learning the differences between sailing and motorboats. There were a lot.

Rigging and sheets referred to the ropes that now seemed to be everywhere.

Elyse covered the physics of sailing and how a boat could sail into the wind. "Tacking, beating, and jibbing—terms describing methods of maneuvering—result in the wind blowing from different directions across the boat. That means sails and booms move—often violently. Crew communication is the only thing that will eliminate accidents and injuries."

By the time they wrapped up for the day, Steve's head felt ready to explode. He wanted to fall into bed to prepare for another long day of lessons.

"Not so fast, Cap'n Bligh," Jen said when he collapsed on their bed. "We haven't had that Cuban dinner we talked about all day yesterday. Today is our last day in town. Screw the cartel. I'm hungry enough I could bite their heads off."

Steve dragged himself up. A taxi dropped them at a restaurant recommended by the hotel's concierge—a second generation Cuban immigrant.

They fell into bed with a load of tamales stretching the elastic in Steve's pajamas. Most of their luggage remained on the boat. A small duffel filled with cash also contained a change of clothes.

A few minutes after midnight, ringing from the phone on Jen's side of the bed startled them awake. She rubbed her eyes, looked at the phone, and turned to Steve.

"Answer it," he said with a shrug.

She picked it up in the middle of the fifth ring. "Hello?" Her eyes widened, and she looked at Steve. "It's your brother, Todd." She handed him the receiver.

Chapter 26

Ft. Lauderdale
April 13

Todd, Steve's younger brother, was the proverbial black sheep. Never able to hold a job for long, he launched into one get rich plan after another. Whenever anything went wrong, it was never Todd's fault. Someone else caused it—because they were assholes.

One of his schemes landed him in a California jail, where he spent two years, after good behavior, for distributing cocaine. Todd said it could have been worse. At least it wasn't an Alabama prison.

Todd did things with flair. No street corner hustling. His clientele were affluent, casual users who placed a premium on privacy. He divulged none of his clients' identities, not even for a plea bargain.

For all his faults, Todd's overriding good quality, besides his infectious humor, was loyalty to a fault. Steve often said that Todd would give the shirt off his back to a friend even if he had to steal it first.

When his parole allowed him to relocate, he moved to Miami for a fresh beginning. Several of his multi-coastal clients, thankful for his silence, provided him with customer referrals in Florida. Before long Todd was back in business on the Southeastern seaboard.

Steve assumed Todd was doing well because he stopped calling for cash. He even paid back some of the loans accumulated over the years. Steve had long since given up hope of ever seeing the money again.

The loans were always a source of friction with Jen, but Steve loved his baby brother and his similar sense of humor. When he could, Steve helped.

Todd blended well with his clientele. He was always well dressed. Thanks to their parents he was well spoken, having always been an avid reader. He could emulate a sophisticated demeanor although his regular humor ran to a more earthy tone.

That humor and urbane look served him well. He never lacked for friends, or for female companionship. Steve noticed, however, that Todd's female relationships were always short term in nature.

"Y'know my logistics expertise helped me through prison," Todd had said in a late night drinking and joke swapping session at Steve's home in Kansas.

"Logishtics expertise?" Steve slurred.

"Yeah, I get things."

"How's that work?"

"I've got a rep as a 'Go-To-Guy'. If someone needs something hard to find, or a difficult problem needs a solution on the QT, they call me," Todd said. "It's difficult to get a job with a felony rap sheet, but prison contacts have made my life better. S'funny how it works. They send you to prison and teach you job skills. But the important skills aren't on the official curlicue—criclun— curriculum."

Steve nodded sagely.

"I'm doing mush gooder than afore I went to prison. And I don't feel like I'm always working with a batch of assholes."

Steve laughed. "I thought you got through prishon on good looks and a big bottle of Vasheline. As far as people not being A-holes—did they change or did you change?"

Alcohol induced philosophy made Todd admit "prolly both." He lifted his glass to Steve. "Seriously, bro, if you ever need anything you don't know how to get, come to me. You've always been there for me. If *ever*." Todd belched and raised his empty glass again. "You are my number one guy—f'rever and ever."

A little embarrassed, even in his inebriated state, Steve assured Todd he'd come running to his number one Go-To-Guy.

Since then he'd steered clear of talking of prison, legal or illegal logistics or what Todd was up to. After the call to the Thompsons revealed the break in, Steve thought of the promise made in his cozy Kansas kitchen years ago. He called Todd and left a message.

Steve took the phone from Jen. "Hey Todd, thanks for calling back." Jen looked more puzzled.

"No prob, bro. Is this a Florida number?"

"Yep, Ft. Lauderdale. We're passing through. But we'll be back in two weeks and we'll get together then. I've got a favor to ask before then though."

"Steve, remember what I told you."

"I do, and thanks. This may sound strange and I don't want to go into details over the phone, but I want new identities for Jen and me. Passports, credit cards, etc. Not US. Caribbean, or Central America IDs."

"I can do that," Todd replied. "I know people. But, this is out of line from what I expect from my big brother. Are you in trouble?"

"Right now it's a precaution. I have the cash to cover it. I need to know if you have trustworthy contacts in Central America from who can get things?"

"What kind of things?"

"We're thinking of starting a business down there and could need help with legal aspects and maybe transferring capital. Plans are still tenuous."

"Got you covered big bubba."

"I may need help with other things—maybe guns and ammo." Steve listened to silence for a moment.

"A little out of my normal logistical purview, but…"

"You know people?" Steve said

Todd laughed. "You got it in one. For the credit cards, how big a balance do you need? Keep in mind if you lose the card, you lose the money."

"Two cards. $25,000 on each to start, and ATM access."

"$50,000?"

"Not enough?" Steve asked.

"You can have an elegant Caribbean vacation with that kind of dough. I'll need photos for the IDs. Do you have a digital camera?"

"Yes."

"Stand against a white or light background, a foot away so there aren't shadows showing behind you. Take the picture from six feet away. Include shoulders up. Leave room above the head for cropping."

"Got it. You've done this before?" Steve asked.

"Hm mm. Are you in a hurry? Can you email it?"

"No pressing life or death issues. I can email it."

"Good to hear—about the life or death," Todd chuckled, "Will you have the money when you get back? I have to front this and cash may run low."

"I'll throw cash in an envelope. Is one hundred thousand good for now?"

"It'll grease the machinery." Steve heard tension ease from Todd's voice. "One hundred Gs could be bulky."

"It'll be in hundred dollar bills. Can we meet somewhere tomorrow?" Steve asked.

"Unfortunately, I'm out of town handling business for a client. Won't be back until tomorrow late."

"I can ship it. To your PO Box?"

"Sounds good. To minimize the chance of X-rays spotting it, package it to resemble a book under X-rays."

"You have done this before," Steve said. "I'll send it priority mail."

"I look forward to your call when you get back to town. We need to catch up," Todd said.

"You bet. Love ya, man."

"Likewise."

Steve rolled over and handed the phone to Jen to hang up. Her raised eyebrows didn't surprise him. But it didn't bode well.

Steve smiled at Jen. "Good to hear from Todd."

Jen's voice started calmly. "New identities?" The volume went up a notch. "Contacts for guns and ammo?"

Steve winced. Her look reflected anger. Didn't take a rocket surgeon to figure that out.

"What the hell is going on, Steve?" came out in a hiss.

"The new identities are just a precaution," Steve placated with a raised hand. "We haven't been careful enough. Many expenses were cash, but the hotel on the road and here in Lauderdale are on credit cards."

Jen's angry glare softened into worry.

"We've left a wide trial. If the DEA was looking, with their resources, they'd be here by now." His head shook. "It doesn't mean someone isn't after us."

"Andy said the guy was DEA."

"Whoever it is may have connections," Steve said. "It would be best to vanish for a while. We'll be on the boat for two weeks. Let's become someone else, in a different hotel, when we return."

"Makes sense, but why Todd?"

"Arranging things is what he does. And I trust him. Others... you never know who will cheat or if it's a sting."

Jen nodded slowly, then a radiant smile spread across her face. "OK, let's go to sleep and wake up to a great sailing and learning holiday."

Steve leaned over. "Thanks, babe." He kissed her, got up, and reset the alarm for five-thirty. They had to get money and passport photos to Todd before leaving.

Chapter 27

Tulsa, Oklahoma
April 14

Edgar sat up and reached over the back of the front seat to smack Hector on the shoulder. "What the hell? See that sign? Says *Port of Catoosa*."

Hector, snoozing in the passenger seat, shook his head and looked out at scrub trees sprouting from flat land surrounding the Will Rogers turnpike. "What... where are we? Are we by the ocean?"

"No, man. We're in the middle of fucking Oklahoma, but that sign said Port of Catoosa," Edgar said. "These *cabrones* must smoke good shit. Maybe I didn't graduate high school, but I know there ain't any oceans in Oklahoma."

"It's part of the inland waterway," Juan said from the driver seat looking at Edgar in the rear view mirror. "You'll see a bridge in a while. The McClellan, something, navigation system. They dug a canal from here to the Mississippi. Shipping goes by barge. Don't do that in Mexico, do they?" Juan liked to demonstrate his knowledge to the two hulks that Esteban provided. They were intimidating—big and mean—so he needed to maintain an edge.

He let them know he was smarter—to overcome the feeling they could rip his arm off and beat him to death with it. They were a good team—his brains and their brawn—if he could maintain control. He'd barely kept Edgar from chasing that kid at Henning's. A dead or maimed kid wouldn't help his investigation.

Edgar was squeezed into the seat behind Juan. There was no way he could sit behind Hector who had his seat pushed all the way back and looked as if he needed more room.

"What do you mean they don't do it in Mexico, Mr. hot-shit DEA, college boy?" Edgar said. "I was born in the US, so I'm American, not Mexican."

Hector squirmed around in the front seat, making it creak. He pulled his baseball cap over his face and went to sleep.

Juan continued to be surprised at Hector's ability to sleep any time, any place. It must be military training.

"How do you know this Henning guy took the money?" Edgar asked.

"Local cops didn't investigate," Juan said. "Driver died of a heart attack, so they wrote it off as a single vehicle accident. Didn't track down the highway patrol trooper, like I did. He told me enough to use my street contacts to track the SUV. Standard Operating Procedure—SOP."

"Your contacts? Me and Hector put out the word on the SUV with UCLA plates. *Our* guys, not your guys found where he used to park. *Our* guys got information from their client in the building. You couldn't have done shit without us Mr. SOP."

"My DEA resources traced their credit cards to a gas station and a hotel on the way here." Juan looked at Edgar in the mirror. "I found out the wife's parents live in Tulsa. You laughed when I stole paperwork from the house, but it's leading us right to them."

"We didn't need fancy computers to find Henning," Edgar said.

"It took over a week for you to track them to the house," Juan said. "In only a few days, we're on their trail in Oklahoma,"

"OK, but you're not DEA now. What are you gonna be able to do?"

Juan leaned his head to the side to see Edgar in the mirror, but he'd laid his head back with closed eyes. Juan shrugged, wondering about that question himself, and kept driving.

———

Bob smiled. After Jen and Steve left, Molly peppered him with questions and finally said she wanted to try shooting. He was tempted to remind her he'd suggested it many years ago, but age had taught him the discretion part of valor.

Besides, Molly did things when she was good and ready. If he pushed, she dug in.

They'd gone to the shooting field for the first time yesterday. She broke two clay pigeons out of twenty-five, but at least she hit something. It was enough to make her want to try again today.

He'd taught dozens of people to shoot. There was a den full of trophies that spoke to his own prowess. But, did she take his advice? Begrudgingly.

She broke six today after he suggested she swing the shotgun to track the clay instead of just pointing and pulling the trigger. The results delighted her.

After they finished, she rubbed a shoulder when she thought he wasn't looking. Even though she used his twenty gauge automatic for reduced recoil, a box of shells two days in a row was more than enough.

He shot yesterday and again today with his Franchi twelve gauge over-and-under competition gun. He still had it, he thought with a smile. Twenty out of twenty-five.

"Why don't you see to the dogs while I get the shotguns?" he asked Molly.

"What should I do with the boys?"

Bozo had attacked Captain yesterday, forgetting he wasn't the alpha male in this house. Captain put him in his place. They'd both lost hair and blood, but nothing requiring a vet. They were housed in separate pens now instead of roaming free.

"Bring them up when they're done eating," Bob said. "Bozo lost his head over the new girlfriend, but they've been apart today. He shouldn't be so protective of her now. Put the training collar on him. I don't want to put my hand between them if they go at it again."

When Molly left, Bob retrieving the shotguns and shells from the back of the Jeep. He started to take them downstairs to the gun safe and then thought better of it. Molly was a bulldog when she started something new. They'd probably use them again tomorrow.

He propped the guns next to the chifforobe where they hung their coats and put the shells on the top shelf.

Molly came in trailed by Captain and Bozo. The dogs behaved as if nothing had happened yesterday. She handed Bob the training collar remote control.

"Why don't we order pizza?" Molly asked.

"Perfect. There's a game on tonight. Pizza, beer, and basketball. Game starts at eight."

Molly went to the kitchen to call in the order.

———

Juan drove past the house. Hector whistled. "That is one long-ass gravel driveway. They'll hear us coming for five minutes. I only see the top floor of the house from here. You sure this is the right place?"

"Address on the mailbox is right, and this is the only house on this stretch of road," Juan said.

At a cross street, a half mile away, Juan turned the car around.

"Are we gonna do this now or come back after dark?" Edgar asked. "I'm hungry."

"Let's get something to eat." Juan said. "We'll come back later. Then Hector can persuade them to tell us where the money is."

Hector chuckled and nodded. "My pleasure."

———

Bob stared between his feet at the television. He debated whether to snooze in his easy chair or watch the game. His eyelids would probably decide for him.

The floor creaked when Molly moved around in her upstairs sewing room.

The front porch light was on for the pizza delivery driver, so Bob watched the game—at least until food arrived.

Bozo's head popped up from where he laid, front legs crossed, in front of the fireplace. He stared, sphinxlike, toward the front door. Molly hollered, "Bob, there's a car at the end of our drive by the road."

"Must be a new pizza guy. Can't figure out directions. Do I need to pay him or did you pay with a credit card?"

"They pulled in and the lights shut off. The car is just sitting there."

"Sitting there? Lights off, hmm." He pushed out of the recliner, trying to look nonchalant as he went to the kitchen and opened the chifforobe. He pulled out a box of shells.

"What are you doing?" Molly asked when she walked into the kitchen.

"It's probably somebody who's lost. No sense in worrying."

"So you're going to shoot a lost person?"

Bob chuckled and shook his head as he loaded his shotgun. "This is a precaution. Millers got broken into a few months ago."

Molly breathed a heavy sigh of exasperation and walked toward the family room. She stopped in the doorway. "I saw a shadow move on the porch."

Bob grabbed her shotgun, loaded it, and shoved it toward her. "Take this. Safety's on."

She looked at it, then up at him before she took it. He nodded toward the back door with eyes narrowed then turned to the family room.

It was dark except for the lights from the television, the kitchen, and the front porch. He flicked off the kitchen light. "Stay low," he whispered. He eased out into the family room, eyes flicking across the porch windows, to the front door, and back to the side door where the light was off.

Bozo was on his feet looking at the side door, his head cocked to the side. He crouched low on his front legs, but his low grumbling belied playful intent. Bob saw a shadow move outside the side door. He swiveled in that direction.

The door exploded inward with a crunch, pieces of door and jamb spraying toward him. He flicked off the safety. The shadow moved forward—Bob shot from the hip. Pellets peppered the doorway. The shadow leapt backwards.

Molly's gun boomed in the living room.

Bozo unleashed a roaring bark, the force of it raising his front feet from the ground. The rest of the dogs joined in. Captain sprang to Bob's side, ears cocked forward.

"*Cabron*! They got guns!" Following that shout, muzzle flashes lit up outside, brilliant against the dark background.

Bob fired at the flares of light. Captain sprang up on his hind legs, barking to match Bozo.

"Shit. There's a pack of dogs—giant ones." Feet scrabbled off the porch followed by the receding sound of rapid crunching on gravel.

Bob loaded more shells. He stepped to the side of the doorway and peered around it. Two figures lumbered away up the driveway. Bob glanced right and left before he stepped out and brought the gun to his shoulder. Something slammed into the side of his thigh and his knee buckled.

Bozo's shoulder had hit Bob's leg as he dashed through the door He continued barking at the fleeing men as he raced after them.

A deerhound at full speed is beautiful to see, but not when it is running straight at you, barking ferociously.

One man disappeared over the crown of the roadway. The other turned at the top and shot at the pursuing hound. After the second shot, Bozo's forelegs collapsed, he tumbled head over heels, and skidded to a stop at the man's feet.

The shooter turned and ran to the top of the hill. Bob shot. The man kept running and vanished over the peak. "Damn target loads," Bob growled about the small shotgun pellets and ran after the man.

"Where are you going?" Molly shouted through the door.

"Those bastards shot Bozo. I'm going to shoot them."

"Oh, my God. Be careful."

He reached the crown of the hill. His chest heaved as he tried to suck in air. He fired his last two rounds at the car pulling away. Tires sprayed gravel as the men slammed swinging doors.

Bob dropped to his knees next to Bozo panting so hard he thought his heart would stop. Bozo lay with head twisted, mouth open, and tongue hanging in the gravel.

Bob didn't need to place a hand on Bozo's shoulder to know the hound was dead—but he did. "Good dog. Thank you."

———

"We need to go back and kill those fuckers. They shot at us," Edgar fumed. "I got pellets in my ass."

"Why the hell are you complaining?" Hector shouted from the backseat. "I'm the one sitting in broken glass and I might have pellets in my shoulder, too That bastard shot out the window."

Juan pulled out his phone as soon as he swerved the car onto the asphalt road. "I need another car. This one is shot up... the back window blown out. I need it soon as possible. Need a medic, too. You know where we're staying. Yes, I need this car taken care of... you can pick it up there." He disconnected.

"Are we going back?" Edgar asked.

Juan held up his cell phone and pressed the screen to answer an incoming call. "Hello, this is Juan... more credit card info... OK, let's have it. Uh huh... uh huh... Arkansas, Tennessee, Alabama. Thanks." He disconnected again.

"No, we're not going back. I have a DEA flag on their records. They've used their credit cards and are heading east," Juan said. "We're going after them as soon as we change cars. We know where her parents are if we need them."

"I need to get these pellets out of my butt," Edgar groaned.

Chapter 28

Ft. Lauderdale
April 15

Steve crawled out of bed when the alarm sounded. After getting dressed, he positioned Jen next to a white wall as Todd had instructed. She pointed out it was *off*-white, closer to cream. "Thank you for the decorating clarification. Let's see how this works before we repaint the hotel wall." He took several photos of her.

Jen took a turn behind the camera. "Sit on a chair. I don't want to take a picture up your nostrils. The flash will make light come out of your ears." When Steve grimaced she said "C'mon, that's supposed to make you smile."

He copied the images onto his computer which Jen selected as most flattering and emailed them to Todd for their passports.

The storage unit was the next stop on their early morning agenda. Inside with the door closed, Jen grabbed ten packages of one hundred dollar bills. Steve cut the side from a cardboard box and laid plastic wrap on it.

On top of the wrap he placed money in three rows of two packets each. He distributed the rest of the bills evenly to keep the stacks level.

"What are you doing?"

"Todd said to make it look like a book. The stacks are pressed together with no gaps in case of an X-ray."

"That's big for a book," Jen said.

"Ten inches by twelve," Steve said. "Coffee table books are around this size."

Jen cocked her head and studied the slab of money before she nodded. "OK."

After pulling the plastic wrap snug over the packets, he sliced through the cardboard underneath until it was a quarter of an inch larger than the stacks. He used a pocket knife with a mother-of-pearl handle and a three-and-a-half inch long razor sharp blade. Unlike Steve's other knives, it didn't have a practical clip to fasten it to the edge of a pocket, so it fell to the bottom. Since he carried knives in his rear pocket, he had to fish it out from under his wallet. He suffered through that irritation because it was the only knife Jen had ever given him.

When finished, he bound the cash between two pieces of card board with tape. "Now we're ready for priority mail," Steve said. "Remember, if it fits, it ships."

"You've been watching too much TV."

They were in luck. The post office had a medium shipping box. Soon, the package containing one hundred thousand dollars was on its way to Todd's P.O. Box. Steve didn't purchase extra insurance.

"He'll get it in two days, "Steve said.

"Let's hope it doesn't get lost," Jen said—signing air quotes at the word "lost".

Steve looked at her sharply. She smiled.

"My brother will take care of us..." Steve said, "*If* you don't piss him off."

Jen looked abashed and nodded.

By eight-thirty they arrived at the sailing school by cab. They'd left the SUV concealed in the hotel's basement and took a cab. Steve's last task before leaving was to remove the UCLA front license plate and rear bracket.

Already aboard, Connie and Elyse appeared eager to get under way, which irritated Steve. He'd been scrambling for the last two hours to get things ready for Todd. For the last two nights a dream that something large and evil chased him had disturbed his sleep. He didn't feel cheerful. What he wanted was a nap and a cup of coffee.

By the time he finished three cups of coffee and the substantial breakfast Elyse prepared, Steve's tension had receded. He relaxed into the gentle thrum of a diesel engine pushing a yacht past them through the channel. Golden Florida sun sparkled off rippling blue water flowing up and away from the passing boat's prow.

After walking Steve and Jen through a boat checkout, Connie invited Steve to move them away from the dock. The much greater width of the catamaran, compared to waterski boats he was used to was daunting, but he managed without scratching the paint.

Before Steve could puff up with pride, Connie had him spin the boat around in the channel and back it into the dock. It wasn't smooth, but the dual engines allowed him to do it without damage.

Then Jen took control and performed the same maneuvers. She did almost as well as he had. Experience driving their ski boat onto and off the trailer helped.

Steve silently patted himself on the back for not coaching her. Maybe he could learn that tact thing.

The lesson continued for the rest of the day as the boat cruised toward the Florida Keys. Steve and Jen alternated conning and other seafaring tasks, including anchoring several times, until they felt comfortable.

"You're handling this like an old sea dog," Jen said to Steve.

"I guess that would make you the sea biotch," he replied with a smile.

She frowned and held up two fingers. "I'll give you two chances." She folded her index finger down leaving the middle standing alone. "You used up one, now there's one left."

The lessons moved into the galley. Steve and Jen helped Elyse whip up their first hot dinner at sea. Lunch had been sandwiches on the run. Everyone sat to a dinner of Crab Alfredo over linguini, a fresh Caesar salad, and toasted garlic bread matched with a crisp and fruity Sauvignon Blanc. "We've been pushing hard to fit in the manual sailing lessons," Elyse said. "Once you learn those, it'll go easier."

"I'm exhausted, but this has been so much fun," Jen said when she plopped into bed beside Steve.

"Me too, but I feel like we can do this."

———

The next day Jen and Steve weighed anchor under the teachers' watchful eyes. Jen took the con first. During the day she and Steve kept after each other to use the proper nautical terminology and techniques. When Jen called "Prepare for a turn to the left," the others booed her. She felt her face heat up as she said "Make that a turn to port".

Connie had Jen set the boat on a broad reach, sailing perpendicular to the wind across the open ocean. "Now we can go inside for the lunch Elyse made."

"Sit and enjoy the grouper that swam too near the boat this morning," Elyse said. "Can't get much fresher than this. One of the many joys of sailing."

Connie pointed starboard. "Flying fish."

They followed his finger to see two fish floating through the air before plunging back into the ocean.

"Rare this far north," Connie said. "It's a good omen for your sailing careers."

"Are flying fish good luck?" Jen asked.

"Different legends around the world," Connie said. "They're well regarded in Barbados where it's the national fish. Their numbers are dwindling because of ecology changes. Rare and beautiful. Seeing them on your second day is a good sign."

Jen checked on Elf before resuming lessons. Elyse came along, appearing smitten with the little clown.

"I'll be glad to take him around the boat on a leash while you work with Connie and Steve," Elyse offered. "I heard Steve has a dog too. What kind?"

"Bozo—a Scottish deerhound—always in the way."

"He named it Bozo?"

"I named him after Steve. They're both big and loveable."

Elyse chuckled.

Jen handed her the leash and watched Elf prance away—ears and tail raised high while surveying the boat he would be commanding.

Chapter 29

Ft. Lauderdale
April 15

"Here's the last place they used their credit card," Juan said as he pulled into the hotel parking lot. "Look for a white Toyota Land Cruiser."

Hector and Edgar peered at the parked cars as Juan drove the aisles. "Not here," Hector said as they completed a loop through the lot.

"Two white SUVs but no Toyota," Edgar agreed.

Juan parked in a handicapped space near the entrance and donned his suit coat after getting out. "I'll see what charm and an official looking Federal ID can discover."

Hector rolled his eyes.

"Did Esteban send you charm to go with that fake investigator badge?" Edgar asked.

Juan winked at them. "We'll see."

He straightened his tie before he walked to the main desk.

"How may I help you?" the twenty-something clerk asked.

Juan pulled a wallet out of his jacket and flipped it open to display his ID. "Juan Santiago, Treasury department investigator. Our records show that Steve and Jennifer Henning checked into this hotel. Are they still guests here?" He flashed a smile at her as he shut his wallet on the badge Esteban had provided to replace the one he gave back to the DEA.

The clerk's eyes widened. "Oh. I ahh…"

"Federal government business. The IRS would appreciate your cooperation," Juan said and then flashed a brilliant white smile that gleamed against his olive complexion. "We'll keep this between the two of us. The Hennings don't need to know you told me."

"Hemings?" the clerk asked.

"H E N N I N G," Juan said.

The clerk nervously scanned the empty lobby before keying information into the terminal. "Yes, their reservation is for the rest of the week."

Juan raised his eyebrows. "Room number?"

"Four-thirty-one," the clerk said—again scanning the lobby.

"Please keep this to yourself. And your government thanks you." He smiled again.

———

Five minutes later, Juan and Edgar were outside the Hennings' room.

"You sure you can do this?" Juan asked.

Edgar snorted and turned to block Juan's view of the door handle. "Professional secret." After a few clicks the door swung open. Edgar stepped away and swept his arm for Juan to proceed.

It took two minutes to determine that the room wasn't occupied. Not even a toothbrush remained.

"They may have reservations, but they're not staying here," Edgar said.

Juan frowned. Esteban would cut him loose if he didn't show progress. It had been clear in his exit interview that The DEA would not be a fallback option. "You've lost focus from what was a promising career," his boss told him. "Fixating on incidental investigations, like the cartel squabble in Texas, is counterproductive. Private investigation may be a better fit Good luck in future endeavors."

"I don't need a phony badge to figure they aren't here," Edgar said snapping Juan back to the present. "What's next? No more credit card info from your old job."

A knock sounded. Edgar looked through the peephole and opened the door. Hector walked in. "I found the SUV. It's parked in the basement."

"Basement? This place has a basement?" Juan said.

"A small one. There's a white Land Cruiser. No UCLA logos, but it has Kansas plates."

Juan exhaled in relief. "Let's go see it."

Hector led them to the basement entrance at the back of the hotel. It served as a delivery dock and had four parking spaces. A white Toyota was the only vehicle.

Edgar produced a slim-jim lock pick and opened the passenger door in a few seconds. He opened the glove box, rummaged through, and produced an insurance card. "Henning," he said holding the card up.

Juan smiled as he called Esteban. "Found their SUV, but they aren't here. It's well hidden, so I know they'll be back. I need a radio tracking system—ASAP." He listened for a moment before he disconnected and smiled at Edgar and Hector. "We'll plant it on this car in the morning. Good work." He felt tension slide away.

Hector nodded. "They'll lead us right to the money."

Chapter 30

Florida Keys
April 16

After sailing lessons along the Florida Keys within sight of land, they turned toward the Bahamas across the open ocean. The weather remained vivid, and the ocean shaded from turquoise to a deeper shade of blue, sometimes tinged with gray.

Sailing differed greatly from the powerboat with which Steve was familiar. Instead of the steady drone of the engine, water sizzled under the hull, masts and rigging creaked, and sails popped.

No one had to shout to be heard. Steve imagined he could hear the sunlight glinting from the wave tops.

They cruised past pelicans resting on the surface or diving for fish. Gulls floated on V-shaped wings near the mast, looking for handouts and squealing in disappointment when no food appeared. If Connie hadn't been pushing them so hard, the day would have been idyllic.

After several overnight stays in the Bahamas, the boat turned back to Ft. Lauderdale. Cell phone coverage returned when they sailed to within sight of the Keys. The hard work of sailing had pushed Steve's worries aside. Now he needed to plan their next steps.

"I reserved a storage unit large enough for the car," he told Jen when they were alone. "It's not where the trailer is stored."

"Too bad there wasn't room at the same place," Jen said.

"I did it on purpose. Someone knows about the SUV. If it's discovered, I don't want the money nearby."

Jen's face crumpled with worry. "Oh, I didn't think of that. This week has been so great and we've been so busy. I've tried to forget."

"Me too," Steve said. "Out here we've been in a different world. But we're sailing back to reality. We need to get back on our game."

Jen nodded.

"I found sailboats in our price range along the Mexican gulf coast," he said. "Others are in Belize, Guatemala, and Honduras, but I don't want to go there if we don't have to."

"What *is* our price range?"

"From four-hundred, fifty thousand to seven-hundred—cash," Steve said. "No lengthy negotiation—a quick transaction and then back on the bounding main."

"Good idea. Let's get back to where there're no worries."

"I wouldn't say that. We haven't had any bad weather yet," Steve said. "No pirates either."

"In the Caribbean? That's so Disneyland. The pirates all moved to the Arabian Sea."

Chapter 31

Ft. Lauderdale
April 19

Steve and Todd communicated sporadically via email as the boat sailed in and out of cell phone coverage. "Todd received the money and photos and has two sources pulling together three sets of IDs for us," Steve told Jen. "He'll have at least one set when we land in Ft. Lauderdale."

The Central American contacts were coming along more slowly. But, Steve wasn't concerned. Todd wrote, "It takes time to find reliable and trustworthy crooks."

Nearing the harbor, Steve called Todd and left a message. Within three minutes Todd called back. "Hello, bro. I didn't recognize the phone number. It's not the hotel or your cell."

"Our old phones are at the bottom of the ocean. We got new unlocked smart phones," Steve said. "They're water resistant."

"Good idea for someone sailing."

"That's why I'm the brains in the family."

"No, that would be Jen." Even over the scratchy cell phone connection Steve detected the sarcasm in Todd's voice. "I have one set of IDs for each of you—passport, credit card, and driver's license. You will be Scott Hansen. That name gives you the excuse for speaking Spanish poorly. It also keeps the initials the same if you have monogrammed crap—or buy any. It also matches your nickname, Shit Head. I'll leave them in an envelope at your hotel."

"Nice of you to remember, Turd Head." Steve said. Those nicknames dredge up good memories. "Can you join us for dinner this evening with our instructors? My treat."

"You know my weakness—free dinner. Where?"

"Make reservations for six at a good Cuban restaurant," Steve said. "Call me back with the name and address so I can tell our teachers. Can you pick us up at our hotel?"

"Six?"

"C'mon, Todd. Getting a date on short notice is never a problem for you."

"When you said six I didn't know if you arranged a spare for me, or if I had to bring my own."

Steve laughed aloud. "Like you used to find spares for me before Jen and I met? I never had your gift of gab or flair for identifying likely candidates. If I forgot to say it back then, thanks for the great times."

Next Steve made reservations at a different hotel under the new name Todd provided. It was close to the storage facility for the SUV.

He returned to crewing the boat as it neared their dock. Jen steered it through the harbor, then signaled to Steve. "Will you back it into the dock?" she asked. He was glad to. It was the only area where he exceeded Jen's competence that didn't require strength, excellent balance, or long wingspan.

Elyse volunteered to drive them to their hotel. Jen and Elf got into the front seat with Elyse after Steve folded into the rear seat of her small SUV. Elf kept jumping back and forth between Jen and Elyse's laps—tongue flicking excitedly. Steve was thankful when they arrived at the hotel safely.

Elyse dropped them in the hotel basement where they'd left the SUV. "We'll check out of here and move into a new hotel," Steve told Jen as Elyse pulled away. "Will you put Elf in the SUV while I pay the bill?"

There was a manila envelope from Todd at the front desk when he closed their account. Jen had finished loading by the time he returned. "We'll head to the new hotel, check in and dump this stuff," he told Jen. "While you get cleaned up, I'll move the SUV into storage. It's close, so I'll walk back."

"If our room has a bathtub, I'm going to soak."

"Don't fall asleep. Todd will pick us up at six p.m. for dinner."

"Do we need emergency cash before you put the car away?"

"You mean for shopping in the Keys?" Steve asked. "The three-hundred thousand in our luggage should cover us."

Chapter 32

Ft. Lauderdale
April 19

Hector slumped in an uncomfortable hotel room chair in front of a laptop. The app on the screen monitored the tracking device they'd planted on the Toyota SUV. Edgar napped. Hector felt close to napping, too. Two days had passed since they'd installed the tracking device and the car hadn't moved. Juan had Edgar check the hotel this morning. The SUV was still there under a thickening layer of dust.

Juan was out doing whatever he did after Esteban chewed on his butt. Hector hadn't overheard the conversation, but he'd learned to recognize the expression Juan wore when he'd left an hour ago—somewhere between rage and despair.

———

Juan's anger still boiled as he nursed his second beer at the end of the bar. What the hell did Esteban expect? Juan had tracked the money to Florida. Not many people would have gotten this far in the investigation, this fast—and despite losing his DEA resources.

He admitted Esteban's resources were amazing. Juan asked for a tracking system. No requisition forms in duplicate. No three level management reviews. The tracking system showed up the same night.

Now Esteban alternated accusations of Juan wasting time tracking a wild goose and losing the only lead they had. And threats continued—constant reminders he could cut Juan loose with nothing—and worse.

Yes, he'd reached a dead end with Paco's sister. Juan snorted a brief laugh at the irony of that statement—it had been her dead ending. But investigations often hinged on the smallest clue, dogged follow-ups, and good instincts. He'd been the one to find and question the highway patrol officer no one else thought of. That break through—finding out about the white SUV with UCLA plates—put him on the right path.

Now they were in Ft. Lauderdale with a tracking device on the SUV. And Esteban called him incompetent.

He flagged the barkeep and ordered another beer.

Chapter 33

Ft. Lauderdale
April 19

Hector opened the door to the adjoining hotel room. "It's your turn," he told Edgar.

"Crap," Edgar said as he levered himself off the bed. "I haven't started and I'm already bored." Days of constant monitoring was the most mind-numbing assignment Edgar ever had—worse than his time with the Army in Iraq watching prisoners.

"Yeah, Juan leaves us with this crap job while he goes out to 'beat the bush'—whatever the fuck that means," Hector said as he flopped onto the other bed.

Edgar moved into the room with the unchanging laptop. Juan had caught him playing solitaire instead of watching the tracking screen and threatened to send him back to Esteban. No computer games had been played since.

After a quick glance at the computer, Edgar grabbed a comic book and lay on the bed. He occasionally glanced over at the screen. After a half hour of surveillance his eyelids drooped. Maybe he'd drifted off, but the next time he glimpsed the display his eyes widened. The location of the tracking icon had changed by several miles! He jumped off the bed.

He pulled out his phone and called.

"Santiago here."

"Juan, this is Edgar. The SUV moved."

"Meet me outside. I'll be there in a few minutes."

Edgar woke Hector. Ten minutes later Juan pulled up in the gray Ford. Hector climbed into the back. Edgar and the tracking laptop settled into the front seat.

"Where are they now?" Juan asked.

"Between Colee Hammock and Seven Isles. Near the harbor entrance," Edgar said. "It was stopped for almost five minutes, but it moved again."

"Let's find them. Give me directions," Juan said.

In fifteen minutes they cruised in front of a storage yard. No other traffic moved on the street. A tall, athletic-looking older man striding down the block glanced at them as they passed.

"Are you sure the signal is coming from here?" Juan asked when they stopped.

Edgar looked at Juan with narrowed eyes. "When we were on the street ahead it was pointing north. On the next street over it pointed east." He gestured behind with a ham sized fist. "Back there it was south." Another gesture at the storage yard, "Now it points west—*there*. I don't see an 'X' on the map that says treasure buried here but all the signs say the car's inside."

"OK," Juan said. "Let's wait for the SUV to come out." He slouched down behind the steering wheel and leaned against the door.

Hector grunted. "Hurry up and wait. Like the army."

"It shouldn't be long," Juan said. "What they're doing makes sense. Hide the money in a storage facility and stock up when needed. When they come out, we follow them. With the right technology—that I got—it's simple. Hector can do his magic when we corner them and find out which unit the money is in."

"Why don't we go in and get them?" Edgar asked.

"We don't know enough yet. They may be in their car. I don't want a car chase."

Edgar turned to Hector in the back seat. "Stick close and learn, muscle head."

Hector sneered. "My technology is simple. It made that wrinkled crone sing like a diva until she couldn't sing no more."

Chapter 34

Ft. Lauderdale
April 19

Steve checked into the new hotel as Scott Hansen, the identity Todd had left. When his new credit card was swiped and accepted, the tension across his neck and shoulders loosened.

He carried luggage into their first floor hotel room for Jen to unpack, then drove to the new storage facility.

An older lady was locking the office door when he arrived. "Hello, I'm Scott Hanson," Steve said. "I registered online for a storage space."

"Oh yes, I have your paperwork inside," she said as she reopened the door. "I was closing for the evening. But checking you in will be quick."

Steve pulled the money out of his wallet. "I've got cash for the first six months, and I'd like to buy one of those," he said motioning to a display of heavy duty locks.

She showed him the location of his unit on a map. "And here's the gate code," she said as she wrote it on the map before handing it to him. In less than three minutes Steve walked out with his paperwork and the lock.

After backing the Land Cruiser into the unit, he locked the rolling overhead door. Every place else he'd used had been double locked. Maybe he needed another lock.

As he walked toward the exit he stopped next to the office. It was dark inside. It hadn't taken her long to vacate the premises. He decided he could do without another lock. The SUV's doors were locked.

He punched the code numbers into the pad on the rolling gate. Before it had fully opened, he strode out and turned right.

He was halfway down the block when a steel gray Taurus passed him. It stopped across the street from the reclosed gate. The face of the one in the front passenger seat had been illuminated in the deepening dusk by a laptop. The guy was Hispanic and big. Not the sort of person Steve would associate with a bland Taurus.

Steve shook his head. He didn't want to think of himself as a bigot. There must be lots of Cubans who drive Fords and own laptops. Or maybe Honduras is a hotbed of high technology.

At the corner, he crossed the street and looked back. Three men were still in the car—the glow of the laptop still visible at a distance. He shrugged as his walk carried them out of sight, but worry gnawed at his gut.

Chapter 35

Ft. Lauderdale
April 19

Juan, Edgar, and Hector remained in the car for over an hour. A small car with a lone female driver pulled in through the gated entrance and exited fifteen minutes later. The tracking signal remained stationary.

Juan reassessed. Didn't look like the SUV was coming out soon. "Maybe they're staying inside the unit. Hector, stay here and keep watch. Edgar and I will go to a hardware store. If the vehicle doesn't come out, we'll go in."

They returned an hour later. Edgar relieved Hector on lookout while Juan and Hector returned to their hotel.

They rejoined Edgar after midnight. Juan drove next to the fence. Hector stood on the car's roof and placed blankets from the hotel onto the barbed wire topping the fence and climbed over. Edgar handed him the computer and lifted a ladder over the fence. Then Juan and Edgar followed Hector over.

"Open the laptop," Juan told Hector once inside.

They crept from shadow to shadow using the signal to triangulate on the unit that held the SUV. When they had determined the correct unit, Juan took the computer and handed Hector a three-foot crowbar. "Break the lock if Edgar can't cut it."

Edgar could barely dent the lock with the large bolt cutters he'd brought. Hector strained with the pry bar and the hasp screws gave way so suddenly he lost his grip on it. The clang when the bar bounced on the concrete shattered the silence. The sound echoed from the surrounding buildings.

They froze, but all Juan heard was the continuing rumble from the highway not far away.

Juan pushed the rolling door up. His flashlight revealed the SUV. He hurried into the storage room followed by the others. He looked under the SUV.

"Nothing here," Edgar said from where he stood at the back wall peering through the rear hatch of the SUV.

"Damn!" Juan hissed. He tried the SUV door. Locked. "Break the window," he said to Hector. "Don't drop it this time."

Hector hit the window with the pointed end of the bar and broke a hole large enough for his arm to reach in to unlock it.

The sound of breaking glass had made Juan frown. "Can't you be quiet?"

Hector gave him a disgusted look, opened the door, and looked in the front and back seats. Edgar opened the back hatch and searched there.

"Who's in there? Come out or I'll call the police," a man outside shouted.

There wasn't any money in the car. "Let's go," Juan whispered. He snatched everything from the glovebox, including the owner's manual, and ran with Edgar and Hector.

As they ran toward the ladder propped against the fence, the custodian chased after them. "Stop, stop."

Edgar pulled his pistol and fired. The bullet ricocheted off corrugated metal siding. The custodian dove for protection between buildings.

Good thing Edgar missed. Unnecessary corpses only made the job harder. He and the boys scaled the ladder, left it behind, and raced off in the Taurus.

A mile away at a stop light Juan hammered on the steering wheel. "How in the fuck did they get past us? Where are those *cabrones* now?"

Damn. Only bad news to report to Esteban in the morning.

Chapter 36

Ft. Lauderdale
April 19

Jen caught herself observing Dani, the gorgeous Latina who accompanied Todd when he picked up Steve and Jen for dinner. She resembled Steve's description of the women to whom Todd gravitated—light in the head and heavy in the chest. However, she followed the conversations and asked good questions. Perhaps Dani, short for Daniela, wasn't as lightheaded as the rest. "He'd better watch out for this one," she whispered to Steve. "She may be smart enough to snag him."

Steve shrugged and smiled.

"But if she's smart she won't," Jen added.

Steve frowned at her comment.

Todd and Dani were a handsome couple, each tall and slim with dark curly hair. Todd's cobalt blue eyes contrasted with Dani's deep brown with gold flecks. He wore clothes with a casual elegance Steve couldn't match.

Jen glanced at Steve. He looked better in a suit and tie—or naked. She smiled. The tension of finding a way to move the money out of the US should be harming their marriage. But working in concert had brought them back together at a time when she had been contemplating divorce.

Todd's choice of restaurant, with a priceless view of the Intercostal Waterway, was perfect for their one evening in town. Running lights from a succession of passing yachts reflected off the rippling water as they cruised by.

The waitress placed a mojito in front of Jen and she savored a first sip. Todd had ordered them for everyone. Of course, he wasn't paying. She knew she should stop belittling Todd—he was Steve's only family—but old habits were hard to break.

She still needed to call Mom and Dad and thank them for the nice visit and taking care of Bozo. She'd call them after dinner and give her new phone number.

"Your plan to get back out to sea for another week's practice is excellent," Connie said. "You guys should be able to handle most situations in the Caribbean."

"Just most?" Steve asked. "What should we avoid?"

"Storms. But the hurricane season is a few months away. Watch the weather forecast and run away from any storms."

"Be prepared for the bad times, so you can survive to enjoy the good times," Steve said. "That saying of yours is burned into my brain, Connie."

"A good rule to live by," Todd said. "What about pirates in the Caribbean? Not the Johnny Depp kind. More like the Somali kind. Should my sharpshooter brother travel armed and dangerous?"

"You're planning a trip toward Cancun around the northern tip of Cuba," Connie said. "No known problems there. However, there are piracy reports from further south—Belize, Honduras, and Panama. A means of self-defense isn't a bad idea. Gun control laws are tricky, however."

Steve nodded.

"What's this about being a sharpshooter?" Connie asked.

"Steve was a green beret sniper in Vietnam. They wanted him on the army sharpshooter team," Todd said. "He's still pretty good. What's the farthest you ever shot a man?"

Steve frowned. Jen felt his muscles tense in anger. He rarely discussed Vietnam and never sniping.

"My best prairie dog shot was laser measured at 730 yards two years ago," Steve said—anger obvious in his glare at Todd.

Todd looked at his plate. "Well, what was the longest antelope kill?"

"Four hundred fifty yards," Steve said and wrinkled his brow. "I shouldn't have fired. There's a ninety-nine percent probability of a kill when I stalk within three hundred yards. I don't want to wound an animal and leave it suffering in the wild. It was poor judgment, but this shot was in perfect conditions, game had been scarce, and we were preparing to leave."

"It made good chili," Jen said.

"Do you still break one hundred out of one hundred clays when you shoot trap?" Todd said, choosing wisely to avoid sniper questions.

Jen's eyes widened, and she looked at Steve with new admiration. She'd experienced how difficult that kind of accuracy was.

"No. Once I only hit ninety-four." Steve looked abashed.

"How'd you place?" Todd asked.

"I won. It was a very windy day." Steve smiled and changed the subject. "Jen has started with shotguns. The last time out she hit eighteen out of twenty-five clays."

Jen's face warmed with embarrassment. "Yeah, but I had to shoot two and three times to break some of them."

Todd said. "That's as well as I do, and the shooting guru taught me," Todd said with a nod at Steve. "Jen, that's better than most guys."

"Just call me Annie Oakley," Jen said.

"Let's call it an evening," Steve said. "We have to get up early. I want to clear the harbor before traffic heats up."

"Steve, are you sure I can't take you to the boat in the a.m.?" Todd asked before he dropped Jen and Steve at their hotel.

"Thanks, but we'll grab a cab. We plan on being there by 6:30, long before you wake up."

"Good, but I had to ask," Todd said with a smile.

"We're on our own tomorrow," Steve said to Jen when they got to their room. "Connie and Elyse won't be there for us. Nervous?"

"I'm not feeling much of anything after those mojitos," Jen slurred as she collapsed on the bed. She'd call her parents tomorrow.

Chapter 37

Mexico City
April 20

Esteban's rage boiled. "You lost Henning and the money?" Tendons in his hand creaked from squeezing the telephone receiver so hard.

"He moved the car," Juan said. "But was gone by the time we tracked it down. He *will* be back."

"What makes you so sure?"

"It's in storage. Why go to the trouble when he could just park it and walk away?" Juan said.

Esteban's hand relaxed. That's why he used the old time thick plastic telephone—harder to break in anger. "Is the car your only lead?" He listened to silence. "*Well?*"

"It's the best lead," Juan said.

"Because it's your only lead."

"I don't have government resources anymore."

Esteban detected a whine in Juan's voice.

"I do," Esteban said. He paused for Juan's response. "You think you were the only mole on my payroll?" Esteban said when Juan remained silent.

"Use your resources to find me everything you can about the Hennings' families." Juan said. "I know where her parents are. I need more—brothers, sisters, his parents, grandparents, whatever you can find."

"What good will that do?"

"I won't know until I have the information. I'll find something—a clue, a soft spot. The first thing they did was go to her family. I need to know what family he has."

"I gave you Hector to use on soft spots," Esteban said. "Like Paco's sister."

"Get me information, and I'll get your money."

"Not just the money. I want the thief."

"And Henning."

Esteban hung up. He smiled. Juan kept making progress. Esteban just needed to keep pushing him. If Juan didn't succeed, his other spy was working to make sure that if the hunt for the DEA mole continued, Juan would take the fall.

Chapter 38

Ft. Lauderdale
April 20

Steve and Jen flipped a coin to see who took the con first. Jen won, or lost, depending upon point of view. She didn't relish guiding the boat out of the harbor with a hangover, but at least she didn't have to handle the sheets. Despite her throbbing head, the boat glided smoothly out of the dock and motored through the Seventeenth Street drawbridge before it closed to accommodate morning rush hour traffic.

Steve managed the sheets and Jen turned off the diesels. Wind filled the sails with a loud pop and they began the five-hundred-fifty mile trip to Cancun.

Steve joined Jen where she stood behind the ship's wheel on the fly bridge. He slouched onto the couch that ran the width of the upper bridge and propped his long legs on the forward rail.

"Cancun, here we come," Jen said.

"We have the boat for a week, so we'll get as close as we can in three days before turning back."

"I want to sail there on our first trip, so we can say we did," Jen said.

"We might, depending on the wind," Steve said. "But the important thing is getting practice planning a route and executing it."

"And open sea sailing as a team."

"Now you sound like Connie," Steve said, before heading below deck.

Jen's shift was busy but uneventful. She headed farther out to sea to steer away from two cargo ships and a supertanker. Ships under sail had the right-of-way, but she didn't want to argue the point with a vessel weighing hundreds of tons more than theirs.

"Ready for me to take the con?" Steve hollered at the end of four hours.

"Come up and take over. I forgot to call Mom last night," Jen said as she went below for her phone.

When Steve's shift was over she returned to take the wheel.

"How are Bob, your mom, and Bozo?" Steve asked when she entered the fly bridge.

"I tried a dozen times, but never had enough signal."

"Hmm, we've moved away from the mainland," Steve said. "Do you want to try ship-to-shore radio?"

"Naw, I'll try again later. If nothing else, I'll call when we get back to Lauderdale."

Their voyage continued through the nights. They alternated watches while the other slept. Jen was thankful for the full moon and cloudless skies. She felt like the moon was leading them across the Gulf of Mexico, laying out a golden highway on the water for them to follow.

Cancun appeared on the horizon early on the morning of the third day. The water's transition from dark blue to turquoise signaled land. Sun shone on the white, sandy beach, and the temperature was in the low seventies. As they sailed closer, Jen could hear the waves pound and then sizzle as they tumbled and then flowed up the beach.

"Let's go ashore, walk through the surf, and get brunch before we head home," Jen said.

"I checked the weather," Steve said, pointing out to sea. "There's a small storm building on our track back. We need to avoid it—not wait for it to get closer."

Jen followed his gesture. A few fluffy white clouds hung in the sky. "I don't see signs of a storm."

"Good, that gives a better chance to go around it," Steve said her. "It's still below the horizon."

Jen looked longingly at the beach as Steve swung the boat around.

They missed the worst of the storm—skirting the edge of it. Jen handled the rough seas better than Steve. By the time sunbeams poked thorough dark gray storm clouds, his complexion had taken on an interesting shade of light green. "How are you doing?" Jen asked.

"I was Army, not Navy. I have sea legs but not a sea stomach. Imagine how I'd feel if I hadn't taken Dramamine."

Elf fared better than Steve. He was napping on the sofa when she checked on him. For most of the voyage to Mexico he'd been quiet, but alert. A diminutive, but ferocious watchdog, he had warned off a few supertankers and an oil derrick during the trip.

Despite their wide detour to avoid the storm, they arrived early.

"Now that we have a thousand-mile trip under our belts, let's go to the hotel then pick up the Land Cruiser," Steve said. "Tomorrow we'll be on our way to Mexico to buy a boat."

Chapter 39

Ft. Lauderdale
April 26

Although there were still a few paid days remaining on their hotel room, Steve made reservations at a different Ft. Lauderdale hotel as they cruised back along the south Florida coast. They'd left nothing in the old room and moving locations seemed a reasonable precaution in case the DEA or IRS wanted to track them. Once they squirreled the money away in a safe haven, he'd worry less.

"Do you want to take a walk with me?" Steve asked Jen after checking in.

"I don't know if I can. The earth is moving even standing still."

"I feel the same after two weeks at sea. C'mon, a walk will help us get our land legs back."

"Where to?" Jen asked.

"Pick up the SUV to load for the trip. It's close, and a walk isn't as traceable as a cab ride."

Jen looked at him sharply. "You're still worried about being followed?"

"Less and less as time goes by," Steve said. "Nothing has happened since someone broke into the house, but erring on the side of caution doesn't hurt."

"OK. I hate the idea of being followed," Jen said.

"We'll meet Todd for dinner and get the rest of the IDs he has for us after we pick up the Toyota," Steve said changing the subject while walking away from the hotel. "Then pick up more money to buy our boat."

"Are there still good boats in Mexico?" Jen asked.

"In Playa del Carmen, just south of Cancun," Steve said.

Within five minutes they were at the storage lot. Steve keyed in the code and opened the side gate. At the unit he inserted a key into the lock but it didn't work. He pulled the key out and reinserted it. When wiggling it back and forth didn't work, his brow creased. Fiddling more didn't change the results, and he stepped back and looked at the unit number. It was the right storeroom. The lock was the same brand he'd bought at the office. He was using the key that came with it.

Jen pulled a key from her purse. "I think you have sea fingers, too, or your key is defective. Let's try mine." Her jiggling didn't work any better than Steve's had.

"Let's go," Steve said as he turned and headed for the office. "They sold me this damn lock. Let them open it."

The white haired woman Steve had dealt when he brought the SUV looked up when the door opened. She smiled. "How can I help you?" she asked, rising slowly from the chair.

Steve held up the key. "We rented storage unit 317 and bought a lock from you. Now the key doesn't work. Can you help us get it open?"

"Oh dear. Let me call my husband. He needs to talk to you."

Steve looked at Jen. Her face reflected his confusion and concern. "Is there a problem?" he asked. "I paid cash for three months. There shouldn't be a rental fee problem. We've only had the unit for a week."

"Oh, no, no," the lady waved a hand back and forth in the air. "Nothing like that." She picked up the phone and dialed a few digits. "My husband is up in our apartment. We live upstairs so there's… Artie, the people from 317 are here. OK…" She hung up. "He'll be right down. Can I offer you a soda or coffee?"

Steve shook his head.

"No, thank you," Jen said and moved next to Steve placing her hand on his arm.

The side door opened and a slender, spry looking, elderly man limped in wearing a Boston Red Sox cap. "Are you Mr. Henson?" he asked, extending a hand. Boston was in his voice as well as on his head.

Steve blinked. He'd forgotten that the rental was under an alias. "Yes, Mr.…?"

"Kennedy, Artie Kennedy. No relation to the liquored up, philandering politicians."

Steve smiled despite the churning that had begun in his stomach and held up the key. "Mr. Kennedy, my wife and I both tried our keys on the storage unit lock. Neither works."

"It wouldn't. It's a different lock."

Steve frowned. "Why a different lock?"

Kennedy held up hands palms forward. "Lemme explain. Damnedest thing I've ever seen since Marilyn and I bought this place eleven years ago." Behind him Marilyn nodded agreement.

"The night, or the morning, after you checked in we had a break in. They climbed over the fence, right over the barbed wire on top," Artie said. "A motion detector alarmed in our apartment." He gestured upward. "I came down to check the monitors." He pointed at the front counter. "Although we allow twenty-four access, nobody had used a code to get through the gate."

Steve looked to where the top of the monitors showed above the chipped but clean vinyl counter.

"At first there wasn't any movement, then I noticed an open door. It was your unit," Artie continued. "I grabbed a flashlight and hurried out to see what was up. There was a loud clang then car doors opening and closing. I hollered." He scowled. "It got quiet and then three men ran out toward the fence over there. I hollered stop and took out after them. One of 'em shot at me. I dove for cover. That's how I hurt my knee." He patted the leg he'd been favoring.

Jen's hand covered her mouth. "Was anyone shot?"

"No. Missed. Marilyn called 911 when she heard the shot. They were long gone by the time the police got here. The police checked your car, and I tried to call but kept getting voice mail. I guess you didn't get my message." Artie squinted when he looked at Steve.

"No. We've been out to sea, beyond cell coverage. Got back less than an hour ago."

Artie shook his head. "No matter. You're here now. I wanted to spare you this surprise." Artie tilted his head, and the squint came back. "Police said the car isn't registered to you."

Steve didn't expect that. He didn't know what to say.

"We bought it from my cousin Steve," Jen said. "He's laid off and needed the cash. We travel and figured to use it when we're in town. I get tired of using cabs."

Steve smiled gratefully at Jen as she continued.

"We haven't registered it in our name yet," Jen said. "There hasn't been time and we're hoping my cousin will find a job and want it back."

"Did the police have a problem with the registration?" Steve asked.

"The police checked, and it hasn't been reported stolen," Artie said. "Tags are current. Said they'd come back if a stolen report came in. Haven't been back. Guess it's OK."

"It's not stolen," Steve said. "We wanted to keep it someplace safe—off the streets so it wouldn't get broken into."

Artie looked embarrassed. "Well, the other part I meant to tell—they broke the window to get in."

Jen's grip on Steve's arm tightened.

"They broke the latch on the unit. I fixed it and put a new lock on." Artie extended a hand. "Here's new keys. I feel bad about the window. I'll fix it. My insurance will pay. I checked."

"Thanks, I'd appreciate that," Steve said. "I guess we won't be driving it with a broken window." Steve shrugged at Jen. "Back to cabs."

"I'll see how fast I can get it fixed," Artie said. "Not tomorrow I'd guess."

"That's OK." Steve hesitated. He didn't know what to do, but he tried to stay calm for Jen's sake. If she squeezed much harder, his arm would go to sleep. "We're leaving town soon and need to decide about transportation. I'll call later and let you know if we need the SUV. But right now I want to look it over."

"Let me know if there's any damage I missed," Artie said. "I'm so sorry this happened."

Steve raised a hand and gave a dismissive wave. "Artie, it's not your fault. You were injured protecting our property."

Steve and Jen walked out in silence, but Steve's thoughts churned. It couldn't be a coincidence thieves targeted the SUV and their house. He'd been too complacent. The few things done to throw someone off the trail didn't work. But he hadn't really believed anyone was tracking them. It can't be the DEA. They'd get a warrant. How did anyone find the SUV? The car he'd seen with the computer flashed into his memory.

The new keys from Artie opened the lock.

"What the *hell* is going on?" Jen shouted once inside with the door closed.

Steve put a finger to his lips. "I'm as confused as you are," he said in a normal voice while maintaining the finger to lips. "We just got this car from your cousin. Let's look around and see if there's other damage."

Jen nodded her reluctant agreement. While Steve got on his back and looked underneath, she circled the car.

He began at the rear driver side wheel well, and inched his way forward, examining under the running board, then the metal and plastic surrounding the front wheel. It was dirty, but the dirt wasn't disturbed. Front bumper suspension components—nothing. He pulled himself up.

He lifted the hood and scrutinized the engine compartment. Nothing appeared out of place or extra, but he wasn't a mechanic. Was he being paranoid?

He dropped back to the ground next to the other front wheel but nothing looked suspicious. Rolling onto his back again, he scanned the passenger side running board from front to back. Nothing... wait. A faint flash of red next to the middle mounting strut came again.

He squirmed closer. A small box, the size of a cigarette pack, was next to the support bracket. A light on the side next to the brace flashed sporadically. He reached for the device then stopped. It might be set to signal an alarm if disconnected.

Jen dropped to her knees beside him. "Find something?"

Steve rolled out from under the car and raised a cautionary finger to his lips. "It looked like a new dent, but it has a layer of dirt over it. Not new," Steve said, rising to his feet. "Let's go see Artie again."

"There wasn't a dent. I found a box under the car." Steve said after locking the unit.

Jen's eyes widened.

"I don't know if it records sounds, too. We need to treat it as if it does. Don't want anyone to know we found it."

Steve opened the door to the office for Jen and followed inside. "No damage besides the window," Steve said to Artie. "No rush to fix it. We'll be gone for a week at least."

"Glad there's no more damage," Artie said. "Leave a copy of the storage key and I'll get your car repaired this week. It'll be ready when you're back. I think it can be repaired without moving your vehicle."

"Here's the unit key and my car key, if it needs to be moved," Steve said. "Somebody who'll risk his life for our stuff can be trusted with the keys. Leave the keys in the glove box when you're done. We have another." He turned to Jen who smiled and patted her pocket.

At the door Steve stopped and turned back to Artie. "I've heard that drug dealers are fond of that kind of SUV. Don't risk your life again. If they come back, let them have it."

Chapter 40

Ft. Lauderdale
April 26

Jen walked quietly beside Steve. He didn't say anything for two blocks, but kept scanning the surroundings, occasionally turning and walking backwards. Stress built in Jen's chest until she grabbed his elbow. "Stop".

She bent hands on knees, gasping for breath. Jen hadn't felt so weak and helpless since waking from her last nightmare, years ago.

Steve rubbed her back. "What's wrong?" he asked—brow wrinkled and eyes looking frightened. "Are you hurt?"

"I'm scared," Jen whispered.

Firm hands on her shoulders pulled her upright into his embrace. She clung to him.

"I can't tell you not to be afraid," he said, chin resting on top of her head. "I'm scared shitless. But we can't let it control us. Make us weak." His hand stroked her hair, then tilted her chin up. "Use the fear to raise your awareness."

She sensed his energy as intense blue eyes bored into hers.

He kissed her forehead. "C'mon. We'll catch a cab ahead. It can drop us at the shopping center near our hotel."

She drew a deep ragged breath. "That's what I need—shopping therapy."

"Later. Now, I want to determine if anyone has followed us," Steve said.

Another spasm started in Jen's stomach. "Who?"

"Maybe no one. But we can't lead anybody to the trailer. I think we're safe as long as they don't know where the money is."

"You *think*?"

Steve grabbed her hand and led her toward the nearest hotel.

"Is it the police?" Jen asked.

"Police don't need to break in. They get a warrant." He continued to pull her along. "I'm more worried that it's not the police."

Not the police? Jen stumbled and would have fallen if Steve hadn't had a grip on her hand. He placed his other hand under her elbow for support. In the beginning he'd warned her about the cartel, but nothing had happened so far and he hadn't talked more about it. A chill shuddered along her back despite the warm Florida weather.

"Let's go inside," he said, looping her arm through his, and led her past two cabs into the expansive hotel lobby. He stopped and looked around before heading into an elevator.

"What I found may be a tracking device under the running board," Steve said after the doors closed. "Somebody is trying to find us. We're ahead of them so far. But we need to be more cautious. We can't go back to the SUV."

She wanted to scream, but he seemed so calm. It steadied her jangling nerves.

He pushed the mezzanine level button. "We'll see if they found the trailer, but first make sure no one follows us." The doors opened, and he strode down the wide hallway like he belonged here. There were meeting rooms on both sides. Almost at the end of the hallway he stopped and pulled out his wallet. "Got your phone?" he asked.

She nodded.

He handed her three hundred dollars. "If anyone is after us they're looking for two people dressed like this." He waved his hand between them. "Go to the shop downstairs and buy a different outfit. Different style and colors. Come back to this restroom and change." He looked at the hair pulled back and pinned in a chignon at the back of her head. "Can you let your hair down—brush it out?"

Jen nodded again. "How do you know there's a shop here? And how are you staying so collected?"

"If I freaked out like I want to, it wouldn't help," he said. "Big hotels always have shops for the tourists. There was a sign down the hall to the left of the elevator." He smiled.

Jen shook her head. As long as he remained cool, she'd try to match him.

"After you change, go out front and catch a cab to the Galleria," Steve said. "Call me when you're on the way."

"What are you going to do?"

"I'll go out the back, cross to the next hotel, and catch another cab to the Galleria. I'll buy a change of clothes there."

Something didn't seem right. "You're going to the Galleria and I buy something in a hotel tourist shop?" Jen sputtered. "They have a Neiman's at the Galleria."

Steve laughed, threw his arms out, pulling her close in a hug. "I can count on you to find a flaw in the plan."

Jen's stiffness melted into his arms.

"OK, when you get there, buy a new outfit for tonight. I'll do the same. Do you need more money?"

Three hundred would probably buy two changes of clothes, but Jen held out her hand with a smirk. Steve handed her two hundred more from the money clip in his pocket. She didn't mention the five hundred in her purse.

"I'll call Todd to pick us up at the Galleria after I'm sure no one is following. Don't dawdle. We have a lot to do this afternoon. Be careful."

A feeling of loss filled her. "Do we have to separate?" she asked in a small voice.

Steve nodded. "I don't want to, but it's best." He grinned. "Too bad I don't have the CIA for Dummies book here. Any other ideas?"

Jen shook her head and whispered, "OK, you be careful, too." She looked back before she entered the stairwell next to the restrooms.

Chapter 41

Ft. Lauderdale
April 26

The door to the stairway closed before Steve took a deep breath. He didn't want to separate, but trying to tell if anyone followed her was easier if they weren't together.

He was wearing a tangerine colored Nat Nast silk shirt over a dark brown t-shirt. In the men's room, he took off the over-shirt and stuffed it into the trash. After a hesitation, he pulled it back out and ripped the sleeve with his knife. A perfectly good shirt in the trash could raise questions. There was a twinge. It was one of his favorites.

Now attired in drab brown, he found an exit in the back of the building. Once outside he strolled among the parked cars towards the next hotel. A low wall separated the two hotel's parking lots. It wasn't likely that anyone had enough people on short notice to monitor the front, the lobby, and all sides, but he stopped and scanned back the way he'd come. No one else was in the parking lot.

The wall was two feet tall on this side, but there was a four foot drop on the other. He swung his legs over, hopped down, and strode to the side door of the next hotel. It opened when he tried the latch. He breathed a sigh of relief. Many hotels require a guest room key to enter side doors even during the day.

He ran up the stairs to the third floor and stood back from the window to watch for signs of anyone on his trail. He watched for five minutes with the patience learned as a hunter. There wasn't any sign of a tail. The waiting and surveillance in a tropical setting reminded him of his time in Vietnam with one difference. This time he wasn't armed. He could only observe.

In the lobby, he asked the bellman to call a cab and remained inside until the taxi stopped in front. When the bellman opened the rear passenger door, Steve swooped out of the hotel and into the cab, shoving twenty dollars into the bellman's hand as he passed. "Galleria, please," Steve said before the car door closed.

Almost to the Galleria, his phone rang. "I'm on my way," Jen said.

"You were quick—good job. I'm in transit, too. Say my dog's name if you're OK and your dog's name if there's a problem." He watched the cabbie's eyes in the mirror for a reaction. There was none.

After a short pause. "Most of the time I think you're a Bozo," Jen said.

"Good to hear. Or are you venting?"

"A little of both."

"That's fair," Steve said as the driver stopped in the parking garage. "Call when you get to the Galleria."

Passing through Dillards on the way to Niemen Marcus, he spotted a palm leaf patterned Tommy Bahama shirt to replace the one he'd tossed in the hotel restroom. It was no Nat Nast, but it would do in a pinch, and it would give him a shopping bag to blend in with the rest of the mall crowd. He found an extra-large, then paused before grabbing a size large for Todd, too.

Steve strode into the parking garage until reaching a stairwell. After dashing down two levels and across the aisle, he ducked behind a parked car. He watched through the vehicle's windows for anyone exiting the stairwell. When no appeared after several minutes he returned to the mall.

Steve was aware that he was acting paranoid, but being paranoid didn't mean that there wasn't someone after him. His phone rang as he entered the store.

"I'm outside of Neiman's in the parking lot," Jen said.

"Wait outside for a minute," Steve said as he walked through the store. "I'm getting close to the door... OK, I see you. You can come in now, but don't look for me. Go ahead with your shopping. Wander through several departments, even change floors. When you're done, go into the mall instead of back outside. I'll catch up with you."

Jen shopped, and Steve wandered in an aimless pattern around the edge of the department as if looking for a gift. He continually scanned for people in Jen's vicinity who might pay attention to her or remained too long in the area.

He called Todd while he continued to scan. "We're back in town, little brother."

"I didn't expect you back until tomorrow," Todd said. "How was the trip?"

"Great, but there's a problem with our SUV. Can you pick us up at the Galleria?"

"Bummer. I can be there in thirty minutes," Todd said.

"Ready when you get here," Steve said. "Call when you're close."

He disconnected, called Jen, and watched her answer. "Todd's coming to get us. Finish up and meet me in Dillard's kitchen department." No one appeared to follow her as she left the store, strolled through the mall, and rode the escalator to the second floor housewares department.

As he joined her, his phone rang. "Todd, can you meet us in the parking garage at the second floor Dillard's entrance? Great. See you in a few."

When Todd pulled up, Steve piled into the back of the small SUV and Jen took the front seat.

"Jen, you look lovely," Todd said. "Not like you just fell off the boat."

She smiled at him. "Just some tourist trash I threw together."

At the hotel Steve invited Todd in for a drink in the lobby bar while Jen went to the room.

"So, do you need the name of a good mechanic?" Todd asked.

"Can't fix what's wrong with the car. The people we're trying to avoid tracked the car down. That's all I'll say. I don't want you any more involved." Steve's phone rang, interrupting Todd's response.

"Hi, you big Bozo. I'm in the room," Jen said.

Steve grinned and disconnected. She was safe.

"I'm here for you," Todd said. "But, I won't push. Here's the rest of the ID stuff." He handed over a manila envelope.

"I can't thank you enough for this. We need to get out of the country and lose them. To be honest this car stuff scared the crap out of me. I need another car. We planned an excursion in Mexico. I want to buy a boat down there. That should make us untraceable."

"Can I do anything?" Todd said.

"You've already done a lot," Steve said, patting the envelope. "And it helps knowing you'll be there if we need you again. I'll call when we're in Mexico, *hermano menor*."

Todd squinted. "*Hermano* is brother. I hope *menor* doesn't mean manure."

Steve laughed. "It means 'kid brother'. Jen and I have been practicing *Español*. I may need help tomorrow. I'll find a car online today, and will need a ride to wherever it is."

"Here's an instant solution. I have another car. Drop me at my condo and take this one. I'll meet you guys later for dinner. You can even take this one to Mexico."

"Thanks, but I don't want to involve you by taking your car to Mexico," Steve said

When he dropped Todd off, Steve reached into the Dillard's bag and handed Todd the shirt he'd bought. "I was thinking of you. Pretend it's wrapped." He and Todd hated to wrap presents.

Steve drove away. No use putting it off any longer. The money in the trailer was there, or it wasn't.

Chapter 42

Ft. Lauderdale
April 26

Steve watched to see if anyone followed as he drove. He circled the trailer storage lot three times scanning the surroundings. Unwilling to delay any longer, he entered the code to open the entrance gate and drove through to their unit. Unarmed. Their guns were in the trailer he prayed was still inside.

His hand trembled as he tried the key. The first lock opened with a click. Steve let out the breath he didn't realize he'd been holding. After casting a furtive glance around, he tried the second. It opened.

He was as tense as he'd ever been—at least since piling the money from the wrecked van into the back of his Toyota SUV in the Kansas creek.

Steve bent, grasped the handle, and hauled the overhead door into the air. The trailer tongue came into sight, and then sunlight flowed up the white of the trailer body.

Nothing appeared disturbed when he flicked on the light. To shut out prying eyes, he slid the door down before going to the back of the trailer, unlocking the doors, and swinging them wide. Boxes were still inside.

A quick check revealed they were full of cash. Steve turned around and his legs buckled as he collapsed to sit on the floor of the trailer. Tension had knotted his muscles and left him exhausted.

Relief was short lived. There was more to check. He dropped to his knees, rolled over onto his back, and wriggled under the trailer to hunt for a tracking device. This wasn't like the car. There weren't as many places to look. After a thorough search he decided it was clean.

There was his paranoia again, but better safe than sorry.

Steve counted out two hundred thousand dollars in various denominations, placed it in the Neiman Marcus shopping bag, put the peach colored shirt on top, and locked the storage unit.

Chapter 43

Ft. Lauderdale
April 26

Jen sat at the desk in the hotel room, head in hands, not knowing where to turn or what to do. Something scraped against the door then it opened. Fight and flight instincts battled within as she turned and straightened in the chair, prepared to bolt upright. Steve walked in. Relief washed over her like a cool breeze before her anger boiled.

"Where have you been?" she demanded—more shrill than she intended. "I've been so worried. You and Todd weren't in the bar a half hour ago." She stood. One hand gripped the desk chair and the other clenched by her side. Tears stung her eyes. She knew she was overreacting because of the unknown threat hanging over them, but couldn't help it.

Steve shut the door and put the bag on the floor. "I'm sorry. Todd let us borrow a car until we get another. I dropped him at the condo then, since I was out, I went to check the trailer. I didn't want you along in case something happened."

A tentative smile stretched his lips, and he stepped forward. "Good news. It's still there and everything is in it."

Her eyes narrowed. "You didn't want me there if something happened? What if it did and I didn't know where you were? Aren't we a *team*?" Jen didn't like sounding shrill again. She inhaled before continuing. "You said I'm supposed to cover your back. What were the shotgun lessons for—the pistol practice—the fucking *sailing* lessons together?" Hands clenched into fists, she stamped a foot in frustration.

Steve raised hands as if to fend off her anger. "You're right. I would feel terrible if I couldn't find you. I'm sorry my greed got you into this." His contrition was palpable.

"I don't want to be right," she exhaled in frustration. "I want you to include me—don't think of me as a fragile flower needing protection." She looked at him in silence until his head rose to look at her. "We decided *together* to keep the money and hide it. Or were you humoring me?"

"No," Steve said. "I can't do this by myself. Working together has made me realize that. But I want to protect you. It's in my genes." He thumped his chest with one fist. "Bozo protect Jen."

He was a bozo. Her anger drained. She stepped forward and clutched him around the waist. He folded arms around her shoulders and kissed the top of her head as her face pressed against his chest.

She felt tears wetting his shirt. "Steve, you scared me so much. Don't ever do something like that again."

"I can't promise never to be stupid, but I promise to keep you in the loop from now on. If I'm scared and worried, I should realize you are, too. The tracking device I found on the SUV made me afraid to check on the trailer. But when the storage unit was on the way back from dropping off Todd, I made myself go to it." Steve sighed. "You know how I prevaricate when I don't want to do something, so I forced myself to do it."

"OK, as long as you realize you're a bozo," she said into his wet shirt, then looked up at him.

He kissed her forehead, then her lips, and drew back. "Let's get busy. We've lots of work ahead of us. I'm sure one thing you'll want to do is put a new face on. It's streaked. We meet Todd in two hours for dinner."

"What are we going to do about a car?" Jen asked as she pulled out her makeup kit. "If we don't leave soon, we'll be too late for the turkey hunt and won't be able to bring our shotguns into Mexico."

"Find a used car on the internet, of course," Steve said. "I'll find a private seller. Buy for cash. No negotiating."

"How different life is now," Jen laughed. "When it was so crappy a few weeks ago, who'd have thought we'd buy a new car on the spur of the moment. Like buying a new dress."

————

Todd arrived for dinner by himself. Jen was disappointed. She had held hope for their relationship. Dani was the first of Todd's women that she liked.

"Where's Dani?" Jen asked as Todd sat. "Already dumped you?"

Todd's face flushed. "Out of town on a modeling job."

Steve must have seen something in Todd's demeanor. "You serious about her?"

Todd's face burned brighter red, and he ducked his head. "Yeah, kinda."

"Are you going to ask her to marry you?" Jen asked.

"I did. Before she left."

"What did she say?" Jen asked.

"She hasn't. She'll give me an answer when she gets back."

The embarrassed expression on Todd's face made Jen sorry she'd asked. Looking to Steve for his reaction, she hoped he'd cover her faux pas.

"I found a year old Toyota Highlander on line," Steve said. "We pick it up in the morning."

"You like those Toyota SUVs," Todd said.

"Technically this one is known as a Crossover Utility Vehicle—a CUV. I looked at US cars, but they come with miniature spare tires. If we have a flat in the wilds of Mexico, I don't want to use a doughnut."

"Why would you be in the Mexican wilderness?" Todd asked. "You want to buy a boat."

"I'm going to shoot one of those constipated turkeys," Jen said, glad the conversation had turned.

Todd looked a question at Steve.

"Ocellated turkey, Jen," Steve said, looking at Todd with a wry grin. "It's the only turkey not found in the US—a native of the Yucatan jungles. Their colors are something like a peacock with bright greens, yellow, and a pastel blue head. The males don't gobble, they 'sing' to attract mates. I'd like to hear that."

"When Jen said constipated, I pictured a pre-stuffed bird. Shoot it, pluck it, and throw it in the oven," Todd said and chuckled. "Yucatan, huh? It's the last place I'd think of for turkey hunting."

"We'll be in the jungle two to three hours outside of Campeche."

"That's a nice, remote place to hide out," Todd said.

Jen's muscles tensed at the mention of hiding out. She hoped Steve didn't notice. She didn't want to appear weak.

"The plan is to leave tomorrow and arrive before the hunting season is over," Steve said. "We'll almost circumnavigate the Gulf of Mexico to get there."

"Speaking of the Gulf, you asked for contacts to help you start a company down there," Todd said. "Mexico is out—too much scrutiny. Belize is the best bet, according to my sources. They speak English and you can buy a 'shelf' company cheap."

Jen refrained from pointing out that Belize wasn't in the Gulf.

"What's a shelf company?" Steve asked.

"It's a shell business with paperwork that has been aging for up to several years—on the shelf" Jen said. "The company name was registered, but nothing else has been done. Purchase one for a nominal fee and presto change-o you have a business that's been around for a while."

"Right," Todd said. "This has names of lawyers Jen can contact to buy one." He handed her an envelope. "They can supply letters of reference and other stuff."

"I appreciate what you're doing for us," Jen said. "Steve really trusts you, and I'm seeing why. Thank you."

The expression of gratitude that passed over Todd's countenance made her glad she said it. He wasn't such a bad guy.

When rising to leave after dinner, Steve clapped Todd on the shoulder. "We both appreciate you." He handed Todd an envelope. "Here's the rest of what's owed plus extra as a down payment. We'll probably be calling for help again."

Chapter 44

Ft. Lauderdale
April 27

Jen laughed. "That girl sure had a funny expression when you plunked down thirty-seven thousand in cash for her car," she said to Steve as he drove the new CUV away from Todd's condo.

"Money talks," Steve said.

"It was shouting at her," Jen said. "It's probably the most cash she's had in hand at one time."

"I tried not to chuckle when she looked at the bills to see if they were counterfeit."

"Your offer to wait until the banks opened and let her take ten of the bills to the bank sealed the deal," Jen said.

"Glad she didn't take me up. It would have taken time and we still need to stop at a hardware store before going to the trailer."

―――――

Before opening the door at the storage unit, Steve removed the spare tire from under the CUV.

Inside the unit, he let the air out of the tire and used pry bars from the hardware store to open it. Next, packets of money totaling two-and-a-half million dollars were laid end-to-end on top of plastic wrap. He folded the plastic over the money—forming a long cash filled tube.

Jen watched as he stuffed the wrapped money inside the wheel, layering it around the interior. While he resealed the tire bead, after spraying expanding insulation into the tire, she asked,

"What was all that for? Why didn't you just put the money in the tire?"

"The insulation will solidify and keep the money from moving around inside the tire. The plastic wrap keeps it from sticking to the money," Steve said. "Now if the police or border patrol were to remove the tire and shake it, bounce it, whatever, nothing will rattle around. I hope that the insulation and plastic wrap will hide the smell of money from any dogs trained to scent cash. This is the real reason I wanted a full-size spare."

"But we'll be traveling thousands of miles without a spare."

"I'll air it up before I reinstall it underneath," Steve said. "It will still be good as a spare for a short distance until we get the flat repaired or a new tire." He groaned when he picked up the tire to put it in the car. "Whew, it must be fifty pounds heavier. Let's hope no one takes it off and lifts it."

Jen helped him load the things needed for their trip including shotguns, hunting clothes and boots. "I've got the documentation for the guns we picked up at the Mexican embassy."

"And I loaded as many boxes of shells as we're allowed to bring into the country," Steve said.

"*Vamos a México, Ándale!*" Jen said.

Chapter 45

Ft. Lauderdale
April 28

Juan's phone rang. He hesitated before answering. It wasn't a number he recognized. "Hello?"

"Juan?"

"Yes."

"This is a friend of Esteban's. He asked me to dig up information for you. I'm at a payphone, so don't bother calling back."

"What's your name?" The voice sounded vaguely familiar.

"You don't need to know. Have a pen and paper?"

"What's it about?" Juan asked while signaling to Edgar that he needed writing material.

"Steve Henning's next of kin."

"His wife Jen, or their kids?" Juan said as Edgar handed him a pencil and the newspaper from the trash can.

"No, his brother, Todd."

"Henning has a brother? Where?" Juan asked. Edgar had moved away, but stopped and turned.

"He lives in Dania Beach."

"Don't know that town."

"It's a suburb of Ft. Lauderdale," the voice said.

"Ft. Lauderdale?" Juan exclaimed. Edgar's head snapped up.

"Esteban said you'd be interested. I'll get info on his kids next."

Juan copied the address in the paper's margin. "Got it," he said. "Got a photo?" There was no reply. He looked at the cellphone screen. The call had disconnected.

Juan pocketed the phone and held up the newspaper. "We've got Henning's brother. He's local. We'll set up surveillance. It's too much of a coincidence that he's nearby."

Edgar's teeth bared in a vicious smile.

Chapter 46

Houston, TX
April 28

Jen was tired of driving. Yesterday's trip from Lauderdale to Lafayette, Louisiana had been wearying. She'd spelled Steve for five of the thirteen hours. They were back on the road before sunup. Highway 10 had taken them close, then far, and then near again to the Gulf of Mexico. Tall scrawny pine trees with green puffs of needles on top dominated the scenery. A few lanky deciduous trees insinuated themselves among the evergreens. Even rarer were the magnificent, sprawling live oaks dripping with Spanish moss.

East Texas featured more of the same.

They were now west of Houston. The four lanes of Interstate highway were far behind. Cattle grazing operations dominated the sides of the two lane road. Scrub trees struggled upward through fence lines. Cows clustered under the spreading shade of random live oaks.

"What do you want to do with the money?" Jen asked.

Steve stared straight ahead. When she'd raised the question in the past, he hadn't wanted to discuss it. Said it might bring bad luck.

"Help family," Steve said after a few moments. "Liz is studying to be a nurse practitioner as a fallback. Now we can afford to send her to medical school like she wanted."

"Mark hasn't found a job since graduation and wants to get a master's, too," Jen said. "Now he can."

"What about you?" Steve asked.

"Dad and Mom's oil well production fell off a few years ago. Their savings are OK, but not enough to travel. I want to send them to Europe while their health is still good," Jen said. "Also, I want to set up a scholarship fund for battered women. Many stay in abusive situations because they don't have anywhere to go."

"Speaking of your parents," Steve said. "When are you going to call them?"

"Damn. With everything going on, I forgot again. Wonder how Bozo and his new girlfriend are doing." Jen said with a smile as she pulled out her phone.

Steve chuckled. "Me, too."

"Hi, Mom…"

"Jen, I didn't recognize this number. I'm so glad you finally called. I have bad news. Bozo is dead."

"Bozo's dead?" Jen exclaimed. "What happened?"

"Oh, no," Steve groaned and pulled the car to the shoulder of the road. "Damn sighthounds are so fast, drivers don't see them."

"Somebody shot him," Molly said. "I'm so sorry."

"Shot!" Jen exclaimed and looked at Steve. His mouth dropped open in surprise.

"Let me put Bob on. He can tell you better," Molly said.

"Jen, I'm sorry about Bozo." Bob's voice boomed from the phone. "I wish I had buckshot instead of target loads when I went after those bastards. They wouldn't be messing with this or any other Indian again." Half Osage, Bob referred to himself as an Indian when he got excited, although the other half was Scotch-Irish.

"Bozo and Mimi were getting along great, but he and Captain got into a fight the day before. So I had the two boys in the living room—trying to socialize them," Bob said. "Deerhounds aren't the best watchdogs, but Bozo heard someone outside."

"Who?"

181

"Don't know. They had guns, but Bozo's strange behavior made me suspicious. Got my shotgun before they tried to break in. Between Molly and me, we chased them off."

"My god, Dad," Jen said. "That's so frightening."

"Bozo went after them. One shot him—twice. I tried to run after them, but they jumped in a car at the end of the driveway. I blew out their back window. But I don't think the birdshot hurt anyone."

"Are you and Mom OK?" Jen asked.

"We're fine, and Bozo didn't suffer. Dead when I got to him. Called the police. Haven't found them or the car. The yard lights were on, waiting for the pizza guy, but all I could tell was there was two big'uns and a small guy. Little one drove. One shouted some Mexican when I shot."

"I'm glad you and Mom aren't hurt. Do you know what they wanted?"

"Graysons had a burglary a few months back. Police come by every once in a while now—keeping an eye out."

"I'm glad." Steve stared at her and looked as if he wanted to grab the phone.

"Bozo might've been protective of Mimi, like he was when he fought Captain. Whatever—I think he saved Molly and me. Now the shotgun's by the back door—filled with buckshot. Deer rifle at the front door. Loaded pistols in the bedroom and kitchen. I carry one when I'm in the yard."

"This is so scary. We'll miss Bozo, but I'd miss you a lot more," Jen said as she stroked Elf where he lay in her lap.

"Good thing is, I think he'd already covered Mimi," Bob said. "So, we should have little Bozos on the way."

"I better go. Steve's going to have a cat listening to one side of this call," Jen said. "Bye, I love you guys. Be careful."

"What happened?" Steve exclaimed as Jen disconnected.

Jen repeated the news.

"Jimmy said three men—two big and one small—broke into our house."

"Do you think it was about the money and not a burglary?"

"Might be. We have to be extra careful," Steve said.

"Should we warn the rest of the family?"

"And say what?" Steve asked. "The government might be following us? Robbers keep showing up wherever we go? The best thing to do is not contact anyone until we get the money out of the country."

"We've seen Todd."

"Todd's a big boy. He's played with rough people before. He can take care of himself."

"Shouldn't we warn him?" Jen asked.

"Yes, but I can't call him in case someone is tracking our phones. I'll send him an email tonight."

Steve reached to start the car and stopped. "How can someone shoot a dog like that? I'll miss him, but I'm glad your parents are OK."

"Dad said there will be little Bozos."

"It won't be the same. He was my first. The only dog that was only mine, not my family's."

Jen felt sorry for Steve. He must be hurting. He never expressed feeling like that. She picked up Elf and hugged him.

Chapter 47

Campeche, Mexico
April 30

Crossing the border from Brownsville into Matamoras took longer than normal because of the paperwork for guns and ammunition. The documentation Jen handed over was in order, so border guards let them through without checking any further. The weapons were a good distraction, given the stash of cash hidden below the car in the spare tire.

The land grew greener as they traveled south along the Mexican coast. Farms and orchards appeared productive. Blue-green waters beckoned beyond. Their route took them south until Veracruz, then east to Tabasco, and finally north toward Campeche as they circumnavigated the Gulf of Mexico.

Steve pulled into a church parking lot a half-hour outside Campeche where they planned to meet their guide, who pulled in next to them three minutes later. "You the Hennings?"

Steve nodded, and the guide signaled for them to follow.

"Was that an Australian accent?" Jen asked.

"Aussie or South African."

"I wonder if shrimp on the barbie is on the menu," Jen said.

She was delighted as the guide showed them around the camp. They'd be staying in safari cabins. Steve had prepared her for pup tents.

"There's indoor plumbing, but the showers are gravity fed," the guide said.

Steve had told her there would only be outhouses. It was typical of him to make it sound awful so the reality was pleasant.

184

There was even a dining room. It was rustic, but nicer than sitting around a smoky fire on campstools—or on the ground as Steve had lead her to believe.

Hunters began returning with mixed success. One third had bagged a turkey, but others were enthusiastic because of the abundant turkey sign. While they celebrated or commiserated with each other over post hunt beverages, the chef prepared a tasty dinner of grilled turkey breast, shot fresh that day.

"The jungle is filled with horny turkeys," one hunter said to them as he sipped an *Añjeo* tequila.

————

Before sunrise, Jen and Steve went their separate ways, each with a guide to a designated hunting area.

In the gray-blue twilight, Jen's companion led the way uphill, after putting a finger to his lips. She hitched her pack containing turkey calls, ammo, and water. Then, cradling her shotgun like a baby, she followed.

She tried to walk as quietly as the guide, but couldn't—sliding on the rocky ground or stepping on loose rocks and brittle branches. Her companion smiled and nodded in a friendly manner, occasionally indicating things of interest on either side of the path. At one point he squatted and directed her attention to markings on the ground, then made brushing motions in the air with his middle three fingers. Jen looked closer and saw turkey scratches in the dirt.

His thumbs up gave her a rush of anticipation.

At the top of the hill, he opened a camp stool. She sat with the shotgun across her lap. "Strut track," he said clearly enough to understand his accented whisper.

He turned and pointed up the hill to her right and then swung his arm to the left and nodded again.

She was in the center of a horny turkey freeway.

The guide nodded when she held up the turkey call with a question in her eyes. She gave it a thrum. He nodded and held a hand to his ear. Morning silence lingered. He shrugged, squatted, and motioned for her to call again.

She continued intermittently. Nothing responded except the call of a mourning dove and the growing golden morning light.

As the sun lit the eastern clouds a rosy pink, a call echoed back. She rose from her seat, but he raised a hand, palm toward her, and motioned to the right. She sounded the turkey call again.

Bongo-like bass tones quickening in cadence and volume sounded nearby. After a raised thumb, he pointed at her shotgun.

She rose, put the gun to her shoulder, then with a shake of her head lowered it and flicked the safety off, before assuming a shooting stance.

Another call thrummed. Staring intently along the shotgun, she watched the turkey stalk into the open. Iridescent blues and bronzes and its baby blue head reflected the clear dawn light. It resembled a peacock.

She hesitated and dropped the barrel toward the ground. The bird was so beautiful, how could she shoot it? Then remembering what Steve had taught her, she pulled the gun back up, aimed, and squeezed the trigger. The bird sprang into the air with a spray of feathers and flopped out of sight.

The guide scurried down the hill and stopped where the turkey had disappeared. "Good shot. You kill heem."

Jen walked over to view her first kill. She looked at the turkey, fearing what she would see and feel. Expecting to see a sea of blood—instead it lay limp on the ground. It's head was turned away—colors still vivid. Then she looked at her escort.

He smiled widely. "Good turkey." He made the OK symbol with his thumb and finger.

Her mouth stretched in a smile. She felt a glow of accomplishment. Her first kill. One shot. None of her brothers had shot an ocellated. Steve and her dad would be proud.

Chapter 48

Campeche, Mexico
May 2

"Sorry you didn't get a turkey," Jen said the next morning as Steve drove away from the hunt camp.

"I wanted to—but I'm happy that yours was the best bird of the week. Besides, the main point of the hunt was as an excuse to bring our guns in-country," Steve said. He didn't add that her kill was more important than any trophy he could bring back—proving she could shoot living things. "How was the experience of bagging your first?"

"I almost didn't shoot. But then I remembered you said anyone who eats beef, pork, or chicken is indirectly responsible for the animal's death. So, I pointed the shotgun and training took over."

Steve nodded encouragingly. A hunter's initial kill is an event saturated with varying emotional textures for different people.

"I didn't want to look at it," Jen said. "But when I did and it wasn't drenched in blood—just lying there with those gorgeous colors—I was overcome with…a sense of accomplishment. I hit it on my first shot."

"It's a fine-looking bird. It'll look terrific on the mantle. We'll call it mom's turkey," Steve said and then winced.

"Then I'll have two—you and the one on the mantle."

"I regretted it as soon as I said it," Steve said with a chuckle.

"It was nice we could donate the meat to local families."

"Yeah, I didn't want to keep it on ice while we shop for a boat," Steve said.

"Is the boat still in Playa del Carmen?"

"It better be. I made a full price offer pending inspection," Steve said. "I called a few minutes ago and told them when we'd arrive."

"Is it just like the Lagoon 440 we sailed in training?"

"Better," Steve said. "It's got radar, extra sails, and upgraded diesel engines."

————

The boat owner met Steve and Jen at the entry to the marina. He wore a navy sport coat and maroon tie appropriate for greeting buyers with a full price offer. Steve brushed his hands on the black t-shirt he wore before shaking hands.

The owner began with a tour of the expansive saloon. It looked like their training boat, except for the upholstery colors, which Jen complimented.

Steve wanted to see the equipment working. He activated winches, asked to see the radar in operation, crawled into engine compartments to check for leaks, and examined fluid levels.

When Steve came out, Jen was discussing the required paperwork and registrations with the owner.

"I'd like to take the boat out tomorrow for a test sail," Steve said.

The owner's face stretched in a wide smile and he nodded.

"If it sails as good as it looks, we'll pay cash and be on our way," Steve continued.

The owner's brow wrinkled in question and he shook his head.

In a combination of Spanish and English, Jen tried explaining that they would pay in US dollars—folding money—to conclude the deal.

The man's expression turned troubled. "Not good idea. Tax…"

He tried several Spanish words which Steve didn't understand and, given her befuddled expression, Jen didn't either.

"I'll pay ten thousand more to cover the tax," Steve said.

The man shook his head and waved his hand side-to-side in front of his face. His eyes looked haunted. "Tax…tax," he repeated several times.

"Fifteen thousand," Steve said.

The owner turned and shuffled sideways, keeping an eye on Steve as he climbed off the boat and hurried away up the pier.

At a loss to understand the strange behavior, Steve looked at Jen.

She shrugged. "Apparently cash is a problem. Perhaps he thinks we're with the cartel. Your last offer really spooked him."

"Damn!" Steve said. Cash was usually a good thing in a transaction. He hadn't expected this. "There's another boat nearby. It's not as well equipped, and the price is higher. It was plan B. I'll call and set up a meeting."

"I thought he might jump overboard and swim away," Jen said when Steve started the car.

"There was always the possibility of snags," Steve said. "That's why I identified several boats in Mexico and farther south. But I don't understand why he behaved so strangely."

"Let's hope the others are more rational. Let's get a good night's sleep and start over in the morning."

"Not yet. We've almost circumnavigated the Gulf of Mexico and haven't had a good seafood dinner," Steve said. "I found the perfect place nearby."

They shared *ceviche* to start. Jen's entrée was a grilled lobster marinated in a mix of citrus juices served with *axiote* sautéed potatoes. Steve chose shrimp marinated in a tangerine chipotle sauce. They washed down dinner with margaritas prepared with *añjeo* tequila. The finale was a flambéed crepe filled with banana and mango accompanied by coffee with tequila, Kahlua, fresh cream, and cinnamon.

Dinner didn't make up for losing the first boat, but it came close.

"There are other boats," Steve said when they arrived at their hotel.

"Should we test the chef's claim that some of the ingredients at dinner are aphrodisiacs?" Jen asked.

"I think so. Let's hurry and check in."

Chapter 49

Playa del Carmen
May 3

In the morning, they arrived at Steve's plan-B boat, a thirty-eight foot catamaran advertised as customized. The middle-aged owner met them wearing a turquoise silk sport jacket, a pale yellow shirt, and a rose ascot.

His fluttering hands pointed out the boat's features.

Steve stopped the man's recitation of the list of amenities. "We're offering full price, but first let's discuss arrangements."

The owner looked nervous. "What arrangements you want?"

"To pay in cash—US dollars."

The man's eyes flared wide. "I think maybe you want credit. Credit—I could do—but no paper dollars." He waggled an index finger.

"Why not?" Steve asked.

"Too much money. Tax and drug *policía* ask many questions. Maybe put me in jail. Jail not good for old *maricón*, me." The man pressed the fingertips of one hand to his ascot.

Steve threw his hands out. "How can it be too much money? It's the price you asked."

"Too much... dollars... what you say cash. Now not good time in Mexico—drugs, fighting, guns. Everyone suspicious. Sorry, no paper dollars."

This boat wasn't the best choice, so Steve didn't want to argue the point or increase the bid. "OK, *gracias* for your time," Steve said.

In the car, headed back to the hotel Jen laughed. "Boy, wasn't he flamboyant? What did he call himself?"

"*Maricón*. It's slang for gay in Spanish. Like someone in the US calling himself a queer."

"Oh yeah, I've heard that from our friends, Jeremy and Clark," Jen said. "I wondered if they do it for shock value, or if they're comfortable with the term."

"Can't help you there. I'm an engineer, not a psychologist," Steve said. "Now we have two strikes in Mexico. I didn't expect that, but I prepared," Steve said. "We have visas for Honduras and Guatemala, too."

"Do we have to start from scratch?" Jen asked.

"There's a boat on the Rio Dulce in Guatemala. It's more than I wanted to pay, but the seller is motivated. The price has dropped several times."

"That could be good or bad," Jen said.

"It's a fifty-footer, the next size up from what we sailed, and it's fully equipped. Upgraded diesels, radar, solar battery charger, extra sails, main sail reefer, yadda-yadda," Steve said.

"OK, make arrangements. I sure hope this plan works," Jen said. "What if it doesn't?"

"It was plan D. Plans A, B, and C were in Mexico, but they haven't worked. Now we need backup plan E. Speaking of plans, where are we on the International Business Corporation?"

"I contacted the Belize-based IBC broker Todd provided. He said our business will be ready within two days of paying the fees. I picked a company name that's two years old. Not having Belize passports is good. No Belize based IBC can conduct business in-country. Non-Belize passports make that presumption easy to construct."

"Great," Steve said.

"I said we'd supply an initial investment of two-hundred-fifty thousand. Is that still possible with the more expensive boat?"

"Yes, perfect. Knew there was a reason I married you. Besides the sex—," Steve said.

Her eyes narrowed and brow furrowed.

"But the sex is good, very good," he hurried to say.

She smiled.

"Believe me Esquire," Steve said. "I couldn't do your part as well. Thank's for handling that end of it."

"The broker is a fellow lawyer so we speak the same language, although he sounds like the Belize version of an ambulance chaser," Jen said. "It's nice English is the official language. Fewer hand gestures required. Makes phone calls simpler."

"Let's head for Belize city. I'll get in touch with the Guatemala boat seller while you finalize arrangements with your ambulance chasing friend."

"Excuse me. He's Todd's acquaintance, not mine," Jen huffed.

Chapter 50

Belize City, Belize
May 3

The hotel in Belize City had a Tudor exterior. "This isn't the architecture I expected in South America," Steve said as they pulled up.

"Belize was colonized by the English," Jen said.

Inside there was little old-world charm, but the rooms were clean. When offered a room on the first or second floor, Steve opted for the lower. It turned out that they had tile floors instead of carpet. In a tropical climate that was a plus. The room would be cooler.

The main reason Steve chose this hotel was the secure parking inside a fenced lot.

Jen left to meet with the business contact and Steve called the yacht broker. "Hello, I'm calling to see if the Lagoon 540 in Rio Dulce is still available. I'm in Belize City and want to look it over."

"My goodness. Let me check with the seller. What price did you see for the boat?"

"I've been looking at several," Steve said. If the broker wasn't sure of the price, Steve would throw out a low ball bid. "If memory serves, it's just under seven hundred thousand US."

"I believe it is near his asking price. Let me get back to you."

If that's in the ballpark, the seller must be desperate, Steve thought as he hung up.

His cell phone rang within fifteen minutes. This time a strong New York accent boomed across a scratchy connection. "Steve Henning? I understand you're in the market for a boat."

"Yes. Are you the man with a Lagoon 540 in Rio Dulce?"

"Yes, sir. I'm Ira Gorlich, captain of *The Starched Shirt*—one of the best equipped 500's you'll find. She's two years old, been through the canal, and up to Vancouver and back with plenty of stops along the way. We were heading back to New York when our situation changed. Stopped here in Rio Dulce because we like it and needed to weather our storm."

"A hurricane?" Steve asked.

"No, a personal storm. Our plans have changed, and we decided to sell. You want to look her over? When can you be here?"

"We're in Belize City. I wasn't sure if you were in residence or just had it docked in Rio Dulce. As long as you're on board, can I talk you into bringing it to Belize?" Steve asked.

"Well…"

"Or we could meet in *Punta Gorda*," Steve said.

After a long pause, "I don't think that's a good idea," Ira said.

"I'm certain we can reach an accommodation," Steve said. "We'll be in Belize City for several days. I want to try it on the open ocean. If we like it, we'll buy it. Can we meet?"

Another long break. "It's not that I don't want to—I can't."

It was Steve's turn to hesitate. "Why not? Some kind of legal problem?" There was a sinking sensation in his gut. Plan D was going up in smoke.

"I can't move it," Ira said quietly. "Oh, she works great, but… I can't move it… right now."

Steve's confusion converted to anger. "I'm looking for a functioning boat," Steve snapped. "A stationary boat won't do me any good."

"She moves like the wind. But I'm in a channel here and I need the diesels to move her out. And... well, I'm out of fuel."

"Don't they have diesel fuel there?" Steve asked.

"Well... I'm out of money too, otherwise I wouldn't sell her. She's my life's dream... but I have to."

Steve heard a catch in Ira's voice over the raspy connection. "I'm sorry for your troubles. Can't you trade something for fuel?"

"We've traded everything we can without taking the boat apart," Ira said. "I've been trading for food. That's why the price is so low. I've run out of options."

"I'm glad you mentioned price. The broker was vague. I plan on paying cash. Does that present any problems? Oh, and I heard that the price is just under seven hundred thousand."

"You're killing me!" Ira exclaimed. "Seven hundred for my beautiful boat? That fucking Madoff, he's lucky he's in jail or I'd kill him. I couldn't take less than seven-fifty for her."

"Bernie Madoff?" Steve asked. Now he was really confused.

"Yes, my good friend, my investment angel. My stores did his laundry for twenty years. When I sold the business, I gave the money to him to invest for our retirement. Now he's in jail. My money's kaput. *The Starched Shirt* can't move."

"I'm sorry," Steve said—at a loss for any other reply.

"We're ready to starve to death. My darling Effie ran the diesel out. Couldn't wait for the solar to charge the batteries for the AC. No, she had to run the generator."

Steve searched for a solution to the dilemma.

"Cash you say?" Ira said switching gears. "What is it—small bills?"

"Mostly hundreds and some under," Steve said. "Takes up less room. How can I convince you it's not counterfeit."

"After running drycleaners for most of my life, I know counterfeit. I've seen the best, but I spot it every time. I'll be able to tell if your money is real. You realize that seven hundred for this boat is stealing? Can you live with yourself if you take advantage of an unlucky couple? See, I'm concerned for your welfare."

Steve considered Ira's position for a few moments. "I can offer you this. We bought a year old Toyota Highlander for thirty-seven thousand and drove it here. I'll throw it in and pay you seven-twenty for *The Starched Shirt*—but you have to bring it to Belize City. You will have the car to get back to the States."

"I told you I can't move it. Paddling isn't an option," Ira said.

"I'll wire you a hundred dollars for fuel," Steve said. "Tell me where."

"You'd do that? That's more than my kids will do."

"You have kids who won't help?" Steve asked, incredulous.

"They blame me for losing their inheritance. It wasn't me. It was that crook with his Ponzi scheme. The kids think I have money hidden somewhere. They won't help until I tell them where it is. If I do, they'll take it and I'll still be here in Rio Dulce. Can you make it five hundred?"

"Five hundred?" Steve said. "If it needs that much fuel to get here I don't think I want it."

"I owe people," Ira said. "They'd be upset if I left without paying them."

"When we have an agreement, let me know where to send the money."

"I'll call you back," Ira said.

Chapter 51

Belize City, Belize
May 3

"OK, we have a deal, but could you make the wire advance seven hundred dollars?" Ira asked when he called back. "While looking for somewhere to wire the money, a fellow reminded me of another bill I'd forgotten to settle."

"OK, seven hundred. Better stay on the boat until the money comes so you don't receive any more reminders," Steve said.

"Good idea. After the money arrives, it'll take a couple of days to reach Belize City."

"We'll be waiting," Steve said.

While Jen went to wire cash to Ira, Steve brought the spare tire into their hotel room. The foam insulation had dried hard. More than a few curses and scraped knuckles resulted before he had removed the money and cleaned the tire enough to function again as a spare.

Cream colored insulation scraps from confetti to fist-sized covered the floor when Jen walked in. "What happened? Did the tire explode?"

"Very funny," Steve growled. "I'm glad we have a tile floored room. Bring the wastebasket. This will take several trips to the dumpster."

Steve was nervous. Would this Ira guy show up? Steve had made a strong case to Jen for buying a bigger vessel for seven hundred twenty thousand plus their car instead of spending four hundred-and-fifty for a boat they were familiar with. Now they both were eager to see Ira's boat. He dreaded the letdown if they had to start over again.

"It's another stunning day in the Caribbean," Steve said the next morning. "I can't sit around waiting for Ira to call. Let's take Elf for a walk, pretend we're tourists, and see what Belize City offers."

The wet season had begun. The drenching rains the night before had left everything crystal clear after the morning steam burned off.

"This town is a combination of rundown and colorful," Jen said as they strolled along the boulevard.

Many buildings glowed in the sunshine with bright pastel colors. Others were dowdy with pastels, faded to almost white, failing to completely cover graying wood. High over everything, palm trees swayed in a light breeze.

"Some of these buildings look like they received their last coat of paint during colonial times," Steve said.

An alligator lay sunning on one beach. Elf's frantic barking didn't faze the armored lizard.

The river running through the center of town was a constant presence.

Steve enjoyed listening to the mixed Caribbean lilt of English, Spanish and Creole. In the commercial center near the swing bridge there was a mix of shops. Butcher shops with chickens and ducks hanging in the windows abutted souvenir stores selling Mayan crafts and shell jewelry. A few places displayed diamonds in the rough or rings and other jewelry.

Ira called after lunch. "We've left Rio Dulce. Expecting to arrive tomorrow morning."

"Why don't we meet at the Radisson hotel dock?" Steve said.

"I remember it. I'll call when we get close."

Steve disconnected and signaled thumbs up to Jen. "They're on the way."

Elf had been a hit with the locals while they strolled through the shopping areas, but with his short legs he grew exhausted. Steve had been carrying him when he offered Elf to a butcher, which drew chuckles from the locals, but a frown from Jen. She handed Steve the packages she had been carrying and took Elf from Steve drawing smiles from the citizenry.

They returned to the hotel to let Elf rest.

―――――

The Hennings were enjoying coffee and croissants while watching a silver, pink, and blue sunrise climb toward a long cloud bank in the east when Ira called. "We'll be at the Radisson by ten forty-five."

"Excellent," Steve said. "We'll be waiting."

Steve and Jen were on the dock as *The Starched Shirt* maneuvered toward them. It was exciting to watch the automatic reefing winches lower the main sail as the boat glided in to the landing.

A tall, sturdily built gray-haired man manned the helm and an attractive graying woman deployed fenders on the port side of the boat.

Steve moved forward. The smiling woman threw him a line as Ira reversed the diesels to bring the boat to a stop. Once alongside, he boomed "Mr. and Mrs. Henning I presume?"

While Steve made his line fast, Jen moved aft and caught the next line Effie threw.

Ira strode up to the rail. "Come aboard so I can show you my beauty." Then he glanced at Effie with a smile. "And so I can introduce you to my other beauty."

Once on board, Steve and Ira shook hands. They were close enough in height that they saw eye-to-eye. Ira clapped Steve on the shoulder. "You're going to love the headroom on my baby—

only a few places where you'll need to duck Let's take the grand tour."

During the tour Steve and Jen kept nudging each other. The boat was far better equipped than what they had sailed. The master suite which took up the entire starboard hull, seemed twice as large.

"It's bigger than our master bedroom at home," Jen whispered.

"It should be. This boat costs more than our house," Steve replied.

"I wouldn't travel the Caribbean, South America, or most of the rest of the world without armament," Ira said as he opened a closet with a shotgun resting in the built-in gun rack. "We've never had a problem, but better safe than sorry."

"Have you ever had a problem with customs?" Steve asked.

"I always declare it," Ira said. "When they see shotguns they let me keep them. I can lock this cabinet. They might want to keep the key while we're in port, but that's not a problem."

"Good to know," Steve said—his mind generating ideas.

Ira pointed out each of the electric winches. "We couldn't sail it by ourselves without the power options. It has a lot of sail to haul by hand."

Effie showed Jen the clothes washer and dryer and the dishwasher. "Sailing isn't camping. No roughing it."

Everything down to the hundred horsepower diesels with feathered props to reduce drag showed the pride and care Ira and Effie had put into planning this vessel.

"Do you and Jen want to take her out now?"

"We will, but let's grab breakfast here at the hotel first," Steve said. "Our treat."

Ira and Effie looked at each other with obvious relief. "We haven't eaten since yesterday morning." Ira said. "I hope it's a buffet. I'm ready to eat my weight."

Steve caught Jen's eye during breakfast and winked. If Ira kept up his pace it was conceivable that he might eat his weight, but he stopped at about a leg-and-a-half with a deep sigh.

The boat handled easily in the light morning wind. Past the islands separating Belize City from the Caribbean, the wind picked up, and the ship leapt like a dolphin—slicing through the deeper blue water.

"So do want the boat?" Ira asked after Steve brought it back to port.

"Let's do it," Steve said. "But don't you want to look at the car first?"

"Is the money in the car?"

"Nope. I didn't think parking a car in the middle of Belize with seven hundred and twenty thousand in it was a good idea."

"Less seven hundred bucks," Ira said.

"I'll chalk that up to a finder's fee. Besides it saved me from driving to Rio Dulce. From the map, it looks to be one of those places you can't get to from here," Steve said. "How do you want the money?"

"How did you get it here to Belize?"

Steve described carrying it in the tire.

"Ha! What a great idea," Ira said. "I'll do it the same way."

Ira and Effie accompanied them to the hotel. Jen handed Ira two backpacks filled with the money and invited him to count it.

He did and inspected a number of bills while he thumbed through the stacks. He finished and smiled at Jen. "I knew you were too pretty to push fake money. This is Uncle Sam's finest."

"You should stay at a different hotel," Steve said. "It might draw attention if you remove and replace the tire here, since I did the same thing last night."

Jen used a different attorney than she used for the IBCs to prepare the boat and car paperwork since they were using their real names for the sales. "It may not matter but I don't want to explain why we're using two sets of names," she said.

Ira and Effie dropped Steve and Jen back at their hotel. They unloaded the car, exchanged hugs, and wished each other well. Steve watched Ira drive their new car up the Northern Highway to find a different hotel.

Chapter 52

Belize City, Belize
May 4

Steve arranged their gear aboard *The Starched Shirt* while Jen took a cab to town for provisions.

When they finished and Elf was settled, Steve started the diesels and steered the boat out of the slip. Jen plotted a course through the barrier islands that populate the magnificent coral reef for which Belize is well known in the diving community.

"Why don't we spend the night beside an unpopulated island before we head back?" Jen asked. "We've been running scared—constantly on the move. Let's stop to smell the roses on a white sand beach with no one around."

The sun had traveled past midday. Steve considered Jen's suggestion as he looked into the waves sliding by—supposedly the clearest turquoise waters in the Caribbean. It was late to start back, and they had enough time to find a nice spot. "OK, a half-day vacation. We'll unwind on a deserted stretch of sand and snorkel the reef."

"Wonderful," Jen said. "I'll look at the charts and find our idyllic spot."

Before leaving Belize City cellular reception, Steve called his brother. "Todd, we bought a boat."

"Is it the kind you pedal with the little paddle wheel in back?"

"Even better than I had hoped for. It's a Lagoon 540 with upgraded everything. It's called *The Starched Shirt*."

"Unusual name," Todd said. "Are you going to change it?"

"We haven't decided. Bought it from an interesting guy. I'll tell you when we get back," Steve said. "What I need from you is the name of a good cabinetmaker. Somebody who is tight-lipped."

"I don't know if boats are different, but I found one for a client who was refitting a jet last year. Will that work?"

"Give me his info. I'll call him."

Todd looked up the contact information and read it to Steve.

"Thanks," Steve said. "See you in a few days."

Jen plotted a course toward an island that showed on the charts as unoccupied. The miniscule islands they passed were peppered by a surprising number of houses, shacks, and boat docks. The first island Jen chose turned out to have a ramshackle tin and bleached wood structure that, judging by clothes flapping on a line in the breeze, was occupied. By late afternoon, they found a small uninhabited island that rose eight feet above sea level at its highest point.

White sand beaches surrounded a thick grove of palms and mangroves. The beach varied in size from a few feet between the water and tree line to several yards.

The depth finder showed fifteen feet, but the bottom appeared to be no more than a foot away. There were fish gliding and crabs scurrying—a perfect spot to relax.

He dropped anchor next to a pristine beach that stretched inland twenty feet before palms leaned out to drape fronds above the sand. "Last one in the water has to make dinner," Jen hollered as she came up from the berth below wearing her swimsuit.

Steve shrugged, kicked off his shoes, and dove in fully clothed from his steersman position at the top. He hit the water before Jen stepped over the railing.

"Asshole," Jen shouted as she jumped in.

Steve laughed so hard he went under and swallowed water. He resurfaced coughing and spitting up water.

"Serves you right," Jen said with a grin "Are you OK?"

He controlled his hacking enough to climb back aboard, change to his swimsuit, and gather the fins, masks, and snorkels Ira had left.

Paddling through the water, they watched gaily colored fish dart around them and across the coral reef. A gliding manta ray cast an ominous shadow startling Steve until he realized what it was.

Starfish, anemones, and coral formations formed a fantasy kingdom. An hour of exploring left Steve and Jen weary but more relaxed than they'd been in weeks. Whenever he or Jen popped to the surface, Elf pranced along the side of the boat. He gave a shrill bark as a ray passed under the boat. Steve chuckled. Elf behaved as if his barks had frightened it off.

Before snorkeling, Steve had loaded both shotguns with the idea they might shoot a fish for dinner tonight. After sliding over the coral fantasyland, he decided not to chance it, concerned the shotgun pellets might harm the reef. It was too spectacular to endanger, so when he climbed back aboard he replaced the guns in the bedroom cupboard.

Instead of the fish dinner he had contemplated, Jen fixed a plate of chicken sausage, cheeses, fresh fruit, and a crusty French bread loaf along with a crisp sauvignon blanc. Over dinner they watched a golden sunset shade the approaching cloudbank to pink, then to silver, and gray.

"I'll shower before getting into bed," Jen said.

"OK, I'll follow you."

Jen was massaging shampoo into her scalp when Steve opened the shower door, squeezed in next to her, and took over. He finished with the shampoo and conditioner and soaped her body, paying particular attention to her chest.

"Let me return the favor," she said when Steve finished.

The part she gave special consideration to made Steve gasp. "Let's christen the boat," he said, shutting off the water, and leading her to their bunk.

Afterwards, they shared a pair of Steve's pajamas, Steve wore the bottoms and Jen the top. He fell asleep with her back pressed to his chest and his arm across her waist.

Chapter 53

Deserted Caribbean Island
May 4

Frantic barking woke Steve. It was pitch dark outside.

"What is it? Is he trying to frighten away an alligator?" Jen mumbled.

When Elf kept it up, Steve rolled out of bed and grabbed his shotgun out of the cupboard. It was still loaded from his aborted fishing plan.

He handed Jen her gun. "It's loaded with three shells. Ira said better safe than sorry. But please don't shoot me when I come back."

He walked toward Elf's frantic sounds at the back of the saloon. Light rain pattered in the moist dark night. Elf's white patches floated like ghosts on the starboard side as the effort of his ferocious barks raised his front feet off the deck.

Steve moved forward cautiously until he received a hard jab in the back.

"Drop the gun," a Creole accented voice growled. "Raise your hands."

Steve set the shotgun butt on the deck, leaned the gun against a counter, and lifted his arms.

A jab came again. "Move away."

Another man entered the room carrying a rifle. The dim light was enough to display the white teeth in his broad smile.

Steve moved to the left and the man behind him picked up the shotgun. "Naise showtgun," the man said as he hefted it and placed the pistol into his waistband. He motioned toward the main cabin. "Go there." He was shorter than Steve, but broader. He followed Steve in the dim light down three stairs.

Steve shuffled into the dressing area leading to the stateroom. He looked back to see the two men following. This time the poke was with his shotgun. "Don't try anything."

Steve flicked on the dressing room light. The bedroom was still dark. He could see Jen sitting in the bed. "It's an Elf night," he said hoping she picked up on the code they had used. His comment resulted in another hard shove in the back. Steve dropped to the floor.

———

After Steve left, Jen heard the sound of someone else's voice in the saloon—not Steve. She chambered a round, flicked off the safety, and laid the gun beside her on the bed, pulling the sheet over it.

Steve stepped into the cabin and flicked on the dressing room light. Another man entered behind him. Steve shuffled through the light into the dark stateroom.

Steve said something about Elf then fell out of sight below the foot of the bed when the stranger shoved him. The man was silhouetted in the light from the dressing room. He raised the shotgun to his shoulder and pointed it at Steve.

Fear and anger flooded Jen. The shotgun came to her shoulder as Steve had taught her. She squeezed the trigger, aiming at the man's head.

With a deafening boom, his head blossomed in a cloud of red mist.

The force of the shot pressed her back against the headboard. In the smoky haze, she saw a second man enter and bring his rifle up while pivoting toward her.

The man hollered something her stunned ears couldn't hear. She aimed at his open mouth and pulled the trigger. He flopped backward.

A hand rose from the foot of the bed and waved back and forth. Steve's head followed. He shouted, but she still couldn't hear over the ringing in her ears.

Steve dove low and crept up the stairs to the saloon carrying his shotgun.

When she realized there was only one shell left in the gun, Jen rose from the bed to get more. She stopped when she saw the bloody corpses lying on the deck. Her shoulders and hands trembled. She had killed them. Jen clenched her jaw in determination. They would have killed Steve. She retrieved two shotgun shells from the closet and reloaded.

Steve crouched as he entered the saloon, gun at his shoulder swinging side to side. There was movement at the port stern. Someone with a long gun climbed into the boat. Steve fired. The blast blew the man off the back of the boat into the sea.

Steve stepped forward and looked over the side. Two men in a small fishing boat were pulling away, the engine whining. The man he'd shot sprawled across the back of the boat. Steve shot twice. The man at the wheel fell forward, pushing the throttle closed. The other collapsed to the deck of the small craft.

The boat bobbed fifteen yards away after nosing down to a stop. The three bodies didn't move.

Steve searched the rest of *The Starched Shirt*. No one else was on board. The fishing boat still floated off the port side. A fine rain misted the warm, velvety darkness.

He returned inside.

Jen sat on the bed in the master cabin with legs crossed, gun across her lap. Steve climbed into bed beside her and wrapped his arms around her shoulders. "How are you doing?" he asked. Killing a human was a whole different thing from shooting a turkey.

"I was shaky and nauseous at first." She held up a slightly trembling hand. "I'm still shaky, but now I'm thinking I should feel bad, but don't. A little numb. But inside that—I'm good," She paused and frowned. "That bothers me. I killed two humans and I don't feel awful. I don't even know who they are. Are they the ones who've been following us for the money?"

Steve looked at the bodies, which were out of Jen's view from where she sat at the head of the bed. "I'd like to think so, but they they're probably pirates. They don't fit the description of our house burglars or your parents' invaders." He smoothed hair out of her eyes. "Because of what you did we're still alive and not captives or dead. It's very good to be alive. Thank you."

Jen flashed a small smile.

He leaned in and kissed her temple. "And those were two good shots. Unfortunately, we'll never be able to tell anyone. Pirates aren't human. They're scum of the earth, preying on people who haven't harmed them," Steve said. "Instead, think of them as a mess we have to clean up. I'll haul the trash out."

Steve snatched a towel out of the shower and wrapped the bloody mess that had been the head of the bandit. He grabbed the body by the shirt and trousers and lugged him to the port side of the boat and dropped him on the rail with his head hanging overboard.

He retained the towel and used it to carry and prop the remaining carcass on the railing next to the first one with minimal blood leakage.

Jen came out with him. In the moon she looked gray. Was it a delayed reaction?

"Will you take the con and pull our boat next to that one floating on our port side?" He pointed. He needed her help but if she was on the bridge, she wouldn't see the men she'd killed hanging over the rail.

Steve jumped into the buccaneers' boat when Jen pulled close. He walked it hand-over-hand along the sailboat's rail until it floated below the two corpses. He grasped their shirts and pulled. They landed in the craft with the other bodies. Then he tied their boat to a cleat on *The Starched Shirt*, climbed back aboard, and directed Jen to take it out to sea. The fishing boat dragged behind.

When they reached deep water, Steve climbed back into the skiff and dumped the bodies into the ocean. After the last one disappeared, Steve clambered up to their sailboat's deck and cut the empty pirates' boat free.

"Let's head for Ft. Lauderdale," he said when he returned to the con with Jen.

"Do you think they'll float to shore?"

"The sharks were already circling. With blood in the water, I don't think there will be much left," Steve said. "Their empty, bloody boat will run aground somewhere. Let it be a warning to family and friends."

Chapter 54

Ft. Lauderdale
May 4

Juan, Hector, and Edgar had tailed Todd Henning for six days without any indication of contact with his brother Steve. It was time to change tactics. "Where's the equipment you use to make people talk?" Juan asked Hector.

"In the trunk," Hector replied and rubbed his hands together.

"The brother's home for the night," Juan said. "Go get Edgar while I watch here. Pick up a pizza on your way."

"What do you want on it?"

"I don't care. I need the box—in good shape—don't mess it up. Grab a ball cap, too." Juan said.

Hector shrugged. "OK. I'll get the meat lovers."

Juan smiled and nodded. "Perfect."

———

Juan walked up to Todd Henning's condo carrying the empty pizza box. Hector and Edgar had eaten every bit of meat and cheese. The boys positioned themselves to either side of the front door—pressed against the stucco wall.

Juan tugged the brim of his baseball cap lower, raised the pizza box high, and pressed the doorbell. The peephole darkened. After a moment, he heard the metallic click of a bolt.

Todd Henning opened the door a foot. "Can I help you? I didn't order any…"

Edgar slammed the door open, knocking Todd backward. Hector rushed in behind him.

214

"What are you...?" Todd didn't have time to finish the sentence. Hector punched him in the nose knocking him to the floor. Edgar kicked him in the ribs. "Aaaagh," Todd groaned as the air was forced from his lungs.

Hector lifted him by one arm as if he were a child. Edgar grabbed the other, and they dragged a gasping Todd into the kitchen.

Edgar held him up while Hector grabbed a kitchen chair and shoved it against Todd's legs. He collapsed backward.

Juan followed with Hector's black bag and admired their brute force choreography. He set the bag on the table, while Hector pulled handcuffs from his back pocket, wrenched Todd's arms back to the sound of another moan, and clenched the cuffs hard around his wrists.

"What the fu...," Edgar stopped Todd's question with a backhand to the nose that slammed his head around like an owl looking backwards.

Juan leaned forward until he was inches away. "Where can I find Steve Henning?"

Todd flinched away. His nose was flattened and splayed to the side. Blood ran along his chin and dripped onto his shirt. He shook his head and tried to glare through eyes already swelling.

"We'll change that attitude," Hector said and wrenched Todd's nose to the side.

Todd screamed and fainted.

"Wake him up, Hector," Juan said. "Edgar, find his cellphone. See if he has a number for his brother and check his call log. I'll check his computer."

Chapter 55

Caribbean Ocean
May 7

Steve cleaned the bloody mess in the master cabin while Jen sailed the boat toward Ft. Lauderdale. When he finished, no signs remained except a few pellet holes in the woodwork. At short range, most of the pellets struck the pirates' heads, necks, and chests.

The Caribbean warmed, brewing storms in their path. When it calmed again, he found that rain had saved him the trouble of washing the blood off the back deck and side of the boat.

Remembering his and other snipers' reactions after their first kills, Steve kept a careful eye on Jen. She appeared to be dealing with it, but he awakened twice on the first night to find her thrashing in nightmares. He patted her hip. "It's OK." He whispered close to her ear. "The bad guys are gone. I'm here and everything is good." She relaxed, never waking up.

———

"How are you," Steve asked the next morning.

"OK," Jen replied and then frowned. "Why shouldn't I be?"

"In my experience, a lot of guys find killing someone to be traumatic. If you need to talk, I'm here."

"He would have shot you. I had to. It took less thought than the turkey did. They'd have killed us both. I've had nightmares that I didn't shoot and he killed you and the blood in the cabin was yours. I'd do it again to prevent that. No regrets."

She sounded like a mama bear protecting her cubs. It's good he was one of hers.

———————

Steve's cellphone showed two bars as they neared the Florida Keys, so he made an appointment with the cabinetmaker Todd recommended. Calls to Todd ended in voice mail. They'd be together in less than a day, so he didn't leave a message.

After arriving in mid-afternoon, Steve caught a cab to Todd's condo while Jen stayed on board.

Steve climbed the condo stairs. Yellow police tape hung across the doorway and fluttered in the breezy open air hallway. He stopped to make sure it was Todd's place—across from the elevator. Had Todd been busted for "facilitating"?

The door was opened half a foot, so Steve pushed it farther. "Is anybody home?"

"Stay out," a voice called. "I'll be right there."

A tall, middle-aged man with thinning hair, dressed in a navy blazer, gray slacks, no tie, and a light blue shirt walked into the living room. "Can I help you?"

"Todd Henning's brother, Steve. My wife and I arrived in town. I wasn't able to reach Todd, so I came over. Is there a problem?"

"Mr. Henning, I'm detective Art Cohen. We've been trying to contact you since yesterday. Didn't you get my messages?"

"We were out of town," Steve said as he pulled out his phone. "Poor cell coverage." There weren't any messages. "I changed carriers recently. Maybe you called the old number. Why did you call?"

The detective looked to the left, out of Steve's view, and shook his head. "I'll come out there." He ducked under the yellow ribbon. "I'm sorry to inform you that your brother has been the victim of a crime."

Relief that Todd wasn't in jail was momentary. "What crime? Is he OK?"

"No, he's in Broward General."

"What happened?" Steve asked. "I talked to him a few days ago," he said—trying to get a rein on a chaotic surge in emotions. Concern and fear for Todd's wellbeing was salted with anger at the criminal that caused it.

"Breaking, entering, assault—for now."

"What do you mean—for now?"

"He's in the ICU." detective Cohen shook his head. "I hope he'll recover," he said after a pause.

"I need to go to the hospital," Steve said, reaching for the phone in his pocket. "I'll call another cab."

"I'll take you to the hospital. We can talk on the way over."

"Thank you."

"Can you tell me more," Steve asked when he was in detective Cohen's car.

"Your brother's fiancée, Dani, arrived—she had a key and let herself in. Three men had your brother strapped to a chair in the front room. She did the smart thing and ran out—screaming bloody murder according to one of the other tenants."

"Did she get away OK?"

"Yes, she did. She may have saved his life. From the marks on your brother, it appears he was tortured."

"Holy shit." What had Todd gotten into this time?

"Another tenant, the one who overheard her screams, stepped out to the sound of a shot fired," Cohen said. "Then three men ran out, piled into a car out front. We ran the license plate. Found it abandoned six miles from here. Stolen. Wiped clean of prints."

A sense Deja vu made Steve's gut sink. "Do you have a description of the men?"

"Three Hispanics, two big, and one little is all anyone remembers. One had a pony tail."

That big and little description again. Could this be Steve's fault? "You said a shot was fired."

"They shot your brother before they left. Didn't kill him, but he lost a lot of blood."

"Tortured and shot—my God," Steve said. Was this done by people looking for Steve? A feeling of weakness washed over him.

"Are you aware of your brother's activities which would attract attention from people who'd do this?"

"As a real estate broker?" Steve said, remembering Todd's cover story. "Not unless a buyer or seller was unhappy with the deal they got. I understand there's underworld influence in southern Florida. Perhaps he pissed off the wrong client."

"Real estate broker, huh?" Cohen said. "There were credentials on his office wall, but we haven't found a firm he works with."

"Todd dealt freelance. His clients value discretion. If their names got out, speculators often bid the price up. So he fronted for them as a buyer's agent."

"I'll check it out."

Todd had his broker's license for the reason Steve had told Cohen. The story could be confirmed.

"Here we are," Cohen said. "Yesterday a nurse said he might be stabilizing. He owes his life to the girlfriend. She broke up what was going on, called 911, came back to stanch the bleeding, and administered CPR until the EMTs showed up."

"Do you have Dani's contact info?"

Cohen raised his eyebrows. "You don't have it?"

"I just met her. I knew that Todd had asked her to marry, before we left, but she hadn't given him an answer."

The detective pulled a small notebook from a coat pocket, copied information, ripped a sheet out, and handed it to Steve. "Your brother's lucky to have her. How can I get in touch with you if needed? Where are you staying and are you in town long?"

Steve gave his new cell number. "We're staying on our boat. Planned to be here less than a week. We're on a sailing vacation. Now I don't know what our plans are. I'll stay if I can help Todd."

Cohen gave Steve his card. "Call me if you leave town, please."

"Are we suspects?"

"No, I don't think so. But is there anyone who can vouch for you?"

"We were in Belize. I have docking receipts. I made a phone call as we left. You can check my international phone records. And I tried to call Todd when we hit the Keys. They might have location records."

"We'll check it out."

"Thanks for the ride," Steve said and got out of the car.

Detective Cohen leaned toward the passenger side and looked up. "I hope your brother recovers. Sorry it happened."

Chapter 56

Ft. Lauderdale
May 8

Todd was still in a coma when Steve arrived at the ICU nurses' station. The doctor stopped by a few minutes later and Steve introduced himself.

"The bullet punctured a lung and broke a rib on the way out, but that damage was repaired," Dr. Elizondo said. "His real trauma is from the torture."

"What did they do?" Steve asked.

"Repeated and excessive shocks. The police said there was an automotive battery in the room, but they took any other apparatus used. The scorches are much worse than from a car battery. His body was covered with burns."

"My God. Poor Todd."

"His mouth and head were the worst. They shoved wet steel wool into his mouth. It acted as a conductor. They moved the other electrode around on his body so the current traveled from where they touched him to the mouth. I picked steel wool shards out of the mucosa and from between his teeth."

"That's enough to cause a coma?"

"Head and ears were worst. Numerous burn marks around eyes, temples, and deep inside the ears. I believe that caused his coma. He may have brain damage. If he recovers, I don't know how well he'll function," the doctor said.

Steve spent time with Todd, but there was no response. The pain of remorse grew worse the longer he sat.

Before leaving, he had the bills for Todd's care sent to him. On the cab ride to their boat he watched the surroundings without noting any details. His agony intensified as he realized he may have caused this.

———

Jen sensed something was wrong when Steve walked into the saloon. He slumped on the sofa and stared between his knees at the floor. After a long pause, he looked up. "Todd's in the hospital. He's been tortured, shot, and in a coma."

She was stunned. She slumped onto a galley stool. "Oh, my God. Tortured? Who? Why?"

"Three men. Hispanics. Not unusual for south Florida. But there were three in our storage unit—three at our house—and your dad said three were there when Bozo died."

Jen's head lowered into her raised hands. She didn't want to face that they might be the cause. "Two big men and a little man?" Her voice felt weak.

Steve nodded.

"Was he attacked because of us?" she asked.

"At first I assumed that Todd's business put him up against people who could do this," Steve said. "But I'm afraid I've been fooling myself. I didn't get away with the money scot-free. Someone is after us."

Fear caused Jen's stomach to drop. "They're attacking our families. How can we stop it?"

"I don't know. We can't do anything for Todd," Steve said. "They aren't sure if he'll wake up. Or if he'll even be the same person if he does."

Jen heard the catch in Steve's voice—saw tears glisten on his eyelashes as he shut his eyes tight. She was shocked. She'd never seen him cry. Not even when his parents died. "I'm so sorry. But we have to do something."

Steve opened his eyes and cleared his throat. "We should stick to the plan and hide the money. I have no idea who they are or how to contact them. But we can't wait around until they catch us. We could end up like Todd before giving them what they want. We can't even dump the money. They'd keep coming after us."

Jen knew he was right, but she felt so helpless.

"Besides," Steve said. "Todd will have medical bills. I took responsibility with the hospital. We need the cash to help him. I don't care about being rich. Just want to care for our family and ourselves. God help us if we end up like Todd, but with no money. We'll be worse off than before."

Jen thought of her brothers, both aging baby boomers who had retirement plans yanked out from under their feet. Their golden years turned to tin. What if whoever it was went after them too?

"OK, let's keep on plan, but we need to be more careful." Her mind churned—looking for solutions but finding none.

Chapter 57

Ft. Lauderdale
May 9

Steve greeted Jen in the morning with a handful of papers. "I've been wracking my brain where to hide the money on this boat. Ira's shotgun cabinet gave me an idea."

Steve spread the papers on the counter. "I want to build a real gun safe into the closet near the bathroom. Look at these diagrams. We don't need a place for guns, but I want the space behind the safe." He poked at the drawings he made. "Because of the hull's curvature, there's an irregular volume behind these flat walls. I measured and calculated, and there's enough room for most of the money."

Jen examined the illustrations and chuckled. "You're such an engineer. Sometimes I wonder if I shouldn't lock you away from real people."

"Engineers are the most practical," Steve said. "That makes them more real."

"OK, Mr. Real, how are you going to get to the money once the safe is built in?" Jen said.

"The safe will be secure, but moveable. We can lock it in place when the boat is moving, but the safe will be on rollers." His finger roamed over the drawing. "These bolts and braces can be removed, and the safe rolled out when we need to get at the money behind it." He continued to describe his concept in the drawings until she smiled and nodded.

"If this works it will be brilliant," Jen said.

"Good, there's a cabinet maker coming over in an hour to see these drawings and build it."

"But where will I put the evening gown collection I planned for that closet?"

"This is not a formal trip. Strictly shorts and flip flops."

———

Steve met with the carpenter, and afterwards ordered a gun safe for delivery the next day. Then he and Jen went to see Todd.

Dani was in Todd's room and had tears in her eyes when they arrived. Jen wrapped her arms around the taller woman. Steve inadequately patted her back.

Dani reached out and held Steve's hand. "I'm so sorry I couldn't stop them—only run away."

"You saved his life," Steve said. "In their hurry they missed a killing shot."

"But the doctors don't know if he'll recover," Dani said and sobbed.

"They called you his fiancé," Jen said. "Does that mean you said yes?"

Dani nodded as the tears continued to run.

"He has to recover," Steve said and held Todd's hand. "See how much he has to live for."

Dani's mouth twitched into the semblance of a smile.

"Why don't we get coffee," Jen said. "Let's give Steve a few minutes with his brother."

Steve spent twenty minutes with Todd, holding his hand, begged for him to wake up, and told Todd how sorry he was he brought this on him. He didn't expect a response but he still had to say it.

When he arrived in the hospital cafeteria, Jen was sitting alone with a frown. "How's Dani?" he asked.

"She was ready to move in with Todd. That's why she had a key. I told her to go ahead if she wants to. She may not want to after this."

"Yeah. Tough decision." Steve said. "Call and tell her we'll make the payments. It'd be nice if she was there for Todd when he wakes up."

"She said the two big guys looked hard, like gang bangers," Jen said. "The third guy looked more sophisticated."

"Sophisticated?"

"Her words. I didn't ask for an explanation."

"They could be the ones that broke into our house. The little one came back in a suit and tie. Claimed to be with the DEA," Steve said.

"I hate that we brought this trouble to Todd."

"Me too. I'd give the money back if we could make it stop," Steve said. "But I don't know how. Who do we call? I don't even know which cartel. If we give it to the police, we don't know that whoever is after us would stop coming."

"If they find us would they kill us?"

"What do you think after what they did to Todd? We don't have an alternative. Without the money, we don't have any resources to keep going." Steve said. "We have to keep pushing forward with our plan."

Chapter 58

Ft. Lauderdale
May11

Steve rolled the almost 400 pound safe out of the space with ease. He rolled it back in and locked it into place with the push bolts and slid and locked down the baseboard that hid the rollers. Next, he grabbed the safe door and threw his weight backward and forward—to see how much play there was.

It didn't budge.

"It's locked in. Even a hurricane won't make it slide or tip," the carpenter said with obvious pride.

"That's my biggest concern," Steve said. In actuality, his main concern was a customs officer detecting that the safe wasn't permanently built in. "It's perfect."

When the cabinet maker left, Steve slid the safe back out. Behind was a flat wooden panel. Removing it revealed a hidden space between the panel and the curved hull which was fourteen to twenty-two inches deep, twenty six inches wide, and eighty-one inches tall.

"I did the math and we should be able to get four thousand packets of money behind here," Steve said.

"Of course you did the math," Jen said. "Was algebra involved?"

He felt his face flush. "A little calculus to take the curvature into account," he said quietly.

"Calculus. Of course. How much can we put in there?"

"All the hundreds and fifties. Maybe some of the twenties."

"Let's fill her up and check your math."

Steve took a cab to the Toyota SUV's storage. As he walked by the office, Artie came out "Mr. Henson, hello. Your SUV window is repaired. Sorry it happened. You be in town long?

"No. I'll use the car today and then we're off again. We stopped to pick up groceries, then we're sailing again.

Artie shook his head. "It must be enjoyable to have extra time at your age. What are you—fifty?"

"Fifty-nine. Sixty soon."

"Maybe we'll sell this place in a few years and take time for our dreams. Always wanted to travel the country in an RV."

"How old are you Artie?"

"Sixty-eight, but I feel younger in Florida than I did in Boston. The winters are murder on old bones. There's bugs and rain here but the winters make up for everything else. Bought a little place nearby a few years ago. Rent it out. Thought we'd make a killing a few years ago, but the value has dropped."

Steve smiled and patted Artie on the shoulder. His story sounded so familiar. "The economy will turn around. In two years, you'll be seventy. Plenty young enough to enjoy your golden years. Now I need the car to run errands. Be back with it later. Thanks for fixing it."

Inside the storage unit Steve pulled out his wallet and retrieved his knife from where it had fallen to the bottom of his pocket. Knife in hand, he crawled under the car, sliced and pried loose the glue holding the tracking device in place, and put the tattletale electronic bug into a corner. A quick search failed to turn up anything else.

Next, he drove the SUV to the storage unit with the money. After checking the trailer over once more for any electronics, he hooked it up and towed it to the boat.

He was so busy watching in the rear-view mirror for anyone following that he came close to rear ending a car at a stop light—braking so hard he left skid marks and the trailer fishtailed—threatening to hit a car in the next lane.

At the marina where the boat was docked, he found a communal pushcart, and rolled the boxes to the sailboat—six boxes per trip—and then carried them into the master suite. Although the slip wasn't far from where he parked, his paranoia ran at peak efficiency. Every movement in the area, whether it was a seagull, a flapping flag, or a person set his heart racing.

While he hauled the money boxes onboard, Jen stacked packets in the hideaway. There was even enough room for Steve to squeeze in his handgun with little room to spare.

When finished with the woodwork back in place to conceal the carpenter's handiwork, Steve breathed a great sigh of relief. "It's tight, but nothing should rattle," he said.

"If customs finds the gun, what will they do?" Jen asked.

"They'll find the money too. I don't think weapons will matter if that happens."

Jen looked the safe cabinet over closely. She grabbed the safe's handle and shook it, pushing and pulling fiercely. "It looks and feels built in. I wouldn't have any idea it wasn't permanent if I hadn't seen it. Great job." She gave him hard hug. "Occasionally being an engineer has its good points."

"I was aroused until that back handed compliment."

Jen frowned. "Anything I can do to turn that around?"

A slow smile stretched Steve's lips. "Come to bed and let's explore options."

———

Steve and Jen shopped for final provisions for their trip, visited Todd again, and picked up the new registration number decal

Steve had ordered. He applied the new numbers over those that had served Ira. He would have liked to change the name of the boat, but there wasn't time. He'd get the name he and Jen had agreed on—*Caribbean Layoff*—painted on the stern later. For now it remained *The Starched Shirt*.

With a lighter heart, Steve joined Jen on the bridge as she backed their sailboat out of the slip. "We're almost home free," he said. "Soon we'll be out of US waters, and there's no way whoever has been following us knows where we're going. Once the cash is in a bank, they can't steal it from us."

Jen frowned. "We didn't think anyone could find us before."

She was right. He didn't want to be naive again. His chest tightened in anger. Look what it cost Todd. He wished he knew who was trying to find them. He wanted to punish them for what they did to his brother. Maybe it was better if he didn't know.

Chapter 59

Ft. Lauderdale
May 11

"Have you found their boat?" Esteban growled over the phone.

"Not yet," Juan said. "We don't even know if it's still called *The Starched Shirt* like Henning's brother told us."

"How will you find it if they change the name?"

"Registration. If Henning puts the boat in his name, it'll have a new number," Juan said. "You have tentacles everywhere. You got anybody in the Florida tax collector's office? They have registration records." He listened to silence for almost half a minute. Had he finally pushed Esteban too far?

"Maybe. I'll get back."

Juan looked at his phone. The call was disconnected. Obviously Esteban had never learned phone etiquette.

"What do we do now?" Edgar asked.

"Keep looking. You said the reward for finding the boat would be enough to get it found your people on the street."

"Yeah, but there are a lot of boats in Ft. Lauderdale—in Florida," Hector said. "It's gonna take time. It would be better if we knew the model."

"It's a Lagoon, Henning's brother told us that before he passed out and that girl came in before we could revive him," Juan said.

"There are a lot of Lagoons—lots of different models and sizes."

"What if they find out we're looking for it?" Hector asked. "the brother is still alive to tell them. You didn't kill him."

"Don't worry. He's not talking. Still in a coma. Checked today," Juan said. "Another thing Todd Henning said—they're going to Belize or Grand Cayman. Not as many boats. Get people there watching for it."

"I'll make it happen," Edgar said. "Are we looking for *The Starched Shirt*?"

"It's the only thing we have until Esteban's source finds out if it has a new number."

Chapter 60

Caribbean Ocean
May 12

Jen came up to the bridge. "The navigation station shows a small storm building north of Cuba. We need to keep an eye on it to see where it blows and how strong."

"Shit. Do we need to go east or west of Cuba?"

"It could be right in our path whether we take the eastern or western route around Cuba. The west is shorter."

"Let's plan on west," Steve said. "If it goes that way, maybe we can hide in the Keys. The solar panels need to be secured before we hit heavy weather. Will you take the helm while I batten them down?"

"Let me finish breakfast first. We have time to eat."

"Don't let me get between you and our meal. I feel like Ira this morning. I could eat my weight. It must be this sea air. What are you cooking?"

"Eggs, southern fried potatoes, bacon, ham, French toast, syrup and cantaloupe."

"Babe, you know the way to my heart."

Jen's eyebrows went up. "Last night you said sex was the way."

"That was my night time heart. I'm wearing the morning heart now."

"After all this time, I'm still learning the rules."

"Thank god I'm not the only one constantly bemused after all these years," Steve said.

Jen pulled his head down and kissed him. "I love the mystery, don't you?" She smiled up at him, batted her eyelashes, and patted him on the butt before returning to the galley.

———

As they sailed down the coast toward Cuba's north shore, the storm grew and stalled between the Florida Keys and the Bahamas—right in their path.

"Run for the Gulf through the Moser channel," Jen said. "That'll put the Keys between the storm and us."

As they cleared the channel, weather radar showed the tempest turning west, chasing them. It weakened briefly as it crossed the Keys, and then picked up strength as it entered the warm waters of the Gulf of Mexico—hot on their trail.

Jen came up from the navigation station and joined Steve on the bridge. "It's picking up strength. Forecast is a force eight storm—a lot more than we've ever seen and it's catching up with us. We can't outrun it."

"We should have taken shelter in the Keys," Steve said and turned to look back with a glare and thumped his fist on the console.

"Don't forget what Connie taught us," Jen said. "In most cases it's better to meet the storm in the open seas than to have your boat beat to splinters in a dock."

As the storm bore down, dark grey clouds loomed higher. The light that reflected off their tops disappeared as they rose higher and ate the sun. Under the darkening clouds the sea took on a grey-green tinge. An approaching wall of rain moved toward them faster than the boat could run.

Steve and Jen rushed to drop all the sails and deploy the parachute anchor.

The anchor dragged the stern around away from the wind to point the boat directly into the oncoming gale. They rode prow first, up and over the waves heaping up in the sea around them. Froth blew directly at them off the tops of cresting waves. Rain and wind-borne spray rattled and splattered their windows with increasing intensity as the gale engulfed the boat.

Shut inside the saloon, although they monitored radar and other navigational aids, they were sailing blind. It was like being in a howling, dank, dark dungeon. Black clouds had obliterated the afternoon sunlight.

The boat pitched and dove over oncoming rollers. Wind speed reached and exceeded forty knots and wave crowns began to break over. *The Starched Shirt* climbed atop the waves, pausing briefly before plunging to bury it's prow in the ocean valleys.

Steve held her. "I'm sorry I brought you here," he shouted over the banshee wail outside.

Jen shook her head. "She'll ride this out fine. It's what she was built for." She hugged him back, hoping she sounded more convincing than she felt. "This is an adventure we'll talk about when our grandkids are drinking wine with us."

"I'm not made for this," Steve said. "Remember my landlubber stomach. I'm depending on you to keep on your feet if I have to hug the porcelain goddess."

After hours that seemed like days, the storm abated and late afternoon sun turned the tops of the shredding clouds to gold.

They pulled in the parachute anchor, unfurled the sails, and turned the boat southwest around the Dry Tortugas for the run past the western tip of Cuba through the Yucatán strait.

Jen went to the galley, returned to the bridge carrying mojitos, and handed one to Steve. They watched the sun set over the storm clouds which continued their journey to the northwest. The light faded from gold, shading to pink, to silver, and finally gray.

Jen raised her second glass of mojito. "Here's to our first big storm and to a fast trip around Cuba. It sure feels good getting through it successfully."

Steve clinked his glass against hers.

"On, and congratulations on keeping everything in your stomach," she said. "Cheers captain."

Steve raised his glass. "Here's to my first mate. Mate—that raises a thought. You know that's a verb as well as a noun and a good way to celebrate?"

"Have you changed hearts again?" Jen said. "I hope it raises more than a thought."

The rest of the trip to Cayman Island was uneventful, although they spent the first hour in their cabin while the boat cruised on autopilot.

Chapter 61

Grand Cayman Harbor
May 16

Jen was still grinning as they neared Grand Cayman. Steve had been relaxing and reading at the front of the boat on the trampoline that spanned the two hulls. Suddenly, he stood and waved for her to join him. "Come see our friends," he hollered The bridge sat too high for her to see what had stirred his interest.

After she treaded the narrow walkway between the saloon and the edge of the boat she saw him face down with his head and shoulders hanging over the edge of the trampoline. She walked up and saw that he was reaching down to porpoises leaping out of the water between the hulls.

"Aren't they fun?" He said. "They don't have a care in the world. Look how they jump and twist."

She knelt next to him in time to see one leap high enough to brush its back against his hand. Steve laughed.

Jen reached out and then pulled her hand back. "Will they bite?"

"Let me look. 1...2...3...10," Steve said holding his hands up. "Still all there."

Jen reached toward the porpoises then screamed and wrenched one hand back.

"Oh my God. Let me see your hand!" Steve pushed himself up to his hands and knees and reached for her.

She held her hand up with the back facing toward him with only the thumb, index, and forefinger showing. "He got me."

C. Michael Lance

Steve's expression turned from anxiety to chagrin. His face wrinkled in exasperation when she laughed and straightened her other fingers. "When he really does bite you, don't expect sympathy from me," he said.

Jen and Steve spent a half-hour watching the dolphins frolic between the twin prows. She felt a sense of loss when they left to do whatever porpoises do when not entertaining fledgling mariners.

Jen steered the boat to a stop at the Georgetown harbor and they dropped anchor. They waited for the customs tender to arrive for inspection and the traditional filling of the forms.

"Why do you carry shotguns?" the customs inspector asked when he saw the weapon entry on their declaration.

"We hunted turkeys in the Yucatan. My wife shot a beautiful specimen. I can show you pictures. We left it to be mounted," Steve said. "I was also advised that travel near the mainland in the Caribbean can be dangerous and we should carry them for protection."

"I must see them."

Jen followed as Steve lead the inspector to the cabinet with the safe.

"Please open it," the inspector said.

Steve punched in the combination. Jen struggled to maintain composure. If the inspector discovered the money behind the safe, all their work and planning would come crumbling down.

The inspector carefully looked over the safe, guns, and ammunition. He didn't touch the small pile of money on one of the shelves. He pulled out the shotgun shell boxes and hefted them; reading the shell types. "Buckshot and turkey shot. An interesting combination," he said as he turned to look at Steve with narrowed eyes.

"In addition to the hunt, where Jen bagged the best turkey, we carry them for self-defense. That's why we have buckshot," Steve said. Jen thought he was talking too fast, like he was trying to hide something.

"Who told you this?"

"The former owner of this boat," Steve said. "He said pirates aren't as bad as off the coast of Somalia, but we were told it's better safe than sorry."

"Of course there are none in the Caymans, but if I were traveling in some places in the Caribbean I would consider myself wise to be armed. And since your lovely wife also has shooting skills, then it is wise that both are armed."

"I've heard that around Belize, Guatemala, and Honduras pirates are more common," Jen said.

The inspector nodded and smiled at Jen. "If I were to travel there in a boat, I would arm myself, and my family."

"Thank you for your advice," Jen said.

"You may keep the shotguns, however, we must seal this safe while you are in Grand Cayman."

Jen watched the inspector scan the walls, floors, and open and scrutinize the cabinets. It's a good thing Steve and the cabinet maker did such a good job of hiding the shotgun damage and the safe installation.

"Thank you for allowing me to look over your beautiful boat," the inspector said when he finished his scrutiny of the rest of their vessel. "Remember re-inspection may occur at any time. Have a wonderful time in Grand Cayman."

Jen breathed a deep sigh of relief and collapsed on the sofa in the saloon when the examiner's boat pulled away. "I think he watched too much Inspector Clouseau," she said to Steve.

"The way he inspected the safe made me think he suspected something," Steve said. "He checked all the storage spaces and engine compartments. It seemed that he was looking for hidden spaces, but that may be my paranoia over our secret compartment."

"Do you think we'll be re-inspected?" Jen asked.

Steve gestured toward the harbor. "With all the cruise ships docking every day and the number of yachts, it looks like rush hour. I doubt that they have time to revisit many boats. But we need to act like they will, and keep everything buttoned up. Unless we're taking money out, we need to keep the safe secured in place. Rolling it in and out won't affect the tape they used to seal it."

"OK, let's get busy hiding the money," Jen said. "There are over six hundred banks doing business in the Caymans. I'll pick the banks and you deposit the money while I work with local lawyers to establish International Businesses Companies."

"Where are you going to open IBCs?"

"In the Seychelles, Anguilla, Belize, and here in Cayman," Jen said. "The main point of an IBC is tax reduction. You don't pay taxes on business conducted outside of the country, so I'll select several countries to move money back and forth."

"Why those countries?"

"All are English speaking. Apparently a legacy of the empire on which the sun never set is a penchant for tax havens," Jen said. "They have privacy laws to attract business from around the world."

"Get to work so I can begin squirreling away our money," Steve said.

"Slave driver."

Chapter 62

Grand Cayman Island
May 17

As soon as Jen opened an IBC and its associated bank accounts, Steve loaded up a rolling briefcase with cash and began making deposits. He also stored money in safe deposit boxes to avoid hitting the banks with large influxes of cash and drawing attention.

While Steve took care of the physical movement, Jen became an expert on electronic transfers, using remote banking havens as transit points to further obfuscate cash trails.

After a week, most of the money had been deposited. Steve and Jen sat in the saloon luxuriating with a bottle of good red wine, not the cheap wine they'd become used to. They celebrated the christening of their chosen name, *Caribbean Layoff*, which had been painted on the rear today to replace *The Starched Shirt*. "I'm not wasting a good bottle of wine by breaking it on the bow," Jen had said. "Let's toast to it instead."

"How much more time do you need to get the money distributed as you've planned?" Jen asked. "All the IBCs and bank accounts are established."

"Two more days should do it. Day after tomorrow we can head back to Ft. Lauderdale. I want to see how Todd is doing.

———

Steve finished the last bank deposit of the day. The briefcase was empty and easy to pull. He walked down Edwards Street admiring another day in paradise. The sun was well past its apex and the crystal clear light had softened. The temperature lingered in the low seventies. Mare's tail clouds were painted across the blue sky in white brush strokes.

He dressed for business, Cayman style, with olive linen dress slacks, and a hemp colored short-sleeved silk shirt. Ahead, near Heroes Square, was a bus stop where he could catch a ride to the boat docks, where he'd meet Jen for a celebratory glass of wine before going out to dinner. She wanted to go to Margaritaville. What better way to celebrate finishing their work than a cheeseburger in paradise washed down with a Margarita?

They hadn't done much cooking on board while in the harbor. Were they becoming less frugal now that they were moving millions of dollars around physically and electronically? They needed to make sure they didn't become too used to their new found wealth. It was too easy to lose it again.

A gray panel van passed him and parked in front of the library a block ahead. The passenger door opened and a large man with a pony tail stepped out onto the sidewalk. He slid the side cargo door wide and looked inside with his hands resting on the roof. Another big man came around from the driver side and opened the rear doors.

As Steve approached, the man on the sidewalk turned to look at him. Steve nodded and smiled.

The man backed away from the van and blocked Steve's path. Steve sidestepped to go around and the man moved in front of him again. Hearing footsteps from behind, Steve glanced back. The dance he and the large Hispanic man were doing probably blocked the sidewalk.

The second man had come up on the walkway from behind the van followed by a third smaller man.

Alarm bells went off in Steve's head. When he turned forward, the man in front grabbed for Steve. He let go of the rolling briefcase, flung his hands outward and blocked the hands reaching for him, and then rammed a straight jab into the point of the man's jaw with the heel of his hand. The man stumbled back.

Steve crouched and snapped a side-kick at the knee of the other Hispanic man coming from the back of the van. He connected and the man stumbled. It hadn't done any permanent damage, however.

Without dropping his leg, Steve kicked the man's nose. Something crunched. That felt like damage.

The third assailant slowed and reached his hand back at waist height. Steve stepped forward to grapple before the man could draw what was probably a gun.

A blow slammed into the back of his neck. Steve staggered and his head exploded with stars and special effects. The blow rattled him to the roots of his teeth.

He tried to shake it off, but the man on his knees lunged forward and clutched Steve in a bear hug. Another blow slammed into the side of his head. His knees wobbled. A third blow and everything went black.

Chapter 63

Grand Cayman Island
May 24

Steve awoke face down. When he pried his eyes open, he saw a painted metal surface. His head and shoulders ached. He tried to roll over but his wrists were secured behind. Twisting and wrenching his hands only made the bindings dig in. The floor swayed and bounced.

Someone patted his butt on both sides. Steve attempted to writhe away and received a sharp punch in the kidney. As pain immobilized him, he felt his wallet wrenched out of the right pocket.

He slid a few inches and rolled on his side. The floor movement paused. He was in a vehicle. It had stopped.

A hand patted his other back pocket again and then grasped his elbow and pulled sharply, almost dislocating his shoulder. Steve grunted as he was hauled onto his back.

He looked up into the face of a man with a newly broken nose. The man from the van in front of the library. Broken-nose checked Steve's front pants pockets, pulling out his keys. He grabbed the cellphone out of Steve's shirt pocket, ripping it.

The man's nose was swollen and off to one side. He had blood on his face and the front of his t-shirt. Probably a reason to be less than gentle.

The van's side door slid open and the small man who had reached for a gun looked in. "He conscious? Bring him inside." He walked to a steel door in a peeling, white-painted concrete block building and went inside.

Hands gripped Steve's ankles and dragged him toward the rear van door. His head bounced and sharp metal edges on the van floor cut his hands as he slid toward the sunlight. When he was halfway out the door, they dropped his feet and he slid to the ground—striking his head on the bumper.

"Walk," another large man said. 'I'm not carrying you."

He could stand, but felt off-balance and dizzy. Blurry vision revealed a small parking lot enclosed on three sides by painted cinder block buildings. The van blocked his view of the street.

The men seized him by the elbows and shoved him toward the door. He heard his brief case rolling behind them.

He was fucked—but at least Jen was safe on the boat.

As his eyes adjusted to semi-darkness, he scanned the room. Dingy white painted walls. Piles of rags and collapsing cardboard boxes were stacked along the wall to his left under painted-over windows. A beige, rectangular table stood in front of the boxes. A rolled up blanket lay beside two folding chairs.

Broken-nose held onto Steve's arm while the other large man grabbed the edge of the blanket-wrapped object and heaved back and up. Something in the blanket rolled out.

The smaller man stepped forward. "See, she's still alive."

"Jen..." Steve stepped toward her as she wriggled onto her back. Both big men grabbed his biceps and pulled him toward a chair. He struggled to go to her. One spun him around, the other kicked his legs out from under, and he fell into the chair which almost tipped over when he landed.

Steve turned toward Jen. She tried to sit up despite the fact her hands were bound. Blood streaked her swollen face. Anguish that he'd caused this washed over him.

A gun barrel slammed into his temple lighting new stars. "Hold still or we'll hit her again."

Someone shoved Steve's head forward, grabbed his tied hands, and wrenched upward—pulling them over and behind the back of his chair. The pain in his already injured shoulder made him weak.

The other big guy knelt in front of Steve. He looked Hispanic or Indian. Hair pulled back. Tattoos completely covered both arms up to his shoulders where they disappeared under his sleeveless shirt. Using plastic zip ties, he strapped Steve's ankles to the legs of the chair.

The smaller man, also Hispanic, set one hip on the table next to a fresh cardboard box. He wiggled the fingers on his upturned hand at Tattoo, who reached into his pocket and placed cash in the little man's hand.

He turned and grinned at Steve and then at Jen. "He bet me she'd suffocate before we got back." His smile broadened. "It's been a good chase, but now I have you."

While he talked, Broken-nose opened and searched through Steve's briefcase.

Tattoo moved the other chair six feet away and facing Steve. Then he seized Jen by her shirt front and waistband and heaved her onto it.

Her feet were also bound. One eye was swollen almost shut. Blood caked her nostrils and misshapen upper lip.

A flame of anger ignited and burned through the despair Steve had been feeling.

"I am a very good investigator," the little one continued. "Esteban hires only the best. I was the best in the DEA. From the smallest clue—your UCLA license plate—I tracked you to your home. Then I traced your credit cards, but you were smart and stopped using them because you have so much money now. But we found her family, then your brother. We got what we needed."

"Who is Esteban?" Steve asked.

"The head of the Medina cartel." He shook his finger at Steve. "You picked the wrong man to steal from. You think you're rich? You aren't. Esteban has billions and would spend it all to find you. He has threatened to replace me three times." Little-guy shrugged. "If not me, someone would find you. Esteban is obsessed—he won't quit. You might as well take the easy way and tell me where the *dinero* is."

Steve looked at Jen. Mouthed, "I'm sorry," and received a slap to the side of his head that slammed his face away from her and made his ear ring. Anger flickered brighter.

"Now we have you—and her," the runt said. "You will tell us where it is." He snapped his fingers at the bigger men.

Broken-nose threw Steve's wallet and keys into the briefcase and shook his head.

Tattoo had a blackjack hanging from his back pocket. Blood on was on back of his pants next to where it dangled. Steve guessed it was blood from where he'd hit Steve with it. Tatoo went to the box sitting on top of the table and pulled out Steve's and Jen's laptops.

"My name is Juan Santiago," the little guy said as he stood. "I assume the information I need is on these laptops since Edgar didn't find it in your briefcase. Or maybe it's in the safe on the boat that you so cleverly changed the name on—but it was too late—we found you before the change." He gestured at Jen. "She wouldn't tell us the combination. Look at her face. She is loyal like your brother. But he discovered pain destroys loyalty. She will, too."

"Hector," Juan gestured at Tattoo. "Is an expert at dealing pain."

Chapter 64

Grand Cayman Island
May 25

Steve studied Hector. He'd sworn vengeance for the brute that brutalized Todd. Hector was tall, about Steve's height, but much heavier. A layer of fat shrouded massive muscles. Despite his bulk he moved well. Not catlike—but with contained power—like a sumo.

Hector pulled the blackjack out and slapped it against his palm. "It's already tasted your blood. Hungry for more," he said with a smile.

His long hair was tied in back. Jimmy said one of the guys from the Henning's house had a pony tail. A snake tattoo wrapped around Hector's arm. The tail disappeared under his shirt. The open-mouthed head ended at his wrist, and a red forked tongue stretched across the back of the hand holding the blackjack. Steve committed those markings to memory.

"Hector spent time at Bahgram airbase where he learned specialized interrogation techniques," Juan continued. "With the CIA, right?"

"Don't know," Hector answered. "Said if they told me, they'd have to kill me."

Edgar giggled.

"They were serious," Hector said.

Juan turned back with a chuckle. "When he finished with Estralita, we were sure she knew nothing about Paco's whereabouts.

A chill went up Steve's spine. He knew those names. They were both dead.

"Paco was the man in the van you took the money from," Juan continued and then pointed at Broken-nose. "The one whose nose you treated so unkindly is Edgar. He's a cartel enforcer. When we get the money, he may take Paco's place."

Edgar's eyebrows raised and he smiled. Edgar was as large as Hector—with less fat—but he moved like a weight lifter. He wouldn't be as much of a challenge.

Steve shifted in his seat. He felt his knife in his back pocket! It had fallen to the bottom of his pocket and no one rechecked for anything more in it after they removed the wallet.

"Those guys at Abu Ghraib worked magic with a car battery, a condenser, and a few pieces of electronics. You'll get to see how it works—starting with her," Hector said.

Steve wanted to rip the menacing smile Hector gave Jen off his face.

"Your brother was strong, but he still told us the name of your boat," Juan said. "We had to turn the juice up to get that and he passed out. But with the boat name, the possible destinations he told us, and Esteban's Interpol contacts I tracked you down." Juan grinned.

Steve shifted in the seat so his hand could work the knife up his pocket as Juan verbally patted himself on the back.

"I still need a battery," Hector said. "The other equipment I used on his brother is here." He pulled components out of the cardboard box on the table.

Steve opened the knife, moving only his hands. It was slow going operating only by touch and keeping his arms still. He couldn't drop it.

"Get everything ready while Edgar finds a battery," Juan said.

"I want some jumper cables and steel wool," Hector said. "I need a good ground."

Steve sawed on the plastic ties on his wrists. The knife nicked his forearm. He kept sawing as the warm trickle rolled toward his palm.

Juan motioned to Edgar, they both went outside, and the door swung shut.

Hector picked up a gallon jug of water from under the table. He poured half over Steve. "Skin resistance to electric current is high. They taught me well at Abu Ghraib. Water increases conductivity."

He knelt in front of Steve, placed the jug on the ground, and grasped the front of Steve's shirt with both hands and ripped it open. "So I can attach jumper cable clips to your nipples. Think of how much fun I'll have with hers." He licked his lips as he leered at Jen.

Steve's hands came free behind his back as the plastic tie split. His thumb went over the end of the knife hilt to prevent it from slipping. He grabbed Hector's hair and pulled down, twisting his face to the side. Hector reared back, but Steve held on and slammed the knife into Hector's neck, below the jaw, forward of the hinge—at the pulse point.

Hector bucked. Steve held onto knife and hair, pulling back and sawing with the knife. He had aimed at the carotid artery.

Blood fountained under Steve's hand as the knife sliced then pulled free. Hector straightened when Steve released his hair.

Steve rose from the chair.

Hector stepped back. Blood sprayed from under the hand clutching the wound in his neck. With the other he reached for the gun tucked in the front of his pants.

Steve lifted the chair free of the tie on his left leg. The tie on right, wrapped above the rung, clung tight. As Hector raised his gun, Steve whipped his right leg in a roundhouse kick with the chair attached. It knocked Hector down and the pistol out of his hand.

Hector landed, knocking the grip on his wound loose. Blood spurted. His movement toward the gun slowed.

Steve sliced through the wrap on his right leg. He turned toward Jen, agonizing because he wanted to go to her. Instead he hurried toward the door to secure the perimeter first. He looked back at Hector's gun lying beside the twitching body. He should have grabbed it. If both came back he'd have surprise on his side, but they'd have guns. He adjusted his grip on the bloody knife and stepped to the hinge side of the door. The handle turned.

Chapter 65

Grand Cayman Island
May 25

The door opened. Through the slot between door and frame, Steve saw the van pull out of the lot. Only one man to deal with.

Steve kicked the door closed with the force he'd used to win board breaking contests. Juan caromed off the wall and Steve followed, slamming two quick punches.

Juan staggered back and reached behind his back for a gun. Steve kicked him in the side of the knee and heard a crunch. It felt good after what these bastards had done to Todd and Jen.

Juan dropped like a sack of maize, screaming and clutching his leg.

Steve grabbed Juan's shirt, flipped it up, and snatched the pistol from the holster at the little man's waist. He slammed Juan face down and knee-dropped onto his back. Juan's breath expelled with a rush.

Gripping Juan's collar, Steve dragged him beside the table and then pawed through the box on top for more zip ties. He fell to his knees beside Juan and shoved the gun barrel into his mouth—chipping teeth. "Raise your arms over your head."

Juan's eyes went from squeezed tight in pain to wide and staring. Steve strapped Juan's wrists to the folding metal table legs support. Then he hauled on Juan's good ankle and bound it to the legs at the other end of the table.

Steve flipped the table over and dragged Juan on top. Juan screamed and fainted.

Time to free Jen. "OK babe, you turn," Steve said.

First he kicked Hector in the side. No response.

He knelt and cut Jen free.

She tried to stand, but her legs failed. "Oh my god. I can't move."

"You'll be OK," Steve said, caressing Jen's face on the side with the good eye. "Sit. Move your legs. Get the circulation back. I'll work on Juan."

He retrieved his cell phone from the briefcase, pushed a few buttons, and handed it to her. "The voice recorder is on. Make sure it doesn't shut off."

Steve walked to the table. Juan had revived and looked up with panicky eyes. He grabbed Juan by the hair and dragged him along with the table to face Hector. "See what I do to people who piss me off?"

Juan yelped then screamed when Steve jabbed the knife into his butt. He ran the knife down the back of Juan's pants, slitting them open. Juan wriggled and groaned.

Then Steve sliced Juan's underwear from the waistband to the crotch and pricked his exposed scrotum.

Juan's groan turned into a scream. "No!"

"Tell me about Esteban," Steve said. "If you don't tell me what I want, I'll cut one nut off. Then I'll cut off the other. Keep lying and I'll slice your dick like sausage."

Steve pricked him again. "My brother is in a coma because of you. I'm in a hurry. Where can I find Esteban?"

Between screams, Juan became extremely articulate. In a shaky voice he told Steve about Esteban's office in Mexico City—complete with address—as well as the living compounds there and in Monterey, his private jet number and hangar address. He even supplied the names of Esteban's wife and children.

Steve had to twist Juan's injured leg to help him remember the private number he used to contact Esteban.

"Jen, did you get all that?"

She looked at the display, pushed a button, and nodded.

Steve had the information he needed from Juan. He heard a car door outside slam. Jen stood. He handed Hector's gun to her. "Shoot Juan in the good knee if he makes a sound. Safety's off. Imagine he's a turkey."

When Edgar stepped in, carrying the battery, Steve wrapped an arm around his neck and shoved Juan's gun barrel into his ear. "See your friend Hector?"

Edgar gasped.

"Hold still or you'll end up with your brains splattered on the wall. Understand?"

Edgar's head bobbed up and down.

"Put the battery down," Steve said. He pulled the gun out of Edgar's holster and stepped back. "Stay bent over. Put your hands behind your back." He bound Edgar's hands and shoved him toward an iron pipe running from the floor to the ceiling. Steve lashed Edgar to the pipe, then yanked the table on which Juan lay. Juan screeched once and fell silent. Steve yanked Juan's arm up to bind it to the pipe. His arm felt limp. Juan had fainted.

Steve jerked on the pipe. It was solid. "C'mon Jen. They'll be here for a while. Maybe months."

She came to him on wobbly legs and he enveloped her in his arms. "Sorry you had to watch that, but I hate what they did to you," he murmured looking over her tearful, battered face. He scowled and kissed her undamaged forehead. "Let's get out of here." He held up the keys he'd pulled from Edgar's pocket. "Our ride awaits."

While he put the laptops into his briefcase, Jen picked up the blanket she'd been wrapped in.

"We don't need that," Steve said.

"I'm not surprised you don't recognize the comforter off our bed."

Steve squinted when he looked at it, then he shrugged.

Jen laughed then grimaced when it stretched her split lip. "I'm ready."

"Let me collect their cellphones first so they can't contact anyone from in here. We'll dump them in the ocean."

Chapter 66

Grand Cayman Island
May 25

Steve opened the door slowly and scanned the area. He had two pistols and Jen had one, but they didn't need them. No one was in the parking lot.

Steve drove the van back to the harbor, parking it two blocks from the docks. They walked to where he'd left the tender tied up. He dropped the three pistols overboard as they motored back to the sailboat.

Jen went to their stateroom while Steve readied for departure. She returned still wearing her bloody blouse. Tears streamed down her cheeks.

"What's wrong?" Steve asked. Was another of the cartel goons below?

"I think they threw Elf overboard. I can't find him. He wouldn't stop barking at them, and one of them kicked him. He screeched—then stopped. They wouldn't let me go to him. Just laughed."

Steve pulled Jen to his chest.

"I thought I'd at least find his body."

"Fucking bastard. I should have killed all of them." Jen's tears soaked Steve's. "Did you check all the cabinets and lockers?"

She looked up and nodded her swollen face—lips and chin trembling.

"Let's search again," Steve said.

Jen searched the staterooms and heads. Steve looked in all the lockers and storage areas. They met in the saloon when finished.

Jen shook her head at him. She looked even more miserable through all the swelling.

Steve had already checked the all the cupboards in the galley, even the refrigerator. He opened the dishwasher. No Elf.

With a sob, Jen went below to the bedroom.

Steve turned in a circle, looking for anything he may have missed. He frowned and opened the oven. Elf lay on a rack, unmoving. He pulled the rack out and touched the small dog with his fingertips. Elf whimpered.

"Jen, here he is! He's hurt but alive."

Jen ran to him and touched Elf's head and legs. He lay still until she touched his side and he screeched.

She placed Elf on a cushion. "We need to get him to a vet."

"First we need to get you to a doctor," he said.

"I'm no worse than a lot of battered women I've helped. I'll live. Elf could die."

Jen threw on another blouse and Steve drove the tender to the harbormaster's office where they received directions to a nearby vet. Steve ignored suspicious looks Jen's battered face received.

X-rays revealed two broken ribs, but no other internal damage. The vet wrapped Elf 's middle in elastic bandages and gave Jean a supply of painkillers.

Once the *Caribbean Layoff* was out to sea, Steve checked on Jen and the canine. "How is he?"

"Resting peacefully. Drugs are wonderful," Jen said. "Did you finish with the money?"

"No, there's close to a million in safe deposit boxes and two million in the safe. It can wait. First we have business in Mexico with a cartel leader."

Chapter 67

Grand Cayman Island
May 25

Jen watched Steve as he steered their sailboat toward Mexico. After ensuring she didn't need stitches, he prepared a cold compress for her swollen face, fetched aspirin and water, and insisted she lie down in the saloon when she refused to stay in bed. He placed a cushion for Elf on the floor beside her and made sure the little dog had pain medication for his broken ribs.

Now his behavior concerned her. He'd plotted their course, checked and cleaned the shotguns, and manned the con, all without a comment to her. Usually he told her what he was doing, cracked jokes, and asked her opinion. After he'd been so solicitous in caring for her, he'd acted like an automaton. The term "cold fury" sprang to mind. She'd seen him angry often enough. His anger was usually hot and self-directed. He'd curse and sometimes throw things when he made a mistake, like the time he ran the lawn mower without oil and froze the engine. This was different and a little frightening.

Did he blame himself for their situation, for her injuries? She touched her face. The swelling had gone down. Time to see what was going on. He wouldn't holler at her, would he?

Up on the fly bridge, she draped her arms around his shoulders and kissed his neck. "Tell me about our business in Mexico with a drug lord."

Steve shivered after the kiss. "I was stupid to think no one could identify me when I took the money," he said. "Then I thought we could evade and lose them if we kept moving."

"But they tracked us to Grand Cayman," Jen said. "Me on the boat and you walking along a street. That's scary."

"Run, hide, and they still find us," Steve muttered. "Esteban has way too many resources. Juan said he's just one of the crooked cops on the cartel payroll. Hell, Esteban's living in the middle of Mexico City. He must be paying cops to look the other way. You heard the list of his connections—DEA, Interpol, credit card companies, boat registration. He has ready access to sophisticated tracking electronics. Who knows what else?"

"And you think you can do business with him?" Jen said, trying not to sound skeptical.

Steve turned his head—his smile without humor. "The business Uncle Sam taught me. Esteban has an army. To slow it or defeat it, you remove its heart—that's Esteban. You heard Juan—we're Esteban's obsession. When I stop him—they lose their drive to kill us."

"When *we* stop Esteban," Jen said.

Steve studied her eyes. "Yes, we."

Chapter 68

Caribbean Ocean near Cancun
May 26

When they rounded the Yucatan peninsula and picked up cell signals, Steve called the "go-to guy" Todd had recommended before they left for their turkey hunt.

"*Hola*, Arturo. Todd Henning gave me your name and said to count on your help while I'm in Mexico."

"Todd Henning, a good man," Arturo said. "We have worked together to assist mutual customers. And your name is?"

"Did he mention the name Jason Martin?"

"Are you *Señor* Martin?"

"Call me Jason," Steve said. "Todd and I are *compadres*, and you are Todd's *amigo*, so I hope you can help me."

"*Bueno*, Jason. What can I do for a good *compadre* of Todd's?"

"I need a hunting rifle," Steve said. "A Remington Model 700 XCR Tactical rifle set up for 300 Win Mag cartridges mounted with a Nightforce NXS 8-32×56 scope." It was the same as his primary hunting gun and one US snipers preferred, but he hadn't wanted to bring a rifle registered in his name into Mexico.

"I'll need four boxes of Hornady ELD-X two hundred grain, expanding tip bullets and a Harris HBRS bipod." Although he wanted one, he decided not to ask for a suppressor.

Steve listened to a long pause. Was Arturo writing the information down?

"You are hunting big game in Mexico. What—may I ask?"

Steve's mind scrambled to think of what required heavy bullet, long-range shooting. "Big Horn sheep."

"So I have time to acquire the weapon, since the season starts in December."

Damn. "I'm scheduled to practice with an outfitter. He wants to ensure I am capable of the long-range shot required. I need it as soon as possible. I also need a Nikon Monarch Gold laser range finder.

"And a bore-sight tool," Steve added. With the tool, only a few shots would be needed to fine-tune the gun-scope combination.

"This will require inquiries and arrangements." Arturo said. "I will call when I know how long and the price."

"Price is less important than receiving them quickly. Incorporate a rush charge in your price."

"For a friend of Todd Henning. How can I contact you?"

"I'll be unavailable for a few days," Steve said. "I'll call you back at this number in three days and let you know how I'd like to receive the goods and find out how much it will cost."

"Very well. *Adios, Senior.*"

"*Adios,*" Steve repeated. He found Arturo's questioning and resistance unsettling.

Chapter 70

Veracruz, Mexico
May 28

They docked in Veracruz in the morning. The immigration and customs paperwork was handled on the Internet, including paying fees.

Jen took Elf to a veterinarian to recheck his injuries and board him during their stay. She'd miss and worry about him, but didn't know what was in store for them in Mexico City. Steve had told her his plan would come together after he gauged the lay of the land—as it had on his Vietnam assignments. Would he establish a position of force as a basis of negotiation with Esteban? Esteban wasn't to be trusted. However, going after him on his home turf seemed insane, but Steve was confident he could formulate a strategy.

A gleaming white Mercedes sedan had parked in front when she exited the vet's office. The passenger window rolled down and she turned back toward the safety of the building.

"Don't you want a ride?" Steve hollered.

She bent and saw Steve in the driver's seat. "Where did you get this?"

"Rented it on the Internet while you steered us into port. Had it delivered to customs and immigration. Hop in. I've got our luggage. We can be in Mexico City by afternoon."

"Are you trying to be conspicuous?" Jen asked after she scootched around on the leather seat.

"The opposite. You will be the nurse caregiver to a wealthy but feeble old man. It'll take us five hours to get to Mexico City.

While I'm driving, when you have cell signal, you can rent a wheelchair and find a makeup store to turn me into an old codger. You'll need nurse outfits and a wig, too. Whether you want to get sexy underwear to go underneath is up to you," Steve said and winked.

She'd see what she could do. Steve was behaving like himself again instead of the cold planning machine he'd become since their capture and escape.

"I always wondered what it would be like to be a redhead. Flame or auburn?" Jen asked.

"Surprise me," Steve said with a mischievous smile.

———

An inversion layer similar to what Steve remembered of his grad school days in Los Angeles normally clouded Mexico's capital. He could tell by the puddles on the streets that he and Jen had arrived the day after a rain washed the often hazy pollution out of the air.

Steve had been here several times on business trips. This was the first he'd seen it like this. The view was gorgeous. The surrounding mountains, which often hid in the smog, stood out as if posing for a picture postcard.

Tall glass-and-steel buildings contrasted with the bright pastel-painted stucco popular in many of the older neighborhoods. The multicolored city gleamed in the late afternoon sun.

Their luxury car's GPS guided Jen to drive them past the compound Esteban called home. The buildings sprawled on the side of a hill overlooking one of the many green areas on the city's western side. The verdant swath was an arroyo between two lines of hills. Along the crest of the side opposite Esteban's compound shiny new high rises sprouted.

Steve studied the compound and its surroundings as Jen drove past the walled estate. It was one of a number of large homes nestled in expansive plots of land. Daunting walls surrounded every one. Could it be an enclave for drug lords?

The second time they passed it, he focused on the other side of the greenbelt. Two tall hotels or condos stood facing Juan's estate.

"Jen, can you navigate to the avenue on the other side of the valley? The avenue fronting those two tall buildings?"

"You navigate. I'll drive. What's going through your mind now?"

"The buildings have high vantage points that are well positioned."

"They're too far to see anything," Jen said.

Steve's smile didn't extend to his eyes. "No, they're perfect. A quarter mile. At that distance I've killed... deer."

As they rode along the boulevard, Steve motioned at one of the tall buildings. It was a hotel. "Let's stop and see what kind of view it has."

"You're impulsive today. Are we going to check in?"

"Not today. We'll be in disguise when we check in. I want to look out some windows. No one will know we don't have a room. I need to reconnoiter before renting a storage unit."

"We don't have anything to store," Jen said.

"We need a drop box. I want someplace where Arturo and I don't have to see each other. It'll be safer for both him and me. A storage unit with a lock that anyone can open if they have the combination. I put the money in and he puts the things I need in it."

"Are you adding unnecessary layers?"

"I don't know him, or if he can be trusted. There's safety in separation. After the attack on Todd and our adventure in the

Caymans, I depend upon no one but you." Steve felt frigid anger growing.

————

Inside the hotel, Steve accompanied Jen to the hotel bar where he left her with a glass of white wine and guarding a second for him. He went to survey the hotel's prospects.

Jen was engrossed in the view of the green and rocky ravine out the windows when he walked up from behind and slid into the chair opposite her. His glass looked suspicious. He lifted it and swirled. "They give lousy pours here."

"You took so long—I poured half yours into mine instead of ordering another."

"OK. Either of these hotels, this or the next one, will do," Steve said. "We'll make reservations where we can get the rooms we want."

"What rooms do we want? Rooms—more than one? What are you planning?"

"It's still taking shape. I need an observation point to understand the layout, routine, movements, and the terrain. Those variables shape the plan. I want two rooms, separately reserved, in different IDs—as a precaution. Both hotels have rooms with balconies facing the compound. One has balconies on all the rooms. The other has them only for the room on the ends of the upper stories. We need a room with a balcony facing Esteban."

Chapter 71

Mexico City
May 28

"Let's check Esteban's hangar at the airport," Steve said when Jen finished her wine. "Then we can rent storage units." He took a sip from his glass and signaled for their tab.

A drive around the airport confirmed what Steve suspected. Too much airport security and the position of Esteban's airplane facility made any attempt on him undesirable. Steve could track Esteban to here if necessary, but following his movements should be simpler at his home where he spent more time.

Steve obtained a list of self-storage facilities on the GPS, selected the nearest one, and had Jen drive to it. He returned from visiting the rental office after a few minutes. "Don't have what I want. Drive to the next one."

At the next one, Steve got out of the car, looked around, and climbed back in. "This won't do either. On to the next."

They visited three more facilities, which Steve rejected—two after going inside and a third after just glancing around.

"What are you looking for?" Jen asked—exasperation evident in her tone.

"I want the right combination of storage unit and a nearby overlook, like that hill." Steve pointed. "The unit we rent has to be in an area of the yard where it is visible from above, so I can monitor Arturo when he drops off the goods."

"This is getting a little freaky," Jen said. "Like a spy movie. What's wrong with this place? It has the hill."

"Doesn't have the strategic location I want."

A long ridge loomed over the sixth storage yard they visited. Tall wild grass alternated with clumps of thick brush. The greenery swayed in a light breeze. A small forest of trees adorned the crest line. Steve nodded in satisfaction and walked to the driver's side window.

Jen rolled the window down. "Is it OK?"

"The best I've seen. I hope the rooms are well positioned," Steve said and went inside the office. He returned a few minutes later. "It's a go. Do you want to come in with me or wait in the car?"

"I'm tired of sitting and I'll feel safer with you. I'll come in."

When they were back in the car Jen asked, "Why'd you rent two units?"

"Two back-to-back—even better than side-by-side. Provides more flexibility."

"That's troublesome if they're on different sides of the building," Jen said.

"Only a problem if we're really going to fill them. What I want is to be able to access one from the other, without anyone knowing I can. This transfer has bad vibes. I've learned to trust my instincts that are telling me not to depend on Arturo. Now I want to view the inside."

An overhead light operated by a pull chain illuminated each unit. The walls were four foot wide corrugated metal panels, fastened with rivets. This part of the operation was coming together.

"OK, secret agent double-oh question mark, I'm hungry," Jen said when Steve returned to the first unit where she'd waited while he inspected the other. "Are you happy now?"

"They're perfect. I made a reservation at the Intercontinental hotel in Polanco for tonight. Want to check in first?"

"No," Jen said. "Aren't you famished? We skipped lunch while on our grand tour of Mexico City storage facilities."

"Lots of good restaurants near the hotel. I remember Polanco as a hot spot. Several good Argentine restaurants to satisfy your craving for beef."

"Why were you cruising a hot spot?" Jen asked—eyebrows lifting toward her hairline.

"What happens in Polanco stays in Polanco. I'll drive while you call to reserve a room starting tomorrow at one of those hotels on the bluff overlooking Esteban's home."

After spending a few minutes on the phone Jen said. "We have a reservation for eight days. Northwest facing room on the top floor. Does that meet your needs?"

"Excellent. Call them back after dinner and make another room reservation in a different name. Book it anywhere in the hotel for nine days. A different duration will prevent alarm bells going off later, after we're done. If you get another balcony view that's a plus."

Chapter 72

Mexico City
May 29

"Dinner last night was nothing like I expected," Jen said after showering the next morning. She mentally savored the exotic tastes.

"In the US we're used to Sonoran, Chihuahuan, and Baja style. Mexico City food is much more sophisticated," Steve said.

"The ceviche margarita with scallops, mango, and chopped onion blew me away. And they exceeded themselves with shrimp in hibiscus mole."

"The red wine from Baja was surprisingly good. I didn't know they grew grapes in the Baja," Steve said.

Enough rhapsodizing over the meal. "What next?" Jen asked.

"I'll call Arturo," Steve said. "You put together a list of addresses where we can buy what's needed for our disguises."

He dialed, put the phone on speaker, and held a finger to his lips. "Arturo, this is Jason," Steve said.

"Are you in Mexico City now, Jason?"

"Si. What's the news about my equipment?" Steve asked.

"I will have it all tomorrow. It will be nineteen thousand dollars, including your rush fee."

Jen frowned. That much for a gun?

"Good," Steve said. "I'll call tomorrow with drop point instructions."

"What kind of location are you planning?" Arturo asked. "I can't leave a rifle and ammunition in the open."

"Private and secure."

269

Arturo paused for a few seconds before he responded. "*Bueno. Hasta mañana.*"

Steve disconnected. "Let's go to Home Depot. I need props and some equipment to customize our storage."

"Home Depot?"

"There are fifteen to twenty in the area. Closest is a few minutes away. After I fix up the storage rooms, we'll pick up your items for our disguises."

"All the luxuries of home. How long will you be?" Jen asked.

"Hour-and-a-half, maybe two hours."

"I'll run my errands while you're doing that. We'll need a lot of time for disguises and to check into the new hotel."

"It's not safe for you to go alone. You might be seen."

"Who do we know in town?" Jen asked exasperated again by Steve's protectiveness.

"There were those guys in Cayman."

"One is dead, and two may still be chained to that pipe. Anybody else?"

Steve shrugged.

"Don't treat me like a porcelain doll. We're in this together."

Steve frowned and nodded.

She'd work on him while they drove to Home Depot.

———

Steve watched Jen drive away after she dropped him at the storage facility. He didn't want her to leave his side, but she was right that the odds of anyone finding her in a metropolitan area of twenty million people were infinitesimal—especially at makeup and wig stores.

Her arguments didn't eliminate his concern, but he had things to do. Maybe staying busy would take his mind off her safety. He carried his purchases into the room.

Rivets connected each corrugated sheet to the next and fastened them at the top and bottom. With an electric hand grinder he removed the rivet heads that secured the vertical seam between two corrugated rectangles at the back of the unit. Then he ground down the heads at the top and bottom of one of those panels.

When he finished, fasteners only along one side held the panel in place. He pushed it into the room on the other side until he could squeeze through the gap. He left Arturo's money stacked in the middle of the room, swept up all the rivets that had fallen out, exchanged the seventy-five watt light for a fifteen-watt bulb, and returned through the wall.

He looped a string through a washer larger than the rivet holes, threaded both ends of the string through a hole in the loose panel, and then through the sheet to which it had been fastened. He repeated this in another hole. With the two strings he pulled the panels close, threaded long bolts through the remaining holes, and tightened nuts until the panels were again joined. He cut the string and let the washers drop on the side with the money. In the shadowy light, Arturo wouldn't notice the washers or the two open holes in the corrugated metal—not with twenty thousand dollars to hold his attention.

Jen arrived twenty minutes later as arranged. "Are you done?"

"Finished early. You get everything you need?" Steve said as he settled into the passenger seat.

"Yup. When I get done, you won't recognize yourself."

Chapter 73

Mexico City
May 29

Hungry after working all morning without breakfast, Steve ordered room service for lunch. While they waited for delivery, Jen laid out the supplies she'd purchased.

Steve picked up the gray wig. "This is long enough to wear in a ponytail."

"If you want eccentric, I thought we could do that—or I'll cut it shorter. You haven't shaved in almost a week. Instead of fake facial hair why don't you trim up with a mustache and goatee—a Vandyke beard like Frank Zappa."

"Zappa's was just a soul patch under a mustache. Colonel Sanders had a Vandyke, and it was white, not gray like mine. Too bad it's not longer—I could have a handlebar like Dali. Now there was an eccentric."

"I'll color your beard. It'll appear fuller. You'll have gray hair and a dark beard—the opposite of your appearance."

"Good idea."

Steve washed down his tacos with a Negro Modelo beer, shaved, and then sat for his makeup session. When Jen finished he went to the bathroom mirror. "Holy crap. Is that me?" He leaned close to the mirror and raised a hand to his face.

"Don't touch," Jen chirped. "You'll smear my masterpiece."

"Wow, I look so old."

"I'm glad you like it. All of my practice has been concealing wrinkles. Creating them is new." She handed him a dove gray fedora. "Added peculiarity. Nobody wears them except musicians and licentious old men. Nobody will connect straight laced *you* with the dirty old man."

Steve nodded at his reflection and pulled the brim lower. "Even my wife wouldn't recognize me."

"She died and has been replaced by your nurse doxy."

"Is that your name?"

"No, it's Janice, like on a passport Todd provided."

They left the hotel separately after Jen changed into her nurse outfit and donned a red wig. She picked Steve up three blocks away. He sat in the back seat while she positioned a support boot and wrapped bandages around his right leg.

"What's my story?" he asked.

"You had vein surgery, which is slow healing. It's supposed to be immobilized."

"Thank you, nurse Janice."

In the front driveway of their new hotel, Jen pulled a wheelchair from the trunk and helped Steve into it while the bellhops took their luggage. She raised the chair's leg elevating extension, strapped him to it, and covered it with a blanket. When the concierge offered to push, she waved him off.

While Jen checked them in, Steve patted her butt a couple of times. It didn't hurt to stay in character.

Steve called Arturo from their hotel room. "Arturo, the drop site is ready. The payment is in it. Leave the equipment, *por favor*."

Steve provided him with the address, unit number, and lock combination.

"Is it as we agreed?" Arturo asked.

"I left an additional thousand in thanks."

"*Gracias*, I will see to the delivery this afternoon."

"*De nada*."

Chapter 74

Mexico City
May 29

"Has Arturo got what you asked for?" Jen asked when Steve hung up.

"Yes, he'll deliver today. I want to be there when he does."

"On the hill, watching?" She said, recalling his storage unit requirements.

"If we hurry I can be in the other room. As soon as he leaves, I can go through the wall, get the gun and other equipment, return and seal the panels as good as new. They'll be looking for someone who arrives after Arturo makes his deposit—not before."

"So you don't need the hill?" She said feeling annoyance creep into her voice.

"Maybe not," Steve said. "But it's there if needed."

"You said *we* arrive early. I'm coming along?"

"Yes. The carpets we bought go inside these tubes. The gun and other things will fit inside the rugs. I'll move them for you, Miss Interior Designer. No one will connect us with the gun side when we load the car on the other side of the building. There won't be a sign of weaponry on any surveillance cameras. Just carpet protruding from cardboard tubes."

"Like I stored carpet in our basement at home?" She said, pleased he had copied her.

"Where do you think I got the idea?" Steve said.

"How will you know if Arturo's arrived?"

"If a car is parked in front of the unit I'll watch from the hill instead." Steve said while changing to casual clothes from the suit he'd worn to check in. "I'll leave here first."

After he washed out the mascara she'd used to darken his beard, he looked a different person from the wheelchair-bound invalid. Particularly given the vigorous way he moved.

"You stay in your caregiver character, get the car, and pick me up at the Starbucks we passed," Steve said. "Meet me in ten minutes."

"OK." she said and checked the time as Steve went out the door.

————

Steve had almost reached Starbucks when he saw Jen approaching in the Mercedes. "Need a ride, little boy?" she asked. He climbed in.

"We're early enough No car in front of the other unit." Steve said.

Jen parked in front of the unit on the opposite side.

Once inside, he pressed his ear against the corrugated metal at the back wall. "No one inside," he said after listening for a minute.

Jen inspected the boxes, cardboard tubes, rugs, and other paraphernalia while Steve stood against the wall. After ten minutes, he hissed and held a finger to his lips.

Jen pressed her ear to the wall, too.

Steve frowned when he heard two people speaking Spanish. Arturo had company. The volume of the discussion increased. It was an argument. Steve heard *dinero* several times. Then *arrestar*, and *con rifle*. The voices receded followed by the rumble and slam of an overhead door.

"I don't like this," he whispered to Jen and unscrewed the nuts connecting the corrugated panels of the back wall. He cringed and stopped when the wall creaked. No sound came from the other side. He finished, hesitated for a moment, and then separated the panels.

The dim fifteen watt light bulb illuminated the rifle and other items he'd requested. He handed them through to Jen. He again used string anchored by washers on the far side to pull the wall together. This time, he used a pop rivet gun to align and fasten the panels.

When he'd finished, there were negligible signs he had worked on the fasteners. He turned from inspecting it and saw that Jen had wrapped rugs around the rifle and other items and stuffed them inside the three tubes.

His heart leapt into his throat as he bent to lift the rolling door. He had no idea what he would see. When only their car was outside the door he sagged in relief. He placed two of the tubes in the back seat. Jen handed him the third.

He faced forward as Jen drove out. From the corners of his eyes he noted more people and vehicles in the lot than he'd seen previously.

"Turn left," he said as Jen pulled through the exit. "We need to get to the far side of the hill."

"Let me out here," Steve said when they'd rounded the hill out of sight of the storage lot. "Park over there. I'll be back in a few minutes," he said—pointing at a construction site with several autos and trucks twenty-five yards away. "I need the scope." He grabbed the gun tube and scrambled up the hill through the tall grass and brush.

At the top, he kept the line of trees between himself and the storage yard. When he found a copse of bushes below the ridgeline with a good view of his storage unit, he slid down into them. While he surveyed the location, he pulled the gun mounted scope out. No telling how well it was aligned.

Several people still moved below. Some hung around trucks parked in front of closed doors Steve examined them through the scope. They kept glancing at a space between buildings. He couldn't see what might be attracting their attention.

Steve inserted the bore sight tool. He might as well see how the gun had been set up while he waited for what, he wasn't sure. Sighting on the side of a building, he checked the alignment of the crosshairs with the green laser line the laser painted on the wall. It was remarkably close. A few adjustments and the scope was spot on. He'd need to tune it for longer range, but it was good to one hundred yards.

Two men walked out of the gap between buildings. One—a uniformed officer—appeared to be haranguing the taller man. Could that be Arturo? Why was he with the police?

Steve pulled out his phone, searched for Arturo's number, and pressed call. The taller man lifted his mobile and glanced at it. He held up a hand, stopping the officer's diatribe, and answered. "*Hola.*"

"Arturo," Steve replied. "The plan has to change. I need delivery at a different location."

"*Por que?*"

"I've run into issues. I'll call back with details." He disconnected.

Arturo said a few words, looked at his phone screen, and said something to the policeman. The men standing beside trucks walked toward the two who were again hollering at each other.

It felt like a rock had dropped to the bottom of his stomach. Arturo had turned him over to the police.

Arturo could link the gun back to Todd—and eventually to Steve and Jen. Steve loaded three bullets into the magazine. He had to protect his family—all of them.

The policeman waved at Steve's storage unit. Arturo grabbed the lock and shouted back. Steve rested the rifle barrel on the folded out bipod—noting that flags above the rental office hung limp in the dead air. He squeezed the trigger. Red blossomed on Arturo's chest and he fell against the building—leaving a red streak on the wall as he slid to the ground.

Steve cycled the rifle's lever and fired another shot into the side of the next metal building. It ricocheted several times. The policemen dove for cover. Steve lunged the few short yards to the top of the hill with gun, tube, and blanket. He dove into cover and stuffed everything into the tube again.

Two police officers moved in a squat to Arturo. One checked for signs of life. He looked toward the man who seemed to be in charge, now crouching behind a truck, shrugged, and shook his head. Others came out of hiding and scanned the area. Some were on phones.

Bent low to minimize his silhouette, Steve hustled behind tree cover toward Jen and the car.

Almost to the street, he heard the *whump-whump* of a helicopter approaching. He dove back under the tree canopy and froze. The chopper lowered as it neared the storage lot, disappearing over the top of the ridge. He needed to get off the hill. It was the obvious place to look after they examined Arturo's wounds.

Steve ran to the road. On the pavement, he slowed to a rapid walk. When he neared the Mercedes, the reflection in the side window showed the helicopter rising above the hill. Steve shoved the tube underneath the car. "Come with me," he yelled at Jen.

"*Donde Estadio Azteca,*" he said as he walked up to a group of men standing by the construction project. One sure way to start a conversation in Mexico City was to mention the home of their national soccer team.

Jen stood by his side as several men talked over each other. *"Inglés por favor. Mi Español es pequeño,"* Steve said.

The men stopped talking to peer at the helicopter hovering overhead. Steve turned his gaze toward it and nudged Jen. She looked up, too.

After hanging above them for a moment, the helicopter swung away for another pass over the ridge. Steve listened to the construction crew provide several sets of directions, nodded, and thanked them. "I'll drive," he called to Jen. He retrieved the tube, shoved it in back, and climbed into the driver's seat. Hands that had been so steady on the rifle were sweaty and trembling on the steering wheel.

"What the fuck was that?" Jen exclaimed when he'd driven for a few moments. "A helicopter?"

"Arturo betrayed us. Police were with him."

Jen gasped. "My god, they can track us through him back to Todd."

"Arturo is dead."

"Did you…?"

"Yes."

She looked sideways at him. Eyes wide as saucers, but said nothing for a few miles.

"They'll see the gun is gone and figure out what happened," she said.

"It may take a while if Arturo didn't give them the combination."

"The security cameras will have a picture of our license plate."

"It'll be a picture of the license plate I swapped out before you picked me up." He held up a Leatherman multi-tool. He was regaining control of his anxiety. "Need to exchange it back before they notice it's missing. That will make our trail murky."

Jen shook her head. "You aren't the man I know," she said after a few moments.

"Is it scaring you?" Steve asked. He'd thought this might be a problem.

"No… Maybe. I'm afraid of what I'm feeling right now. Let's get back to the hotel."

Chapter 75

Mexico City
May 30

The next morning Steve slid out of bed without waking Jen. There was a lot to do. He needed an early start. He wasn't sure he could manage it if she woke up. She'd surprised him. Apparently she had a thing for bad boys. And yesterday he did a bad thing, but it was for his family—and he would probably do more. He hoped Jen had left him with enough energy to finish the job.

He used the shower in the second bedroom of their suite. Jen still hadn't awakened when he'd finished. He hung a Do Not Disturb sign on the outside door handle to ward off Housekeeping, picked up his binoculars, and went to the balcony door.

Steve stood at the window and watched Esteban's compound, while jotting occasional notes.

Teams of men patrolled the ten acre grounds that sloped toward the arroyo. In the middle, an elegant stucco, brick, and rock residence cascaded along the hill. A flagstone deck surrounded a large swimming pool on the house's lower level. A waterfall fell from an upper patio before it flowed into the pool.

The upper and lower floors featured massive walls of windows.

A razor-wire-topped rock wall followed the slope up from the wash and encircled the entire compound. The wall alone must have cost a fortune. Despite its massive construction, Steve had a mostly unobstructed view from his lofty vantage.

He studied the compound's front entrance across what seemed like acres of red-tiled roof. Ten-feet-tall wooden gates—two feet shorter than the estates' encircling wall—stood guard over the flagstone driveway that circled the house. The drive continued to a large barn-like structure. It probably wasn't storage for drugs. Perhaps Esteban kept his wheeled toys there.

Steve took notes and sketched the layout—adding dimension and distance estimates.

"Why'd you let me sleep so late?" Jen asked, rubbing her eyes from the bedroom doorway. "What're you doing?"

"No point in waking you. I'm getting familiar with Esteban. Here, take a look." Steve held out the binoculars.

She studied it after he helped her find a sight line. "Wow, so that's what drug money will buy you. The landscaping is beautiful. All those huge pots with bougainvillea and trees and the smaller pots of flowers scattered on the patios must have cost a fortune. Gorgeous beveled glass windows. Is that Esteban by the pool?"

Steve took the glasses back. "No, just one of eight guards I've counted. I'd guess it's uncharacteristic for Esteban to carry an AK-47 while he's getting ready to take a dip."

"He has a gun?"

Steve chuckled. "We notice different things. Your thing is color, décor, landscaping, and beveled glass. I notice guns, surveillance cameras, razor wire, and an absence of guard dogs—so far."

Jen looked back across the arroyo. "You're right I didn't see any of that."

"The rest of the day is devoted to dreary. Why don't we order breakfast? We can eat in bed, then you can go shopping while I continue my tedious task."

"I'd like you back in bed."

"Lord, give me strength."

Chapter 76

Mexico City
May 30

After breakfast Steve resumed spying on compound activity. He kept a log of the security team's movements. It would be useful if he had to go in after Esteban.

A woman in an apron came out on an upper level patio on the right side of the house. It was separate from the other outside entertainment areas. She set a table with silverware, napkins, and placemats before returning inside.

Another woman came out followed by a young girl. Both were slim with dark hair. The girl was coltish. The woman tall and elegant. Before taking a seat, the lady called toward the screen door. After a few moments a chubby teenage boy joined them.

The aproned woman returned with a serving cart and set out bowls and plates of food.

A short swarthy man came out and took a seat after kissing the two females seated at the table and ruffling the teenager's hair. The boy jerked his head away. Was that Esteban? The cozy family scene didn't correlate with a criminal who gave the orders that put Todd in a coma, attacked Jen's mom and dad, or was trying to kill Steve and Jen. Just your everyday drug lord doting on his family.

"What's going on across the way?" Jen asked. She'd showered and now wore her nurse costume.

"A scene right out of the Donna Reed show, if the Reeds had more money than God." Steve held out his binoculars. "Wanna look?"

Jen took his offering.

"On the right side of the house, small upper deck—mom, dad, and two kids."

"I love the elegant rock work on the patio and the landscaping is to die for," Jen said.

"OK, if you can tear yourself away from the aesthetics, track to the right until you find a stone staircase. Follow it to the top and again shift right to their little domestic scene."

"Homey. Oh, there's another woman serving them." Jen said, observing through the glasses. "Is that Esteban?" she asked as she handed them back to Steve.

"I don't know. It's the address Juan gave. It has security befitting a drug lord, but is it him? I've scoured the internet for images, but came up dry."

"Why don't you call the number Juan gave us? If the man on the patio answers, it's Esteban."

Steve smacked his forehead. "I forgot." It was the same trick he'd used with Arturo. He was slipping up. He wanted it to be Esteban so bad, but he couldn't afford to let his anger overwhelm the concentration and instincts that served him so well in war. "That's why I keep you around—to do the thinking when I have brain farts." He pulled out his phone, replayed the recording Jen made in Grand Cayman, and copied the number. "Now I remember why I didn't use it. Juan gave an eight digit number. Countries in North America use ten digit dialing."

"What's the Mexico City code?" Jen asked, opening the laptop.

"With an area code, that'll make it eleven digits."

Jen's fingers pattered across the keys. She looked up and smiled. "Mexico City and two other cities have two digit area codes instead of three. It's five-five here."

Embarrassed, Steve picked up the binoculars and reacquired a view of the small patio—in time to see the door close behind the man as he walked into the house. "I need to wait until he comes back out."

"Will you shoot him?"

Steve closed his eyes, and a vision passed through his mind. "I can't in front of his kids. Maybe his wife, but not the children."

Jen let out a shuddering breath. "Thank God."

Her face was screwed up in anguish when Steve opened his eyes. Apparently a similar scene was still playing across the theatre of her mind. "There will be other opportunities," he said, resisting the desire to cross his fingers, and resumed his observations. The man had not reappeared by the time the rest of his family returned inside.

For two more hours Steve watched the house and jotted new information or checked his notes to confirm them while Jen lay on the couch and read.

"I'm getting hungry," Jen said. "What about you?"

Steve looked at his wristwatch. "Yes, I am. Room service? I have to monitor the compound all day."

"OK, I'll order."

"First, Ms. Makeup Artist, slash Houri, I need to become old and decrepit," Steve said. "I want to emphasize that image for hotel staff. I can't always hide in the bathroom with my wheelchair when they come in."

"Did you call me a whore?" Jen asked, thrusting out a pouty lip as she set out the makeup kit.

"I refer to the beings embodying the Islamic ideal of beauty. The virgins Islamic martyrs are supposed to encounter in paradise."

"Oh... I suppose you expect wild sex tonight after those honeyed words...it might work," Jen said and winked.

"Not in this room."

"Why not?" Jen asked, drawing back from applying penciled wrinkles to Steve's forehead with a disappointed expression.

"We have to leave the impression that the other room is being used. We can mess up that bed."

"Why did we rent that other room? For sex an old cripple can't have here?" Jen asked.

"Didn't I tell you?" Steve shook his head in exasperation. "I'm sorry—my mind has been going a hundred miles an hour."

"I know. That's why I haven't bugged you about some of the things we've done, but the squeal and scraping from grinding gears seems to have grown quieter."

"I hope my brain hasn't burned out," Steve said. "When the action comes down we have to get the hell out of here. Leave the building, the City, the country. But, if we can't, we need an interim hideout—close-by and easy to get to."

"Oh... the room on the other floor is the hideaway. You're thinking of everything."

"I hope it's enough," Steve said. "That reminds me, we need to stock some essentials in that room, change of clothes, toiletries, etc. Are you up for shopping this afternoon?"

Jen cocked her head at him. "Is a bear Catholic...? You did say *clothes*."

———

Jen returned after dark with one bag of groceries and another of clothes. Steve waved and remained at his post. She wrapped her arms around his shoulders, nuzzled his neck, and whispered "Let's go mess up the other bed. You can teach me those Houri tricks."

A smile stretched Steve's lips, and he buried his fingers in her hair. "It's getting too dark to see, anyway. Let's go rumple linen and give housekeeping something to do."

Chapter 77

Mexico City
May 31

Steve placed a hand on Jen's hip and gently shook her awake.

She stretched, smiled, rolled over, and wrapped her arms around his neck.

"Wake up, my Houri, we have lots to do," he said.

"Do I have to?"

Her sexy gaze tempted Steve to give in, but he resisted. "No rest while the wicked drug lord is still after us. I still don't know if the man we saw was Esteban. I need a few accessories from the hardware store, and today we smuggle the rifle into the hotel."

"Accessories and hardware store don't belong in the same sentence."

With a wry smile, Steve climbed out of bed, pulled on the nitrile gloves they wore whenever they were in either room, except in bed, and went to shower.

They purchased a rolling suitcase and a wheeled combination overnighter-attaché case at a luggage store. In Home Depot they bought Steve's accessories, which included a burlap-wrapped bag of sand.

"Accessories?" Jen said with a snort of derision when Steve heaved the bag into the shopping cart.

"The bipod gun support won't work. The balcony railing is too tall. A bag of sand makes a great gun rest, and it's less obvious. I can sit behind the rail, instead of standing like I'd have to with the bipod."

Steve drove to a park. After ensuring no video cameras aimed at them, he distributed Arturo's equipment and the sandbag between their two new pieces of luggage. Then he disassembled the rifle using tools they'd just acquired.

"Why are you taking it apart?" Jen asked.

"Assembled, it's too long to strap to my leg."

When he finished, Jen taped the stock to one side of his leg and the barrel to the other—covering it all with elastic bandages. The pants were snug over her handiwork but didn't look lumpy. No need to fake a stiff leg this time.

He donned the suitcoat, wig, and hat he'd left in the car while shopping. Jen was already in her nurse's outfit. She drove her invalid charge to the hotel. This time she parked in the underground self-park and helped Steve maneuver to a seat in the wheelchair with his leg sticking straight on the extension support. The elevator to the lobby was empty when they boarded. When the door opened on the next parking garage floor, the people waiting said they'd wait for the next elevator car—or at least that's how Steve translated their Spanish words.

Jen rolled Steve across the lobby and backed him into the elevator up to the rooms. Again, they rode alone.

"Get this stuff off me," Steve stood and exclaimed after she pulled his chair into their room. "My leg is itching like fire from the tape. Please hurry."

She helped pull down his pants and unwrapped him. He whimpered when the tape pulled out leg hairs.

"I told you we should have powdered you before we put the tape on," Jen said.

"And you were right, but I didn't want to stop at another store. I wish we had," Steve said as he rubbed and scratched bare spots and red marks on his leg.

"I think pulling your pants off is pointless this time," Jen said.

Steve chuffed out a chuckle as he limped over to the sliding patio door. "If you're talking about sex—I'm more in the mood to shoot someone." For the next hour he alternated watching the estate and reassembling the rifle.

He was ready to carry up the rest of the things from the car to install the scope and check alignment when he spotted motion on the small balcony. The serving lady was setting the table. Steve checked his phone to ensure that Esteban's number was ready to dial.

This time the entire family came out together. The teenage boy and the man he presumed to be Esteban appeared to be arguing. Esteban slammed a hand on the table and the boy cringed and sat. His wife looked angry, but said nothing.

The man continued his diatribe. Steve pressed the call button. The man stopped, patted his pants pocket, and pulled out a phone.

Steve heard "*Hola?*" He raised the pitch of his voice, trying to imitate a teenager playing a prank. "Look up. *Levantas la vista.*"

Esteban glanced at the sky. Steve could see him say something, but Steve had disconnected "Got you, you bastard!" he said to silence.

Esteban looked at his screen, peered around, then tapped the table for a few moments before pressing a few buttons, and speaking into the phone.

A chill slithered up Steve's back. He remembered how well connected Juan said Esteban was. He may have set someone to tracing the call. Steve shut off his phone and removed the battery, eliminating any possibility of GPS or other radios being tracked. He now knew it was Esteban, but at what cost?

Chapter 78

Mexico City
May 31

"I don't think of everything," Steve said.

Jen set her E-reader aside and frowned. What did he mean?

"I called. The man *is* Esteban."

Exultation surged through Jen. She'd come up with the right strategy.

"But I didn't think about the call being traced—even back to the caller's location."

Her stomach fell. "How?"

"You've heard about people rescued by homing in on their cellphone?"

"Yes... they track the GPS."

"They can do that, but mobile phones communicate with nearby cell towers and make the call through the one that has the best signal. If a call is made, it's possible for the telephone company to home in on the caller's location from multiple cell towers."

"You're kidding."

"I don't know how accurate the triangulation is, or even if Esteban could get it done," Steve said. "But he's pulled off a lot of shit through connections that he shouldn't be able to—like having a DEA agent track us, getting our credit card spending information, and the boat registration to mention a few."

"What do we do?" A large rock had settled Jen's in stomach.

"More contingency plans. Number one—dump this phone. It's the one I called both Esteban and Arturo with." Steve dropped it to the carpet next to the sliding door, lifted the rifle, and slammed the phone with the butt—three times—then gathered up the multiple pieces and laid them on the table next to his notebook.

He glanced at the compound. "What's this?" he said.

Jen stepped next to him by the door. A car pulled in through the front gate and two men entered the house. A short while later, those two and Esteban came out on the upper deck and sat at a long table. Esteban sat with his back to the house, facing the greenbelt. Four armed guards took up positions at the corners of the patio. In less than five minutes and Esteban and his guests went back inside with two of the guards. The other two resumed patrolling the compound.

"Missed opportunity. The rifle isn't ready yet." Steve shook his head as he turned to her. "We need a different car. Will you take the Mercedes back and rent another from a different agency? You can drop pieces of the phone along your way to the airport. Dress like Nurse Ratched to return the car. Change to yourself before you rent the new car under a different ID. Pick up a new burner phone for me on the way back, please."

The tension in Jen's nerves eased. Steve was back in focused mode. Dictatorial and harder to live with, but it gave her confidence.

"I'll bring the suitcases up here, empty them of the rest of the things I need to get the rifle ready, and take the suitcases to the other room," he said. "I'll pack, ready to leave."

Disappointment clouded the relief Jen had felt. "After all this planning, it's too bad we're leaving before we finish."

"We're not leaving yet—just preparing for a quick departure."

A whirlpool of conflicting emotions left Jen at a loss for words. Worry won out. "What if they come here to kill us?"

"Even if they zero in on the hotel, there are over a hundred rooms here. The only possible connection is to the Mercedes—it was at the storage facility just before Arturo died."

Jen nodded. Worry receded until it was nibbling at her mind instead of taking bites out of her gut. She looked at the demolished cellphone. "OK, I'll switch cars."

Steve held his gaze on her until she dropped her eyes. "If you want to leave now, we can," he said. "We're partners. It has to be unanimous. I'm not saying it's without risk, but I don't know how hard Esteban will pursue a potential prank phone call."

"I'm sure he has moles in law enforcement in Mexico," Jen said. "But it would be a huge coincidence if they connected the phone that called Arturo with the call you just made." She was trying to talk herself into staying, and what she said made sense. But, other things that had made sense turned out wrong.

"OK, I'm in." She said with a sigh, then packed a change that would allow her to assume her Jen persona, kissed Steve on the forehead, and left for the airport.

Chapter 79

Grand Cayman
May 31

Juan grimaced at the face of his ringing cellphone. Edgar had delivered the new phone this morning. Why did the first call have to be Esteban? Six days had passed since Henning ruined Juan's knee and escaped. Edgar freed them after two days. Juan didn't know how—he'd been delirious with pain.

More days passed with Juan in a drug-induced fog. Then surgery and more drugs. Today was the first time he'd risen from bed. Despite crutches, a leg brace, and pain killers, putting weight on the leg brought tears to his eyes. Now Esteban. Which was worse?

Hector was dead. They'd failed to recover the money or punish the Hennings.

"*Hola*, Esteban."

"Find them," Esteban demanded.

Juan looked at the leg swathed in bandages. "I took my first step today," hating that it sounded whiny. "I don't think I can. Doctor said I need therapy to walk normal again."

"That *pinche gringo culero* stole thirty million from me," Esteban shouted. "You get nothing until you kill them."

"That *gringo* killed Hector, your best enforcer, despite being tied to a chair. He ruined my leg and left us to die." Mention of the money had crystalized Juan's thoughts. "Can't underestimate him again. What are you doing to find him?"

"I hired *you* for that. They've been on the run again for a week. Start today and I'll pay your hospital bills. If not, I'll find someone else."

Juan's face scrunched in a scowl of pain and agony. He hated Esteban. "We have to find their boat. Start people searching the coast. South Texas to Massachusetts. And I need more resources."

"You'll get what you need. Come to Mexico City," Esteban said. "I want constant updates. Do your therapy here."

"I'll begin today." Juan groaned. The door to his room opened.

Edgar walked in, accompanied by a man wearing a lab coat. "What's the plan?"

"We're going to Mexico City," Juan said.

"OK," Edgar said.

The other man lifted a pistol from his coat pocket and unscrewed a silencer. "Now I don't have to kill you." He turned and left.

Juan took a deep breath and exhaled. Coercion wasn't needed. He wanted to kill Henning, too.

Chapter 80

Mexico City
June 1

Steve continued observing the compound. He'd had more interesting days watching paint dry. He scribbled timing and shift changes—complete with names—Bashful, Sleepy, Grumpy, Sneezy, etc. He'd learned the mnemonic for remembering the Seven Dwarfs years ago; two S's, two D's and three emotions. The names suited Esteban's crew. Since there were eight, the bald one was Gollum.

"I got a Ford Edge," Jen said when she got back.

"Good. Businesslike. Change of character from a rich old invalid."

"That's what I thought, but I could get used to the Mercedes," Jen said with a sigh. "What's going on?"

"A whole lot of nothing. Seven dwarfs with assault rifles walking the compound. Normal day at the drug lord garden of paradise."

"Seven dwarfs?"

"I named the guards. Easier to identify them."

Jen shook her head and lay on the couch to read.

The guards walked their routes with regularity—important to know if Steve had to penetrate the compound.

Sneezy always made three circuits and then stopped behind the ten-foot wall in the citrus tree grove for a cigarette. Steve didn't see him, but saw smoke rising from the trees. After five minutes in the trees, Sneezy edged out, flicked his cigarette over the security wall, and continued his rounds.

Doc stopped by the upper balcony every fourth round and a young girl sauntered out with a beverage glass. They'd chat between his sips. He wasn't in a hurry to finish. A lot of smiles and a bit of touching went on. She'd swish her skirts and glance away demurely. Those times when she didn't appear, Doc would wait five minutes before continuing his rounds.

Grumpy seemed to be the lead guard. Whenever he passed another guard, he stopped for a conversation that sometimes resulted in Grumpy gesturing backward and forward along the other guard's route, as if giving instructions, complaining about their conduct, or perhaps he was a tour guide. Sometimes the other guard gestured back, with animation, particularly if the other guard was Doc. Regular meetings were a point of distraction that could be used if Steve needed to go behind the wall.

The day dragged on. Jen made the bed, rearranged the pillows on the couches, and sighed a lot—signs she was going stir crazy.

Patience was a quality that made Steve a good hunter and sniper. He relaxed while awaiting developments—able to focus without his mind wandering. Jen's fidgeting, however, was getting to him. "Why don't you go shopping, or go to the other room— read, rent a movie, or something? What will happen will happen when it happens."

"Thank you for that wisdom. You forgot to add 'Confucius says'."

"Please find something to do—somewhere else—so I can focus. I've never had a jumpy partner on a hunt before. At least not one I wasn't able to lose. I don't want to lose you. Just take your nerves elsewhere for a while."

"I'll see what's on Pay-per-view. Can I check here?"

"I'm sure the TV works as well in the other room."

Jen sighed and flounced out. At least she didn't slam the door.

The sandbag was too big to fit on the railing and it was heavy to move. Steve scooped out half the contents with the hotel's ice bucket and hurled it over the balcony so that the sand fell in a dust mist. He tried to aim for the planter sections. He didn't want anyone investigating clumps of sand on the walkway below. Then he rolled the remains into a tube to use as a shooter's rest and wrapped it with string.

He set the bag on the balcony railing and positioned one of the patio chairs behind it. In the bedroom he moved the king-size mattress to the side. The gun with scope, laser range finder, and ammunition were wedged between the two box springs. He carried them to the patio table, sat in the chair, and lifted the binoculars.

Steve realigned the rifle and scope with the bore sight tool, but that was only good for one hundred yards. He loaded the magazine and used the laser range finder to measure the distance to the seat in which Esteban had chaired his meeting. Four hundred and twenty yards.

He scanned the arroyo for a target at the same distance. What was that? A doll hanging in a tree? A closer look revealed two more hanging nearby. The children's toys appeared old and worn. He didn't want to fire where children might be. He spent twenty minutes surveilling the area but no one was in the vicinity. The dolls were the right distance. One hung in front of a large tree trunk.

Steve checked the estate. The guards' were out of sight—the weak point he'd waited for. Flags hung limp. Leaves still. No wind. Perfect.

He laid the rifle on the sandbag and adjusted the scope for elevation and distance. His breathing took on a shooting rhythm as he cradled the stock to his cheek, took aim, and squeezed the trigger. The boom was loud in the confined patio space. The doll didn't move, but he saw where the bullet had scarred the tree trunk. Left and low.

A guard—Bashful—jogged from the other side of the house, his head whipping back and forth. Grumpy trotted out on this side—scanning. From this distance the sound should be muted. Both looked in opposite directions. No clue where the noise came from.

Steve's smile faded. Bashful stared directly at him. Steve held still—fighting the urge to duck out of sight. Grumpy hollered. Bashful turned, shook his head, and shrugged.

Happy walked out of the garage and shouted. Grumpy responded. Happy threw up his hands and walked away. Grumpy looked... Grumpy.

Steve backed inside, out of sight. He adjusted the scope to account for his miss. In a half hour another interval arrived when the guards were out of sight. He stepped outside, quickly checked that no children were in the area, aimed, and shot. Levering another round into place he shot again at a different doll, rose, and hurried back inside before checking the results through the closed sliding door. The first shot tore the lower half off the doll. The second blew the other doll off its string. The rifle was zeroed in. He might take more practice shots later. The guards' slower responses to this shot let him know they were becoming accustomed to the sound—starting to take it for granted. Gunfire in Mexico City wasn't rare.

Five minutes later *Señora* Medina and daughter took seats on the upper private patio. After few moments, Esteban joined them and bussed each on the cheek. The serving woman brought beverages on a tray. She shook her head and shrugged when Esteban spoke to her. He slammed his hand on the table, leapt to his feet, and stomped inside—returning with his hand locked around the teenage boy's bicep.

Esteban shoved him toward a chair. The boy stumbled against the table, then moved sulkily to a seat.

Esteban sat, picked up his drink, held it up to the family in a toast, and took a long draught.

The family returned inside together. Steve waited for Esteban to reemerge on the lower deck, but only guards crossed the patio. The sun set and lights came on inside. The household appeared to be settling for the evening.

Steve called Jen. "What are you doing?"

"I finished my second movie and I'm looking over the porn channel."

"Without me?" Steve said indignantly.

"No, I'm watching a Spanish language movie and trying to understand what they're saying. Think I'm getting a lot of it."

"Want to get dinner?" Steve asked. "We can leave without our disguises, grab a cab at the next hotel, and find a restaurant."

After they'd ordered dinner Steve asked "Are you sure you want to stay?" "This could go on for days. Like hunting, it's boring waiting for an opportunity. Afterwards is the tricky part of the job—in this case, exiting the room in a hurry, making sure nothing is left behind, and we aren't seen."

"If you want me to leave, I will," Jen said.

"I think how lucky I am you came along with me. I couldn't have done it without you. You handled the business details so well, and you keep coming up with good ideas. I don't want you to leave, but I understand if you want to. But if you stay, you need to remain focused and ready. We're nearing the end game—however it turns out."

Jen caressed his hand. "Let's take our mutual admiration society back to our room. But, which room do we take?"

"Decide on the way back," Steve said. "We need to make them both look lived in, but I only have energy enough to rumple the sheets on one bed. I'm getting old."

Chapter 81

Mexico City
June 2

Steve sat in the shadows of the balcony where he could watch but not be seen. Jen had left for breakfast. He sipped hotel room coffee while he waited for real coffee and a Danish.

He turned his head with a smile when the door slid open.

"Here you go. Two cups of coffee, h*uevos con chorizo* taco, and a cheese Danish."

He rose, kissed her cheek, accepted the plain white coffee cups, and walked into the room. "What do you have planned for today?"

"I can take a hint," Jen said. "PPV movies in the other room." She waggled her e-reader at him. "I downloaded another book like you suggested at the Wi-Fi cafe instead of the room, so they can't trace the hotel internet connection to our Amazon account."

Steve smiled as he set down the coffee. "Good girl." He nuzzled her neck. "Don't come back to this room unless I call you."

"Your paranoia is getting to me," she said and shivered.

He didn't know if it was from his breath on her neck or worry. "Just because you're paranoid doesn't mean someone isn't out to get you," he said with a smile.

"Ta ta," she said as she shut the door.

Steve had noticed she wasn't wearing gloves, so he wiped the door handles, inside and out, and made sure the Do Not Disturb sign hung from the handle before he carried his breakfast back to the balcony. He looked in the brown paper bag. No receipt—no tracks. Good. He wasn't worried about DNA. Neither he nor Jen were in a DNA database, but they both had fingerprint records. No one could match their DNA unless they were captured. If that happened it was too late.

He finished half a cup of coffee along with the taco while Esteban and his family enjoyed a quiet breakfast on their balcony. The pastry Jen brought was a flaky, cheesy delight that he washed down with the other half-cup. The next coffee lasted for an hour-and-a-half—until the liquid was room temperature. Sipping gave him something to do as he monitored the relentlessly boring scene across the arroyo. Watching a house, no matter how grand, generated waves of ennui. Esteban's guard marionettes marching their drill didn't break the tedium.

A stomach growl presaged lunch when he spotted movement on the lower patio. Grumpy strode out carrying an assault rifle. A large man without a weapon followed, and then came Esteban with a small man, about Esteban's size, on crutches hobbling behind.

Steve sat forward. Another guard came last, but Steve focused his field glasses on the one stumping on crutches—Juan. Satisfaction welled up. He was sure the crutches resulted from his kick to Juan's knee. "I hope I ruined it, you son-of-a-bitch."

He shifted the binoculars to the weaponless big one—Edgar.

Esteban bowed and gestured for Juan and Edgar to take seats on the other side of the table. Their backs faced the sun and Steve across the wash.

Grumpy stationed himself six feet back from the table behind Esteban's shoulder. His head swiveled back and forth, watching Edgar and Juan and scanning the surroundings.

Steve sat in the chair beside the railing and rested the rifle across the sandbag. Through the scope he saw Juan's hands wave as he talked. A glance at the flags in front of a nearby building let him know the wind was five to ten miles an hour. He adjusted the scope and centered the crosshairs on Esteban's chest.

Esteban stood and slammed the table with both palms. His mouth stretched in a holler at his guests. He sat down in the chair—back into Steve's crosshairs.

He began his breathing routine. Slowly he squeezed the trigger. The rifle boomed and Esteban's shirt bloomed red as he slammed back in his chair.

Steve chambered another round as Juan leaned forward, hands splayed on the table, head turning, his mouth gaping.

As Steve pulled the trigger Juan dove to the right, disappearing from view under the table.

Steve couldn't tell if he'd hit Juan and knocked him out of the chair or if he dove for safety. He turned to track Edgar's dash toward the house. He centered the reticle on the doorway. Edgar stepped into the crosshairs and stopped to open the door. Steve's shot knocked him forward. His weight pushed the door open. He dropped across the threshold and lay unmoving.

Steve chambered his last round and swung the rifle toward Grumpy who now had his gun aimed at the hotel balcony. Grumpy fired a burst and dove behind a table. Steve heard glass shatter nearby. Steve fired to keep Grumpy and anyone else's head down.

They had his location—time to leave. Steve stepped inside and slid the door shut. From the closet, he grabbed a set of gray coveralls he'd obtained for this eventuality. He left Jen's overalls hanging. A ski mask was in the pocket. He pulled on the coveralls and tugged the mask over his head. At the door to the suite, he removed his gloves and used them to propel the suite door closed. As it swung, he pitched the gloves inside the room. He checked to ensure the Do Not Disturb sign still hung from the doorknob before it closed.

He jogged down the empty hallway to the stairwell. A door in the hallway behind him opened. He kept his face averted as he stepped through to the landing and scampered down the stairs as fast as he could make his feet work.

His scurry had slowed to a shuffle by the time he'd descended twenty floors to the bottom. After he rolled the mask to resemble a stocking cap on his head, he passed into the lobby—immediately turning right. The lobby camera was positioned to focus on people entering the hotel. It would record his back as he strode toward the exit.

Outside Steve stepped behind a row of dense bushes, taller than his head, which lined the length of the building. As he worked his way along the building in a crouch, he ripped off the coverall and ski mask. After bundling them up, he shoved the roll of cloth into a low crook of branches.

The hedge continued around the corner and Steve followed it until he reached another door. He pulled the key to his suite from his pocket by the edges, stepped out, and opened the door. A short hallway emptied into the lobby. No cameras here. He pulled on eyeglasses with a large nose and black eyebrows attached, which Jen had purchased at the costume store.

He felt like he should have a cigar and walk in a crouch. Not much of a disguise, but it would conceal his identity for the brief time he was in range of the lobby cameras.

He ducked into another stairwell and sprinted up to the second floor conference center. The main hallway was empty. Two cameras above the water fountains faced in opposite directions. Hoisting himself on top of the shorter fountain, he stepped up onto the taller. He took two packets of Play-Doh wrapped in cellophane from his pocket and wedged them into the lenses. The plastic and any fingerprints on it went into his pocket.

Inside the restroom, standing on a toilet, he moved a ceiling tile and pulled out the sport shirt, shorts, and sandals he'd hidden there. There were benefits to being tall.

He changed and placed the clothes he'd been wearing along with the glasses, funny nose, and mustache above the toilet and moved the tile back into place.

He wanted to call Jen, but he didn't want his phone to show her number, in case he was caught in the hotel. The Play-Doh was still in place obscuring the camera lenses when he left the restroom and took an elevator to the first floor. Outside the hotel, he asked the bellman to hail a cab.

While Steve waited for a cab, three SUVs raced up and screeched to a stop in front of the hotel. Grumpy and four of the other guards piled out of the first. Doc led the team in the second vehicle. Grumpy glared around. Then he and Doc stalked toward Steve.

Chapter 82

Mexico City
June 2

Steve tensed and reached to his rear pocket for the knife. Sleepy fell in beside Grumpy and Doc as they advanced on Steve… and walked past him to enter the lobby. The rest of the dwarves followed inside. They must be deaf. How could they miss Steve's heart hammering like a bass drum. *Where is that freaking cab?*

An eternity crawled by in the few moments it took a cab to pull up. Steve collapsed into it. The cabbie cocked his head and looked at Steve in the mirror.

"Polanco, *por favor.*" As the cab left the drive, his adrenaline rush ebbed. He was too old for this. He held the cellphone to his chest until his breathing normalized, then dialed Jen.

"Are you ready for lunch?" Jen asked by way of greeting.

"I'm on the way to Polanco."

"You sound tired. I thought you'd call before you left. Is everything OK?"

"Yes, I'm fine. How soon can you be ready to check out?"

"Check out?" Jen exclaimed. "What happened?"

"Not a secure line. I'm on *Avenida Presidente Masaryk* . There's a Starbucks ahead. Check out then pick me up there. Just your luggage. Do not go to the other room—no matter what."

"OK".

Steve could feel her questions overflowing but she was a trooper.

Chapter 83

Mexico City
June 2

Jen stared at the phone after Steve disconnected. What the hell?

She looked around the room. Get out, but get out clean. She stuffed as much as she could into her suitcase. Only a pair of Steve's jeans, a sport shirt, and sneakers didn't fit. If not for his shoes she could have crammed the clothes in, but she didn't want conspicuous bulging luggage when she checked out.

He said to leave his suitcase, but an abandoned suitcase with clothes would call attention to this room. She hefted the almost empty suitcase and carried it two floors lower and left it on a landing before returning to her floor via elevator. It might cause a bomb scare, but it wouldn't be associated with this room.

In the bathroom she lathered a washcloth and wiped the surfaces in the room she or Steve may have touched. She'd pitched the washrag and a hand towel into the bathtub when her phone rang—spiking her heart rate. It was Steve's number.

"I bought you an airline ticket," Steve said when she answered.

"Why?"

"It's more likely that a *gringo señora* will fly home than drive to Veracruz. You'll have an email itinerary on your phone soon. Be familiar with it before you go downstairs. I'm afraid the fan will start spewing shit soon. I want you as far under the radar as possible."

Jen saw flights through Dallas to Kansas City when the travel plan message arrived. Fairly mundane.

The elevator doors opened onto chaos. Guests and hotel staff milled. Uniformed police officers barged straight at her. She stepped aside in confusion and they entered the elevator.

A long serpentine line had formed, waiting for assistance from the front desk. Before she could join it, a man wearing a suit and tie stepped in her path with his hand out. The other hand held a badge.

"Name and room number?"

She gave the name on the itinerary Steve had sent—the same as on her room reservation.

"Passport," he said.

Her heartbeat juddered. What passport did she have in her purse? She handed it over. What if it doesn't match the name she'd given him? Her mind went blank.

He checked the passport and asked in English, "Where are you going?"

"Home… to Kansas." She gasped. She'd been holding her breath. "What's going on?"

"There has been a problem in the hotel," he said. "Itinerary?"

She showed him the flights on her phone—thanking Steve in her mind. Her interrogation finished when the man stepped aside and motioned for her to step into line. The next group he stopped was a family with small children. Another man stopped two women together. It appeared it was a general canvas of the guests.

Someone in line ahead of Jen mentioned a shooting in the hotel and another used the word murder. Word traveled fast.

"You are checking out two days early," the desk clerk said when Jen requested her bill. She turned and nodded to a police officer who approached Jen.

"Will you come with me, *Señora*?"

"What for?"

"There has been a problem in the hotel. We are questioning some of the guests."

"What kind of problem? Why me?" Jen said.

He shook his head. "Follow me."

"I'm in a hurry. My plane leaves in a few hours."

"A crime has been committed in this hotel. You may be in a hurry but we must find the criminal," he said, escorting her into a small office. "Wait here until we release you." He took her itinerary info and passport and went into another office.

An older officer came out. "*Señora,* you are leaving the hotel two days early. Why?"

"I've finished my business."

"What were you doing this morning?" He scrutinized her face. This was uncomfortable.

"I was in my room."

"So no one can confirm your presence or actions?"

"An associate… I am here on business… away from my family. He and I had… breakfast together." Jen looked away, then at the floor. "He has a family." She looked up and arched an eyebrow. "I don't believe there is any reason to involve him."

He smiled knowingly and nodded. The first officer returned and handed him a slip of paper. "Your itinerary is in order. You may leave."

The line waiting for cabs looked like a slow motion evacuation of the hotel. Jen was glad she had a car.

Chapter 84

Mexico City
June 2

Steve was torn as he stood in front of the Polanco Starbucks. Emotions goaded him to return to the hotel, to stand at Jen's side. Logic told him Esteban's men and the police would search for a man and woman together—not the invalid and his nurse—but a couple. She'd be safer on her own. His rational brain won, but it didn't lessen his anxiety.

He needed a large black coffee. Starbucks had pet names for different sizes, but he never remembered how they corresponded. Small, medium, and large worked—except in Mexico. The *grande* he ordered, Spanish for large, was actually medium. Perhaps that was better. Adding caffeine to nerves sizzling near a flash point might not be the best idea.

He wasn't hungry, but wanted something to linger over while waiting for Jen. This Starbucks was a surprise. The menu was more extensive than his home town Starbucks. He ordered a panini cooked to order and a pastry. Next he discovered that the restaurant's three stories included a top floor terrace where he watched the street from behind a low brick wall topped by a wrought-iron fence.

He'd never felt anxiety like this during an operation, but he'd never had so much at stake. It wasn't just his life at stake. To keep Jen safe, he'd walk—no, run—from the money.

Time dragged. He was preparing to return to the hotel when his phone rang. It lay on the table beside him. Jen's number lit up on the screen. Did police in Mexico give prisoners one call? He answered.

"You wouldn't believe the turmoil in the hotel," Jen sounded rattled and the words flowed. "The cops interrogated me. They're not discreet. Ham-handed is a better description. I am so glad you made the airline reservation. I don't know if they'd have released me without it. They checked with the airport."

Steve had waited for her to take a breath. "Are you OK?"

"Yes. I'm in Polanco, driving through a section with a hundred street signs pointing every which way."

"I'll meet you in front of Starbucks."

After he exited the building, a police car pulled to the curb thirty feet to his left. Two officers got out and walked toward him—hands on holstered guns. Steve tried to ignore them, continuing to scan traffic. They approached. Continuing past him—so close he smelled corn tortillas on the larger one—they turned into the coffee shop.

After Steve's heart stopped fluttering, he wondered what replaced doughnuts for police in Mexico. He saw Jen's car and raised a hand.

She pulled to the curb and Steve opened the passenger door.

"I'd have passed you by if you hadn't waved. You're not dressed the way you were this morning."

"This is my third outfit today."

"You drive," she said as she opened the door. "My nerves are frayed."

Steve drove and filled her in on his actions.

"O M G. All the while I was reading and listening to Mexican TV in the background."

"Your thoughts?"

"I'm glad those bastards are dead," Jen growled. "I'd have done it if I could shoot like you. But you don't know whether you hit Juan?"

"He lunged out of the chair as I shot. I couldn't tell if it was a hit or miss. When he was on the ground the table blocked my view."

"I hope you got him," Jen seethed. "He would have killed us—and what he did to Todd. He doesn't deserve to live."

"The important thing is Esteban won't be pushing to find us. What were the police looking for?" Steve asked.

"I'm not sure they know yet. It seemed to be a general canvass. They stopped men and women—old and young. Lots of couples."

"It will be dangerous when the cops and cartel coordinate their efforts," Steve said. "Esteban's guards were at the hotel before I left—and I departed in a hurry."

"Will they work together?"

"Cartels are octopuses—tentacles into everything. Don't forget—Juan was United States DEA working for Esteban. The cartel may not have strong influence with the *Policía Federal.* But it's probably hand-in-hand or hand-in-pocket with the local police. I wouldn't be surprised if half the Mexico City cops are on the cartels' payrolls."

"We have to get out of here," Jen said.

"Five hours to Veracruz."

Chapter 85

Mexico City to Veracruz
June 2

Two hours out of Mexico City, Steve passed a police car on one of the few four lane highway segments. He checked his speed—just under the limit. Nevertheless, the black and white switched lanes and fell in behind his Ford Edge—speeding up to stay within six car lengths.

The patrol car didn't have the distinctive nine inches tall *Policía Federal* lettering of the highway patrol along the side and was several years old—local cops.

Not wanting to be conspicuous, Steve maintained a pace within five kilometers of the speed limit—ranging over and under—but the cruiser remained glued to his tail.

Jen glanced over her shoulder. "What are you watching?"

"Don't look now but cops have been following us for four minutes."

Jen pivoted in her seat to peer behind.

Flashing lights turned on followed by the whoop of a siren. "Which part of 'don't look now' was confusing?" Steve asked while he pulled to the shoulder.

"Were you speeding?" Jen asked.

"No."

"Shit."

One officer walked up on Steve's side of the car—a hand on his pistol.

The other officer stopped behind the right rear quarter panel. In the side mirror Steve watched him flick the safety strap off his gun before his hand came to rest on the pistol grip—thumb on the hammer.

Steve rolled down his window and looked up at the portly cop. "Yes, officer?"

"Step out of the car," the man said in passable English.

A modicum of relief surged. At least he wouldn't be trapped in the car with gun toting *policía* outside.

"License please." The officer extended his hand.

"What's the problem?" Steve asked as he handed it over.

"Speeding. Follow me."

Steve noted that that the other officer pivoted to keep an eye on both Jen and him.

Instead of getting in the cruiser to run Steve's information, the pudgy officer turned and snapped the license against his other fist. "Where are you going?"

"Veracruz."

"You will follow me in your car to our courthouse. If the *Jueza*, judge, is there you may pay your fine. But, you may have to wait several hours."

Steve saw where this was going. "We are in a hurry. What is the fine?'

"The *Jueza* will say."

"What is the most the fine could be?"

The officer's eyes shifted left and right. "Four hundred dollars—American."

"I may not have that much."

"Then you will wait until the money is wired to you."

"If I do have it, can I pay you now and you deal with the judge?" Steve saw a glint of greed in the cop's eyes.

"That could be arranged."

Steve looked in his wallet. "I don't have enough. Let me check with my wife."

"Do you have two hundred dollars?" Steve asked Jen when he bent and rested his forearms on the driver's window opening.

"Of course." She rifled through her purse.

"Smaller bills. We don't want to appear too flush."

He pulled two hundred from his wallet and shuffled it together with the Jen's cash. He counted on the way to the officer who was bouncing on the balls of his feet while he remained standing beside his vehicle.

"Here you are. *Gracias* for doing this for us. We need to get to Veracruz soon," Steve said.

"Pay attention to the speed limit signs," the officer said after he counted the money and handed the license back.

Steve nodded, returned to their rental car, and accelerated away sedately.

"What happened?" Jen asked.

"The Mexican version of the hick-town-speed-trap hustle. I guess we looked like tourists, ripe for the picking. I gave him the money and asked him to pay the judge for us."

"Thank God. I thought the cartel had an All Point Bulletin on us."

"Likewise. I palmed my knife when I got the wallet out."

"Do you think the judge will even see the money?"

"I doubt it."

"My heart is still pounding."

"Relax. Veracruz in three hours, then we'll be running free on the Caribbean."

———

Jen called the vet, and found that Elf was well enough to bring home.

"I'll pick up supplies while you get Elf," Steve said as he pulled away from a toll booth headed into Veracruz.

"Do you know a good *mercado*?"

"A Walmart *super mercado* should have everything we need."

"Walmart?"

Steve pointed ahead to a familiar blue sign.

"Walmart." Jen sighed. "And even a Sam's. It's kind of sad our version of civilization is moving south."

"I'll buy anything I think we need," Steve said as he got out and Jen walked around to the driver side.

"I don't remember what's on the shopping list."

"I don't either, but the sooner we're out of Mexico the happier I'll be," Steve said. "Food, drink, toothpaste, toilet paper, paper towels …"

"Do we need toilet paper?"

"Can't buy it in the Gulf. Better safe than sorry."

Jen nodded. "I'll be back in thirty minutes."

Steve prowled the aisles, pitching necessities into the cart. Mint Oreos, ice cream, granola, yogurt, Kleenex, *Dos Equis*, *Modelo*, toilet paper….

He stopped at a newspaper rack. A picture on the front page looked like Esteban. Under the image, the word *cartel* jumped out at Steve. That was quick. Must be an afternoon edition. The Spanish headline included the word *Asesinado*. Did that mean assassinated? He picked a copy up and dropped it into the cart trying not to stare at it.

Outside, he scanned the parking lot for Jen. He pulled out his phone when he didn't see her.

He'd missed a call. A Florida area code. He didn't know anyone in Florida except Todd. It wasn't his number. Steve listened to the voice mail. Dr. Elizondo asked him to call.

With a heavy sigh Steve pressed the redial icon. He didn't know if could tolerate the frustration of listening to the typical physician's office menu—'which has recently changed so please listen carefully'—just to hear Todd was dead.

"Hello, Elizondo here."

"Doctor Elizondo? Steve Henning returning your call." He'd never had a physician answer a phone.

"Ah, Mr. Henning. Thank you for calling. This is my cellphone. I wanted to give you the news directly."

Steve's momentary hope was dashed. He was surrounded by death today.

"Your brother was responsive today."

Steve's heart surged. "Responsive? In what way?"

"He hasn't spoken yet, but he reacted to questions while awake for a short time."

"Thank God." Steve felt his voice shudder.

"I don't want to create unrealistic expectations. He has a long road to recovery with the possibility of many stumbles, but I thought you would like to know. I'd also like to tell Todd when you can be here?"

"We're about to put to sea on a return voyage," Steve said. "Tell him we'll be there in a few days, depending on weather."

"Very well. Have a good voyage."

"It will be, based on this call. Thank you very much, doctor."

Jen pulled up. Steve knew he had a silly smile plastered across his face but he couldn't wipe it off.

Jen got out with Elf in her arms. "I didn't think you'd be so happy to see him."

Steve reached out and ruffled Elf's head. "It's not Elf. The doctor called. Todd's awake."

"Aww", Jen said and wrapped the arm not holding Elf around Steve's waist and hugged him tight. "That's wonderful. I'm so happy. Amazing that it happened today." Steve felt Jen shiver. *"What if he woke at the same time you shot Esteban?"*

Steve shook his head—speechless for a moment. Then he turned to loading groceries into the trunk. He handed the newspaper to Jen. "Look this over."

316

"I wish my Spanish were better," Jen said as she scanned the article in the Mexican paper. "*Asesinado*—Esteban and one other—Edgar—is assassinated. An American—Juan Santiago—I think it says is injured—*lastimado?*—critically—*severo.* I think that's right, but I'll check the Spanish dictionary later."

Steve gathered the groceries. "Juan made it plain Esteban was the one who wanted us dead. Hector's dead, and now Edgar. With Esteban gone, Juan shouldn't have a reason to come after us—if he lives."

"He won't have Esteban's resources either. So we should be safe?"

Steve stopped in the harbor parking lot, dropped his head, and exhaled gustily. "I don't know how long it will take to make me feel safe again—if ever." Then he looked up at Jen, a smile bending up one side of his mouth. "But we have thirty million to cover our asses."-

Jen laughed and looked at her watch. "Sunset in an hour. One more night in Mexico."

Steve shook his head. "I don't want to wait for morning. We've night sailed before. Let's get the hell out of here and put the cartel behind us."

"Oh, Cisco, let's went!" Jen said.

Forty-five minutes later, Steve backed the boat out and pointed the bow east. The cartel should leave his loved ones alone now, and he counted Jen's family in that category. Now that they were safe, he could use the money to improve their lives—a lot.

Behind them the disappearing sun lit towering clouds on fire as the wind filled the sails of the *Caribbean Layoff*—blowing them home.

The End

Books by the Author

by C. M. Lance
Contemporary Fantasy
The Battle Wizard Saga
Wizard Dawning Book 1
Wizard's Sword Book 2
Dragon Sword Book 3

by C. Michael Lance
Action Adventure
Caribbean Layoff

About The Author

An Aerospace Engineer, Accountant, Product Manager, Operations Director, Sales Executive, and Writer in that approximate chronological order.

He's always enjoyed writing, even though early writings were mostly Product Specifications, Sales Proposals, and Departmental Budgets. Most readers assumed those were fictional.

Currently traveling the US in an RV to visit friends and family with his Interior Designer wife and a Granddog.

Three grown children span the United States from New York to Austin, TX to San Diego.

To find out about other book projects visit:

http://CM-Lance.com

Caribbean Layoff

An indie author's success is influenced by your reviews. Please visit the Amazon pages and let others know what you think, good or bad. Numbers matter.

Thanks,

85509418R00182

Made in the USA
San Bernardino, CA
20 August 2018